Laurie Gilmore is a *Sunday*  author who writes small-tov *Pumpkin Spice Café*, won the award in 2024. Her Dream F townsfolk, cozy settings, and swoon-worthy romance. She loves finding books with the perfect balance of sweetness and spice and strives for that in her own writing.

www.thelauriegilmore.com

instagram.com/lauriegilmore_author
facebook.com/lauriegilmoreofficial

Also by Laurie Gilmore

THE STRAWBERRY PATCH PANCAKE HOUSE

Dream Harbor Series
Book 4

LAURIE GILMORE

HarperCollins*Publishers*

HarperCollins*Publishers* Ltd
1 London Bridge Street
London SE1 9GF
www.harpercollins.co.uk
HarperCollins*Publishers*
Macken House, 39/40 Mayor Street Upper,
Dublin 1, D01 C9W8, Ireland

This paperback edition 2025
1
First published in ebook by HarperCollins*Publishers* 2025
Copyright © Laurie Gilmore 2025
Map illustration © Laura Hall

Laurie Gilmore asserts the moral right to
be identified as the author of this work

A catalogue record of this book
is available from the British Library

ISBN: 978-0-00-871334-8

To F for making me a mom and to V for keeping me on my toes ever since.

You guys still aren't allowed to read this one but thanks for all the inspiration.

LOGAN'S FARM

HAZEL'S HOUSE

FLOWER SHOP

ICE CREAM SHOP

PET SHOP

HOTEL & SPA

DREAM HARBOR

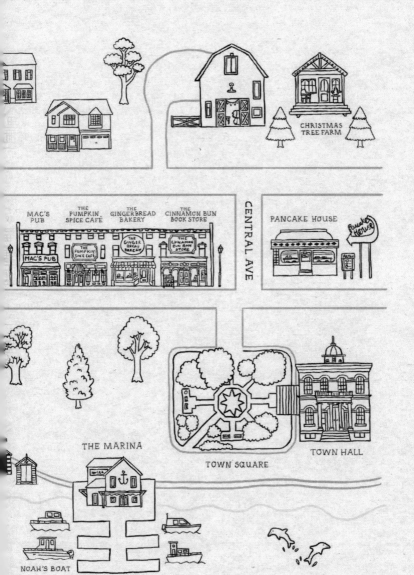

CHRISTMAS
TREE FARM

MAC'S
PUB

THE
PUMPKIN
SPICE CAFÉ

THE
GINGERBREAD
BAKERY

THE
CINNAMON BUN
BOOK STORE

CENTRAL AVE

PANCAKE HOUSE

THE MARINA

TOWN SQUARE

TOWN HALL

NOAH'S BOAT

Playlist

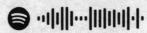

Beautiful Things - Benson Boone ♥
Bed Chem - Sabrina Carpenter ♥
Enchanted - Taylor Swift ♥
Beautiful As You - Thomas Rhett ♥
enough for you - Olivia Rodrigo ♥
Feels Like - Gracie Abrams ♥
Everywhere, Everything - Noah Kahan ♥
Call Me Lover - Sam Fender ♥
Love Me Anyway - Chappell Roan ♥
You Are In Love - Taylor Swift ♥
Grace - Lewis Capaldi ♥
What Was I Made For? - Billie Eilish ♥
Pancakes for Dinner - Lizzy McAlpine ♥
The Night We Met - Lord Huron ♥
Out Of That Truck - Carrie Underwood ♥
Break My Heart Again - FINNEAS ♥
Forever - Noah Kahan ♥
Sleep Tight - Holly Humberstone ♥
Perfect - Ed Sheeran ♥
You've Got The Love - Florence + The Machine ♥
Fast Car - Luke Combs ♥
Young and Beautiful - Lana Del Rey ♥
Nice To Meet You - Myles Smith ♥

Chapter One

Archer Baer had just become a father in the most unimaginable way possible. Not that he'd ever imagined it at all. What was a confirmed bachelor, a workaholic chef like himself going to do with a child? He didn't even have houseplants because he didn't have time to keep them alive. And he was fairly confident that children required more upkeep than a ficus.

But according to the lawyer who had called him a week ago and disrupted his entire existence, Archer had a daughter. A little girl he had never met or heard about in the five years that she had been alive. And that her mother, Cate, had been killed in a car accident and now he would never get to ask her why she hadn't told him about the kid but had listed him as the father on the birth certificate.

It was all still so insane when he thought about it. Even now as he strode down Main Street in this bizarre little town where Cate had grown up, it didn't really seem possible. Archer, a *dad*? It didn't make sense. He shook his head in frustration, trying in vain to wake up. He needed coffee. He hadn't been awake this early in years. Working in kitchens across Paris had left him practically nocturnal. He rarely got home before 1am. How in God's name was he supposed to take care of a little girl?

The lawyer had been convinced that his daughter would be better off with him than her elderly grandmother, but Archer was not at all certain about that.

Wouldn't she be better off with someone who knew what the hell they were doing?

His thoughts wandered back to Cate. Despite having not spoken to her in five years, he couldn't believe she was gone and now he couldn't ask her any of his hundreds of questions.

Cate Carpenter. He'd met her while working in an upscale restaurant in Boston. She was front of house, he'd been a trainee chef. She was beautiful and funny. They'd only slept together a few times. He had been leaving anyway, heading to Europe to chase his insane dream of becoming a Michelin-star chef. Was that why she hadn't told him about the baby? Over the years she could have told him a thousand times, so why hadn't she?

And what would he have done? Given it all up? His dream. His perfect job. His quest to be the best. Would he have ended up in this little New England town sooner? Would he have married her?

Would he have resented her for derailing the plan he'd so meticulously set out for himself?

He swallowed the hot lump in his throat. None of that mattered now, because Cate was gone. Christ, Cate was *gone*, and he was here to meet his daughter. It was all so damn tragic. And Archer couldn't deal with any of it before he had had coffee.

This was the first time since he'd arrived that he'd ventured into the town center. It was … quaint, like something from an old postcard. Quaint, and incredibly *small*. The tree-lined street consisted of a handful of stores and ran all of about two city blocks. And that was it. The commercial area quickly became residential. It was nothing like the pulsing energy of Paris. His hopes of getting a decent cup of coffee were quickly fading.

It was cold today, especially this early in the damn morning. The chill of winter still hadn't let go, and despite the fact that it was only the first week of March, each shop door stubbornly displayed a floral wreath or faux tulips in the window. Every single one had a sign advertising an Easter egg hunt coming soon. It was all a little too … cutesy for him. Was he really going to live *here*? Here, inside this commercial for New England charm. He wasn't sure he could stomach it. He preferred his life to be grittier than flower wreaths and egg hunts.

Store owners were beginning to open their doors, and more and more people filled the formerly quiet street. And, unless Archer was totally paranoid, he was pretty sure most of the people were looking at him.

Wonderful. Just what he needed. Nosy, small-town folks butting into his business, when all he really wanted to do was sort things out with his kid and then head back to Paris, to his kitchen, to his real life. This bizarre street, with its forced, spring décor and its curious townsfolk, was not for him. He already longed for the anonymity of a city.

He passed a pet store, ignoring the bunnies in the window, along with the shopkeeper's friendly wave. He didn't pause at the florist's or the ice-cream parlor. There had to be a goddamn coffee shop somewhere in this place!

Ah, there! Up ahead he caught a glimpse of a sign: 'The Pumpkin Spice Café'. He frowned. They better have something other than overly saccharine seasonal drinks. He crossed the street and took note of the pub next door to the café. That could come in handy while he was here.

The chalkboard sign in front of the coffee shop was advertising a new kale smoothie and lemon blueberry scones. The smell of fresh roasted coffee seeped from the shop and Archer could feel his body perking up. Thank God. He could not meet his daughter, his *daughter*, he still wasn't used to that word, while he was half asleep.

He reached for the door handle, not really paying attention, his thoughts snagging on that word and that responsibility, and on whether or not he wanted a scone, when the door to the cafe swung open and nearly nailed him in the face.

'What the—' His words were drowned out by the woman's shriek, as though *he* was the one charging out of the café with no regard for other people.

'Oh, no!' she yelped and then it was too late. The tray of smoothies she'd been carrying was tumbling toward him and her body was crashing into him and her wild red hair was flying around her face and Archer was steadying her with his hands on her arms.

'Oh, shit,' she groaned, staring at the place between them where smoothie was currently dripping down the front of him, with little green splatters speckling the front of her.

Archer nearly growled. God damn it! He did not have time for this. He didn't have time to go back to the absurd little house he was renting to change his clothes. He couldn't be late to meet his … his … his *daughter*. He had not factored in time to be run over by a human cyclone carrying kale smoothies!

The growl must have escaped him because the woman's eyes had widened in alarm, her cheeks flushing pink.

'I'm really sorry,' she said. 'I was rushing because I'm running late and I wasn't paying attention and—'

'It's fine,' he bit out, even though it was absolutely not fine. He was going to show up to the most important meeting of his life in a smoothie-soaked shirt. A smoothie-stained father was not the kind of father that instilled confidence. And he was desperately trying to gain some of his usual confidence back.

'It's really not fine. Here let me help you.'

It was then that Archer realized he was still holding the woman's arms and standing far too close to her. He dropped his hands and took a step back, hitting the now closed door behind him.

'I don't need help,' he said, his gaze flicking to the café counter and the long line waiting there. He probably wouldn't even have time for coffee at all now. He would meet his daughter with a stained shirt and a caffeine headache. Perfect. Just perfect.

'Here, let me just dab the worst of it off you.'

The woman had grabbed a fist full of napkins from the nearest table and pressed them into his chest. 'This should help. We'll just soak up the excess and then maybe with a little soap in the bathroom or something…' She talked while she worked, a stream of chatter that he found oddly comforting. The press of her hands, roving over his chest, and the gentle curve of her lips as she spoke distracted Archer enough to dissipate his anger. In fact, he found himself wanting to lean into her touch. He wanted to keep talking to this frenetic woman. He wanted to ask her why she'd been carrying so many drinks. Who were they for? She was dressed more for a workout than the office, her tight leggings hugging the curve of her thighs, the tiny, athletic top revealing a stripe of skin around her stomach, skin that was now speckled with smoothie. Skin that he should probably stop staring at.

God, what was wrong with him? He was supposed to be getting his head in the game for meeting his kid, not trying to pick up an, admittedly beautiful, woman at the local coffee shop.

Archer sighed, pulling his gaze away from the dangerous stripe of skin and back to the woman's concerned face. Her pretty lips were turned down in a pout.

Damn it, Archer. No lips either.

Get. Your. Head. In. The. Game.

'Don't worry about the floor!' a woman called from behind the counter, momentarily distracting him from staring and admonishing himself for staring. 'Joe is grabbing the mop!'

'Okay, thanks Jeanie,' the woman still dabbing at his chest called back. 'Sorry about this.' Her hands kept up their assault on his body. She was standing far too close. He could smell her shampoo. Strawberries? Oh God. He needed to go.

'It happens,' Jeanie said with a shrug.

An older couple walked gingerly around the puddle and Archer. 'You gotta slow down, Iris, honey.'

'I know Estelle,' the redhead—Iris, apparently—said with a sigh. She straightened, finally releasing him from her clean-up efforts. 'You're right.'

'You're a good girl,' Estelle said, giving Iris a little pat on the cheek. The gray-haired man with her gave Archer a bemused smile.

'Rough morning?' he asked.

'It's turning into one, yeah.'

The old man laughed. 'Hopefully it turns around.'

'Come on, Henry,' Estelle said, taking the man's arm. She sipped the smoothie in her hand. 'Looks like I'm going to beat Iris to class today. Good thing I bought my own drink.' She laughed as they walked out.

Iris laughed in return, until her gaze landed back on Archer's face and she quickly sobered. 'Well, I don't think I can fix it.' They both looked down at the bright green stain on his white button-down shirt.

'Of course you can't.' He sighed. None of this was helping. His head was a complete mess before this meeting and the last thing he needed was to be lusting after the town's yoga instructor, or whatever she was.

Iris winced. 'I'm really sorry. How about I buy your drink? What are you having?'

Archer glanced at the line again and every single person was pretending not to be staring at him with a million questions on their faces and doing a terrible job of it. So much for getting in and out of this town without attracting too much attention. He turned his gaze back to Iris and her crinkled brow and downturned mouth. The zip-up hoodie she was wearing over her workout clothes had slipped down one shoulder revealing more skin he shouldn't be staring at.

He had to go.

There was no way he was answering anyone's questions today. Or staying any longer in the presence of this woman who'd already thrown his day for a loop.

'I don't have time,' he said gruffly, and turned away from Iris and her shocked expression and the judgemental line of

LAURIE GILMORE

coffee drinkers. He wasn't here to make friends. He was here to do right by his daughter. Whether he was convinced that *he* was the right thing for her was inconsequential.

'Monster!' The little girl took one look at the green splotch on the front of his shirt, shrieked in horror and ran behind the couch. So, the first meeting with his kid was going about as well as he thought it would.

'He's not a monster, love. That's your dad,' Paula, Cate's mom said, smiling fondly at where the girl had disappeared behind the furniture. Archer had never met Paula, just further evidence that what he'd had with Cate had been casual and fleeting.

Paula was breathing with the help of an oxygen tank, the tube in her nose making it perfectly clear that she needed help with this child. With *his* child. His child who he'd only gotten a brief glimpse of before she'd disappeared.

'Then why does he have green gunk spilling out of him?' the little girl asked, still not emerging from her hiding place.

Archer glanced down at his shirt. She wasn't wrong. The smoothie stain did look suspiciously like monster gunk. 'It's uh … it's just smoothie,' he said, and Paula nodded.

'Did you hear that, Olive? Just a little smoothie spill, that's all.'

'I'm not coming out,' Olive, *his daughter, Olive*, said.

'Okay, dear. You can stay there for now.' Paula smiled at Archer. 'Please, sit. Olive can be shy at first.'

'I'm not shy,' came the little voice. 'I just don't like monsters.'

Archer winced. 'I'm really sorry,' he explained to Paula. 'There was a kale-smoothie related accident this morning and I didn't have time to change.'

'Of course, don't worry,' she said even as her own smiling face had taken on a worried expression. 'I'm sure it's all going to work out.' He could see it then. This *had* to work out. This woman had lost her own daughter and now wasn't well enough to take care of her granddaughter.

This wasn't just about him and his own life, his own selfish needs.

Shit.

He cleared his throat. 'Right. Of course it will. I'm sure Olive and I will get used to each other in no time.'

By the look on Paula's face, she wasn't exactly impressed that Archer had big plans to 'get used to' her granddaughter but frankly it was the best he could promise at the moment. Just saying her name, Olive, was a first. He'd avoided it until now as if not saying it somehow kept all this from being real.

But it was real. She was real. And she was terrified of him.

That damn woman at the coffee shop. If she hadn't poured green goo down the front of him then none of this would be happening. And then she'd had her hands all over him, as though those flimsy paper napkins were doing anything. Not that he was still thinking about Iris's hands on his chest (but he might think about them later). At the moment, he had bigger problems.

And he had no idea what to do about them.

The main one being how to get his daughter out from behind the couch.

She was still hiding over a half hour later while he and her

9

LAURIE GILMORE

grandmother made painful small talk and the lawyer went over the paperwork.

'So, Paris,' Paula said, 'Did you like living there?'

'I *do* like living there,' he said, emphasizing the present tense. He was *not* moving here permanently. 'I love it.' Even as he claimed to love it, his words rang false. How could you love a place you'd barely experienced? Archer's life consisted of the kitchen at Beau Rêve where he was the head chef, a few bars he and the staff frequented after work, and his apartment. Did he love Paris, or did he love the idea of being the best there, a place revered for its cuisine? It didn't matter. Paris was part of the plan. Dream Harbor absolutely was *not*.

He didn't really know how everything would work now that Olive was in the mix, but he would figure it out. His life may have been temporarily derailed by this situation, but it would not be permanent. If everyone involved decided that Olive should stay with him, and that still felt like a big IF, then she would come with him.

He refused to think about the fact that he couldn't even get her to come out from behind the couch, let alone move her to France. One problem at a time.

'Okay, Mr. Baer.' The custody lawyer, Ms. Kaori Kim, turned her attention away from the paperwork and back to him. 'I see you've rented a house in town.'

'Yes. And Olive will have her own bedroom.' He'd rented a cottage on a quiet street. He'd moved in and unpacked and set up a bedroom for a little girl, which he was not at all qualified to do so he'd just bought every pink thing he could find. A shitty approximation of home, but he was hoping it would make Olive feel comfortable.

'And what about employment?' the lawyer asked.

Employment. Archer's stomach dropped. Of course. He needed a job while he was here. And he'd looked. He'd spent his first few days in town scouring the nearby areas for an open chef position and he'd come up empty. His search area was too narrow, but he didn't know what he was going to do with Olive while he worked. He couldn't add a long commute or late hours into the mix. And they had to stay in town for now. They'd all agreed that the transition would be easier for Olive if she could stay near her grandmother and her friends and her school. It made sense but it had left Archer stuck and with no good options for work.

'I have the perfect place!' Paula piped in. 'Gladys is looking for a new cook.' She beamed at him.

'A new cook?' he repeated faintly.

'Yes, at her diner!' Paula's face was lit up like this was a great idea.

'A diner?'

She nodded.

'Wonderful,' Ms. Kim said, slamming her binder shut. 'So, we are all set for a temporary custody arrangement. Mr. Baer, you will be Olive's primary caretaker for the next six months, with Paula Carpenter retaining visitation rights. After the probationary period is up, we will reconvene and make a decision based on the best interest of the child.'

Archer just nodded, unable to do much else. His whole face felt numb. A *diner cook*? That was his life now? A suburban dad, diner cook. He felt sick. How the hell would he ever get his Michelin star working at a diner?

Kaori peeked over the edge of the sofa. 'Is that okay with you, Miss Olive? You're going to live with your dad for a little while and he's going to take good care of you. We're all going to make sure of it.' With that ominous line, Kaori sent Archer a stern glare that pretty clearly said the entire town would be watching him. As if he hadn't already gotten that message this morning at The Pumpkin Spice Café.

He couldn't make out Olive's answer, but he was sure it wasn't good because Kaori's face slipped from all business lawyer to concerned friend.

'I know, sweetie,' she whispered, leaning over the couch cushions. 'But sometimes we have to be brave.'

Kaori and Paula both had tears in their eyes and once again Archer felt like shit for worrying about his own life when they'd just lost someone dear to them. It had only been a couple of months since Olive had lost her mom. And now she was stuck with him.

He got up from his seat and kneeled on the couch beside Kaori. He peeked over the edge and found Olive staring up at him with large, brown eyes. Same as Cate's. His heart clenched.

'Hey, Olive.'

She kept staring but at least she didn't run away, so that was progress.

Archer cleared his throat. 'So, I know this is kinda strange, and I know we just met, but let's just give this a try, okay?'

Her forehead crinkled.

'I think your mom would have liked for us to be … friends,' he tried.

'She would have,' Kaori added. 'I knew your mommy, and she would have loved for you to spend some time with your dad.'

Would she? Archer wanted to say. If that were the case, then why hadn't she told him about Olive? But now wasn't the time to ask. Not with Olive looking at him like that, like she was lost and scared, and he had no idea how to help her.

But Archer did not quit. And he didn't fail.

If he could survive apprenticing in some of the most intense kitchens in the world, then he could surely manage one little girl. Right?

He reached his hand out and for several, tense heartbeats, Olive just looked at it. And then, finally, she placed her tiny hand in his.

It was a start.

Chapter Two

I ris pushed a piece of pancake through the thick, imitation maple syrup covering her plate as she went over the math in her head one more time. It didn't matter how she did it, though, the equation kept coming out the same, she wasn't going to make rent. Again. And while her landlady had been incredibly patient about the last three late payments, Iris was pretty sure she was not likely to be as kind this time. Mostly, because last month she had said, 'Iris, this is the last time! I need that rent money.' So that was pretty clear. Iris was out on her butt if she didn't come up with the rent in the next two days.

She sighed and stared out the large diner window next to her booth. Rain trickled down the glass doing nothing to lift her spirits. Gladys, one of her favorite yoga students and owner of the diner, slid into the booth across from her.

'Why so blue today, hon?'

Iris shrugged. 'Oh, you know, the usual. Unable to make ends meet working in the current gig economy.' At the ripe old age of twenty-six, Iris might need to get one of those careers everyone was always talking about. The kind that came with retirement funds and salaries. The ones that paid in actual US currency and not unlimited classes at the Y and free flowers every month. Although she did love the free flowers.

Gladys frowned.

'But don't worry. I'll figure it out.' Iris forced a smile. 'I always do.' She always did. Another new job, another cheap apartment, another questionable roommate. Iris had been making it on her own for a while now. Ever since her mom moved to Florida with her latest hot and heavy fling, Iris had been pretty much on her own in Dream Harbor. Well, except for her cousin, Rebecca, but Iris couldn't possibly crash on Bex's couch again. The woman had three cats and played the trumpet well into the night. The situation was not conducive to a roommate. Iris simply could not handle listening to her jazz ensemble practice until midnight and then sleep with at least two cats draped across her face. Not again, anyway.

A crash followed by a string of expletives from the kitchen startled Iris from her thoughts.

'What the heck was that?'

Gladys gave her a grim smile. 'The new chef.'

'New *chef*? For the … diner?' Iris glanced around at the worn booths and old linoleum floors. She loved the diner, but it wasn't exactly fine dining.

'We're revamping the place,' Gladys said, straightening in her seat. 'And we need a new menu.'

Iris popped the last bite of pancake into her mouth. 'You're not getting rid of the all-day pancakes, are you?'

'Of course not!'

'Oh, phew.' Iris smiled at the older woman over her mug of bad diner coffee.

'Actually…' Gladys perked up. 'I might have a solution to your problem.'

'I mean … I could pick up some waitressing shifts…'

'No, not that.' Gladys waved her suggestion away. Apparently, after breaking multiple plates per shift and eating her body weight in pancakes, Iris wasn't the top contender for waitressing jobs.

'I have a better idea,' Gladys went on. 'How about nannying?'

Iris leaned back in the booth, waving her hands in front of her like she had to physically fight off Gladys's suggestion. 'Nannying children? No way.'

'Why not? You're so energetic and you're a wonderful teacher. You'd be great at it.'

'No, I'm great at teaching *adults*. Adults that are capable of real human communication. Children are a whole other can of worms.'

Gladys raised her eyebrows like she was not buying Iris's deep and abiding mistrust of children. 'Children are capable of communication.'

Iris shook her head. 'They're unpredictable, and I feel like they're always plotting something. And why are they always so sticky?'

Gladys laughed, shaking her head. 'Kids are just people. I'm sure you could manage one little girl.'

Just people? Just small, incoherent people hellbent on destruction. Iris had spent much of her own childhood with adults. Well, adults and Bex, but she and Bex were nearly the same age. Iris had no younger siblings, no little cousins. She never babysat for the neighborhood kids. And she'd had zero interest in baby dolls.

Her best friend growing up was their sweet upstairs neighbor, Josie, who was seventy years old at the time. She would look after Iris after school while her mom worked, and Iris adored her. She told the best stories and cooked the best spaghetti. To this day, it just didn't feel like Sunday if there wasn't sauce simmering on the stove. Josie taught her that.

Old folks were fonts of wisdom. Small children were just …wild.

'Who would I be working for?' Iris asked, not that she had any plans to take this insane job but now she was curious.

Gladys's gaze slid toward the kitchen. 'Well…'

Another crash and a shout.

Iris's eyes widened. 'The man currently screaming at your staff has a small child?!'

'You heard about what happened to Cate Carpenter?'

'Of course.' Everyone had heard. It was a tragedy. Iris had gone to school with Cate, though the two had never been close friends. Still, hearing about something like that happening to someone so young was always stop-you-in-your-tracks terrible, the kind of story that made you question what the hell you were doing with your own life.

'Well, apparently they found her little girl's father.'

'And the father is the maniac in your kitchen?'

'He's not a maniac,' Gladys said with an exasperated sigh. 'He's a world-renowned chef and he's whipping my restaurant into shape.'

'Hmm.'

Gladys shrugged. 'He needed a job to support his daughter. We were the only place looking for a cook.'

'So, you now have a chef—'

'A world-renowned chef.'

'A world-renowned chef flipping pancakes?'

Gladys grinned. 'He's going to reinvigorate the entire menu.'

'And how does Lionel feel about that?' Iris would have loved to be there when Gladys told her husband that the diner would now be run by a fancy-pants chef. The look on Gladys's face told her that it went about as well as Iris would have expected.

'He'll come around,' she said, folding her hands on the table. 'Now, what do you think about the job?'

'Gladys, I would love to help. Really. But I have zero qualifications to be a nanny.'

'Nonsense! You're CPR certified, you're creative, energetic, fun, responsible…' Gladys ticked her qualities off her fingers. 'And most importantly, you are available.'

Iris shook her head. 'No way. I'm sorry.'

'What other options do you have?'

'I'll probably… I could just…'

Gladys's expression grew more smug the more Iris faltered.

'I will figure it out.' She'd pick up some shifts at Mac's or maybe Jeanie needed a new barista at the PS Café or maybe she could sell a kidney or something. Anything but spending her day with a small child. Kira had already promised to hire her again for the holiday season, so she just had to make it another eight months or so. Easy.

'You're being ridiculous. Did I mention it would be a live-in position?'

'Live-in, like I wouldn't have to pay rent?'

That smug smile grew. 'Exactly. No rent. And the girl is in

kindergarten. She won't even be home for a big portion of the day. You could still teach your classes.'

The math was rapidly shifting. If Iris didn't have to pay rent *and* she could keep teaching her classes *and* get paid for this nanny gig she could maybe, finally, for once in her life get ahead on her finances. Maybe she could stop scrabbling by.

Damn that sneaky Gladys and her good ideas.

'So, what would I actually have to do?'

'Well, I imagine you'd be getting her ready for school and picking her up. You'd be in charge in the afternoons, before her dad gets home, but I'm sure you could manage it, Iris.'

'Why are you pushing this so hard?' This whole town was filled with pushers and busybodies, gossips and well-intentioned folk just dying to get into your business, but Gladys wasn't usually the type to interfere. She had her own husband, two daughters, more grandchildren than Iris could count and this diner to run. She didn't have time for other people's nonsense.

The woman's face softened. 'They're struggling and so are you. Why not help each other out?'

She was about to say that she was not struggling, but the look on Gladys's face shut her right up. Of course she was struggling.

'That little girl lost her mother and the man in there is doing the best he can—'

Another crash cut off Gladys's words but her intention to tug at Iris's overdeveloped heart-strings worked anyway. What was she supposed to say? No, I won't help the poor little girl who lost her mother? That would be terrible.

That, combined with the threat of all-night trumpet practice, pushed Iris into saying, 'Okay, fine. I'll do it.'

Gladys beamed. 'Wonderful! I'll tell Archer. Oh, here he is now.' Gladys's gaze slid to the kitchen door as it slammed open. It was *him*. The angriest man Iris had ever seen emerged from the commotion of the kitchen. If it was possible to scowl with your whole body, that was exactly what he was doing. Even his distinguished, white chef's coat did nothing to soften the glower in his dark eyes. Dirty blond hair flopped over his forehead like he'd been tugging at it and it had finally given up. His brow was furrowed, and his mouth was a disapproving slash across his face. Tension radiated off him. It was the same guy who'd looked like he had wanted to murder her for coating him in kale smoothie. Not exactly the nurturing-dad type.

'Archer!' Gladys called, her voice filled with the good cheer of her success. 'I found you the perfect nanny!'

Archer's storm-cloud glare turned to Iris.

She gave her potential new boss a weak smile and a wave.

If he recognized her from the smoothie incident, he gave no indication. 'Send your résumé,' he barked and then turned and stormed back into the kitchen.

What the hell had she just gotten herself into?

Chapter Three

I t was only quarter to six when Archer got in his car in the back parking lot. The diner opened early for breakfast and lunch but was closed by three. So even after cleaning up and making sure things were ready for the morning, he was heading home earlier than he had in years.

Just one more reminder of how upside down his life was since moving here to this weird town. He used to be headed into work at this time of day, not going home to another silent dinner with his kid.

His kid.

God, he still wasn't used to thinking of her that way. Was that awful? Should he have fallen in love with her right away? He didn't know. He didn't know what was normal. Did people love their red-faced, screaming newborns right away? Maybe they did. Maybe he should have felt some biological pull toward Olive, but so far things had just been incredibly awkward.

He blew out a frustrated sigh as he drove down Main

Street, passing all the charming little stores. Gladys was right. The diner needed a new image if it was going to keep up with this picturesque town.

He pulled down the tree-lined side street where he'd rented the cottage. Never once had he wanted to live on a street like this. Never once had he pictured driving home to his green lawn and picket fence. To his family.

This was nice for some people. But not for Archer.

He was meant to be a chef. To be cooking gourmet food for people who would appreciate it. Not flipping pancakes in small-town America.

Ugh. He rested his head on the steering wheel in the driveway. He just needed a minute before he walked into this life that wasn't his. In this house that was not home. To this child who was a stranger.

He groaned.

He was the adult.

He had to do right by Olive.

Eventually, she would start talking to him, right?

Right. Of course, she would. It hadn't even been a week since she moved in. She just needed more time to adjust. And so did he. Archer unfolded himself from the driver's seat and cut across the front lawn to the door. He had the insane urge to knock on this door that didn't feel like his. But it was his, at least for the moment, so he went in.

'Mr. Baer, you're home.' Kimmy, the current babysitter, jumped up from her spot on the floor where she'd been playing Candy Land with Olive. 'See ya, kid.' She ruffled Olive's hair before grabbing her purse and meeting Archer by the door.

'Thanks, Kimmy.'

'No problem. You can Venmo me.'

'Right, sure.'

'Do you need me tomorrow? Because I have drama-club practice. I got the lead in *The Duke and I*. Can you believe it?!'

What Archer couldn't believe was how a high school could perform a *Bridgerton* novel, but that didn't really matter.

'I'm in the process of hiring a nanny, so we won't be needing you as much.'

'Okay, great. See you around, Olive.'

The girl just watched Kimmy leave, her large brown eyes tracking the young woman's departure. When he'd first seen Olive, her resemblance to Cate had startled Archer. She was like a miniature version of the woman he'd once known, half a decade ago. Dark hair that framed her round face and fell just below her chin with bangs sweeping across her forehead, big eyes that seemed to take him in and immediately found him lacking. Although that part was unique to Olive. Cate had seemed to like him just fine.

'So…' Archer stepped farther into the small living room. 'Would you like me to play with you? Uh … Candy Land, I mean.' He gestured feebly toward the board.

Olive blinked.

'Or we could do something else. I could … uh … put on a movie or something? Or we could color.' Color? Archer hadn't even held a crayon since he was eight. But at this point he would do literally anything rather than just stare at each other. Ever since that first disastrous meeting, he got the impression Olive was tolerating his presence, that she wasn't at all convinced in his ability to do this. So that made two of them.

Olive shook her head, crawling up onto the couch. She pulled her ratty old blanket around her. Her grandmother had explained that it was her blankie from when she was a baby and under no circumstances should he try to put it away or wash it, and if it was ever lost, neither he nor Olive would sleep again. So, no pressure there.

Olive hugged her stuffed wombat and grabbed the remote, flipping on her favorite thing to watch, baking competitions.

A small flicker of something lit in Archer's chest.

Maybe she was his after all.

A knock at the door gave him something to do besides stare at Olive. He went to answer it, thinking maybe Kimmy forgot something, but it wasn't Kimmy. He should have known better.

'Hello, Archer!' Nancy, her wife Linda, and the custody lawyer, Kaori, stood on his doorstep. The first time this happened, he had been alarmed that he was already in some kind of trouble, but this was the third time in four days that the three women had shown up. And on the one day they hadn't made it, Estelle, whom he'd met briefly at the café, and Gladys had just 'dropped by because they were in the neighborhood'.

Archer had learned that Nancy was a retired kindergarten teacher who apparently saw the wellbeing of every child in the town, including all her former students, as her own personal business. Linda mostly seemed to be along for the ride and to point out how little progress he'd made. Throw the woman responsible for his custody case into the mix, and they made quite the welcoming committee.

This time Nancy was carrying a casserole dish of epic proportions. How many people did she think he needed to feed?

'Brought you a little dinner,' she said, hefting the dish into his arms.

He'd already failed at convincing them that he was a chef and that he was perfectly capable of cooking dinner, so this time he just mumbled his thanks.

'How's Olive?' Kaori asked, peering past him into the house.

'She's fine.'

'Still not talking to you, huh?' Linda said, shuffling her way past him.

'She'll get there,' Nancy said, patting his arm as she also scooted her way into his house. He didn't fight it. He'd already learned it was best to let them in, to prove that Olive was alive and well, and then they'd be on their way.

He sighed as he watched the two older women coo over Olive, feeling absurdly jealous when she smiled at them and answered their questions about her day, opening up as soon as they flanked her on the couch.

'We're all on your side,' Kaori said.

'Yeah,' he huffed a laugh. 'You all clearly have a lot of faith in me. There hasn't been a day since Olive moved in that someone hasn't checked on her.'

Kaori stared at him like he was missing some critical brain cells.

'Of course we have,' she said. 'We love that girl, and frankly, we don't know all that much about you.'

'Fair.'

'But Cate apparently thought you were okay, so I'm giving you the benefit of the doubt.'

Archer leaned his head back against the doorframe, the evening sun warming his face. 'She thought I was *okay*?'

'Actually, she never talked about you at all.'

He winced. 'Ouch.'

Kaori shrugged. 'The one thing she did say was she thought you were destined for bigger things. She didn't want to stand in your way. Olive was *her* dream. She didn't want to derail yours.'

There were tears in Kaori's eyes when he looked at her again. 'I'm really sorry,' he said.

Kaori sniffed, wiping her eyes with the back of her hand. 'She was a wonderful person, Archer. And Olive is wonderful, too.'

He cleared the emotion from his throat. 'I know. I'm … trying.'

Kaori studied him carefully before patting his shoulder. 'It takes a village to raise a child and we're that village.' She held his gaze. 'And we're watching you.'

'Comforting,' he said, dryly.

Kaori smiled. 'It should be. We're looking out for Olive. And for you, too. Just accept the help, Archer. It makes the whole thing easier.'

She moved past him and got a big hug from Olive. Archer closed the door and went into the kitchen to find space among the other casseroles in the freezer for the latest addition.

Accepting help was not exactly his strong suit, but for Olive, he'd try. Not that he had much of a choice. He was pretty sure these women could take him down, if necessary. He was going to try to make sure it wasn't necessary.

Finding a small space, he shoved the casserole into the overstuffed freezer and pushed the door shut.

There. Help accepted.

28

Chapter Four

The next day, Iris showed up at Archer's house at exactly the time he'd said to. Give or take ten minutes. But by the way he was glaring at her it was like she was an hour late or something.

'You're late,' he said, arms folded across his chest. He was blocking the entire doorway like maybe this ten-minutes-late transgression was enough to get her fired—or not hired—in the first place. She'd only agreed to come this afternoon to meet him and Olive. She hadn't even really agreed to take the job yet. She wasn't desperate enough to just move in with a guy she'd never met. Not again, anyway. The last time had been a guy she found off a flier hung up in the diner. He had supposedly been looking for a roommate but what he actually wanted to do was steal her underwear while she was at work.

She wasn't looking for another panty-stealer situation.

'Sorry about that. My class overran.' She'd barely had time to get out of her swimsuit and get over here. Her hair still dripped down her back in a wet braid and the early spring breeze raised goosebumps on her bare arms. She'd forgotten her sweatshirt at the gym. Again.

She pulled her braid over her shoulder and squeezed it out on the front step. When she looked up, Archer was still glaring. Maybe he was still mad about the whole smoothie thing?

'Olive needs to be picked up from school at two-thirty.'

Iris met his glare with a glare of her own. 'Well, *if* I take the job, I will move my class time to accommodate Olive's schedule.' She tipped up her chin and waited. Was he going to let her in the house or was the entire interview going to take place on his front step?

His eyes lingered on hers a moment longer before flicking down to the wet spot her hair was leaving on her shirt, directly over her left boob. She would have thought he was being a pervert until the stern line of his mouth tightened in disapproval. Apparently, her uniform of a tank top and leggings and perpetually damp hair wasn't meeting his standards. The same thing had happened at the café. She'd thought he was checking her out and then she'd offered to buy his drink and he couldn't have run away fast enough.

Well, good thing nothing had happened since he was about to become her boss. Maybe.

His gaze returned to her face, hard and assessing. God, she could just imagine him in a kitchen shouting at his poor sous chefs like every chef she'd seen in the movies. Demanding perfection. Demanding precision. A small shiver ran over her skin at the thought of what it might feel like to please a man like that.

She shook that entirely unhelpful thought away. If he wanted perfection from her, he was going to be highly disappointed. Iris was curlicues, not straight lines. She was always late, except when she was teaching (she wouldn't do that to her students). She had a trail of half-finished hobbies and partially read books long enough that she couldn't see the end of it. She was good enough, but never perfect. And if her usual pattern held, she wouldn't be at this job for longer than six months. Maybe she should just go now and save them both the trouble.

But he finally relented in his perusal of her appearance and stepped aside. She reluctantly followed him into a narrow entryway that led directly into a cozy living room where a small girl was perched on the couch watching what appeared to be a cake-baking show. Iris kicked her flip-flops off by the door with the other shoes. A pair of particularly tiny sneakers made nerves flutter in her belly. How could she be responsible for someone so small?

This was clearly a bad idea.

The dad was an asshole. The kid was too tiny. And Iris was way too unqualified.

She'd just have to take her chances with Bex.

She opened her mouth to say so when she caught a glimpse of Archer watching his daughter. He looked completely … perplexed. Like a man caught in a maze with absolutely no idea how to get out. He looked sad and a little panicked. He looked like he needed help.

He caught her looking and quickly schooled his features back into scary-boss-man mode.

'Let's talk in the kitchen first and then you can meet Olive.'

'Okay, sure.'

Olive didn't even look up from her show as they walked past her. The kitchen and living room were essentially one room with a small island separating them. Iris sat at the island

and Archer stood facing her, his hands on the counter. His sleeves were rolled up, revealing bare forearms.

'Shouldn't you have a spatula or something tattooed on your arms?' she asked.

His eyebrows rose. 'Shouldn't I have what? Why would I?'

Iris shrugged. 'I don't know. Isn't that like a chef thing? To have a lot of tattoos of kitchen tools and meat and stuff?'

'Meat and stuff?' His mouth twitched, as though he was almost amused but refused to show it.

'Don't pretend you don't know what I'm talking about. The whole bad-boy chef thing? Unless your tattoos are somewhere else…' She gestured toward his body and her hand froze in mid-air at the horrified look on his face.

Good lord, what was she even saying right now?

'Uh … sorry. Never mind.'

'How about we discuss the job?' There was that just barely amused quirk of his mouth again.

Iris nodded, relieved to think about something other than if Archer was in fact a bad-boy chef type and if his broad chest was covered in ink, or maybe his back…

'Iris?'

'Huh?' She blinked back into reality. The reality in which Archer was asking her questions about nannying his daughter. The one that had nothing to do with his body. Not that she cared about his body. Not that she was still thinking about the feel of his firm chest under her hands as she had cleaned up the smoothie. His body was completely irrelevant. As was his face. And his large hands that were still spread flat on the countertop in front of her. Gosh, those were long fingers. Fingers that were probably capable of all sorts of tricks…

Iris cleared her throat. 'Sorry, I missed that.'

Archer was looking at her again with that expression, like he was disappointed he'd even invited her here. He must be just as desperate as she was. Just as desperate as Gladys had said, if Iris was his best option.

'I asked if you had worked with children before.'

'Oh … uh … not exactly.'

'Not exactly children?'

'Well, I work a lot with seniors who are also a vulnerable population,' she said, repeating the line she'd rehearsed with Bex last night with a tense smile.

Archer gave a small nod, as though he wasn't quite sure if he should believe her bullshit. Not that it was total bullshit, just the normal amount of interview spin. She was sure her seniors would just love to be compared to a kindergartener, but as much as she hated to admit it, she could really use this job.

'I teach classes at the Y.'

The *teach* part seemed to get his attention so she kept going. 'I'm CPR and first-aid certified and … uh … I'm creative and…'

What else had Gladys listed?

'And I'm available.' Why did that make her cheeks flush hot? 'I mean, I'm available to start work right away.' She smiled again and met his stare. And for a brief second, his expression softened, and she thought maybe she'd passed the test. Until he tore his gaze away, his mouth reset in its grim line.

'Coffee?' he asked.

'Sure.'

He turned away to pour her a mug, giving her a much-needed reprieve from his stare.

'How do you take it?'

'Milk and sugar, please.'

He set it all out on the counter and as she stirred in her milk and sugar, she noticed he drank his black. With the intensity radiating off this man, she felt that a nice cup of chamomile would be a better choice, but it probably wasn't her place to say.

'So, maybe we should go over the responsibilities of the job?' she suggested as she sipped her coffee.

'Right. Of course.' He set down his mug, his gaze traveling past her to where Olive sat on the couch before flicking back to Iris.

'I will need to leave before five every morning, which is why I proposed a live-in situation, if that works for you. Then you will be responsible for getting Olive up and ready for her day and getting her to school. Like I said before, she needs to be picked up at two-thirty. *Promptly*. I typically get home around six.'

He glanced at Olive again and then lowered his voice.

'She doesn't talk.'

'What do you mean, she doesn't talk?'

An expression like shame mixed with frustration crossed his face. 'She *can* talk. She just doesn't talk to me.' He raked his hand through his hair. 'She's in therapy, and obviously this is really hard and traumatic, and I just want...' Again he looked like he wanted to scream his frustrations but instead swallowed them down. 'I just want some stability for her. I want someone to be here for her when I'm not. It's why I thought it best if you ... if the nanny lived with us... But if that's a problem...?'

He was practically whispering now and they'd both leaned in across the counter. She was close enough to see the worry in his eyes, the crease between his brows, the way his hair stood up from his hands tugging on it throughout the day. And looking at him, worried and tired and scared, something warm and tender settled in Iris's gut.

And Iris always listened to her gut.

'We'll make it work,' she said, the smile soft and gentle around her lips in an attempt to coax out the same from him. The most she got was a slight relaxing around his shoulders, but she'd take it for now. 'I agree that me living here would help Olive feel more comfortable around me. And this way I can't be late for work.'

A surprised laugh escaped him.

Success. Iris grinned.

'Thank you. I really…' He cleared his throat. 'It's been a rough week.'

'I can imagine.'

He was looking at her again, but now there was something just a little bit softer in his gaze. In fact, his eyes, now that they weren't glaring, were actually a quite lovely, warm brown. And when he wasn't tugging his hair back, it flopped gently over his forehead. And she could just imagine that mouth softening even more, smiling and lighting up his face. And then it hit her.

Archer Baer, her potential new boss, was hot.

And that was very bad news.

She couldn't have the hots for her boss! That was bad. Very bad, Iris.

His lips tipped up in the corner, giving her just the tiniest glimpse of a smile, but it was enough. It was enough to show the slight indent of a dimple high on his left cheek.

NO! Why? She'd just agreed to move in with this man and

now he had a dimple?! And kind eyes. And touchable hair. And any number of hidden tattoos just waiting to be uncovered.

Iris had clearly made a grave error.

She sat back abruptly on her stool.

'Everything okay?' Archer asked, straightening again.

'Yes. Okay. Totally A-Okay.'

He was back to looking at her like she was a little nutty, which helped cool her feelings a bit, but then his gaze slipped past her again and his eyes widened in alarm.

Iris turned to see what was causing him such concern.

The couch was empty and the front door was wide open.

Olive was gone.

Chapter Five

Somehow, Archer's shitty day had gone from bad to worse in the blink of an eye. One minute he was trying desperately not to find the new nanny charming, and the next his daughter was missing. Again. One week in, and he couldn't even keep track of the damn kid.

'Oh my God! Where did she go?' Iris's worried voice cut through his thoughts. He would have been more panicked if this hadn't already happened three times since they'd moved in.

'I have a pretty good idea.' He stormed past Iris and out the open door, but he could sense her following behind him. Hopefully she still wanted the job after this little demonstration of what she'd be dealing with.

When Gladys told him she would help find him the perfect nanny, he'd assumed she'd meant someone like herself. Someone older and sweet, someone grandmotherly. Not someone like Iris Fraser. Someone young and beautiful, who showed up to a job interview in leggings and a wet tank top and flip-flops. Someone who'd already had her hands all over him after dousing him in smoothies. Someone who smelled like strawberries.

He didn't know if he should be angry or turned on. No, that wasn't true. He knew he was one hundred percent not supposed to be turned on by the nanny. In fact, he was pretty sure that was the number-one rule of having a nanny. But that rule would have been a lot easier to follow if Iris looked more like Mrs. Doubtfire and less like, well, less like herself.

He raked his hand through his hair as he crossed the lawn to the neighbor's house with the inconveniently attractive nanny hot on his heels. He probably shouldn't hire her. He should find someone else. Someone more suitable. But he was desperate. The diner had been operating on autopilot without him, but he needed to actually start working there full-time if he was going to transform it.

The kitchen was the one place he felt even remotely competent anymore. He needed to get back at it and he needed help with this kid.

He stopped dead in his tracks.

Iris crashed into his back.

'Oh!' she cried. 'Sorry.'

He glanced over his shoulder and found her smiling weakly.

'I wasn't expecting you to stop so suddenly. What's the matter?'

Archer just shook his head, listening. It was a sound he'd only heard from a distance since he moved here. The sound of his daughter's laughter.

It was coming from the neighbor's backyard, so he cut down the driveway and knocked on their wood fence.

'Oh. Hey, Archer. I was just about to escort Miss Olive home.' Noah, his new neighbor, smiled at him. Olive sat perched on his shoulders, the smile Archer was sure she had on her face a moment ago was long gone.

'Thanks, Noah.'

'My pleasure.' Noah peeked around Archer's shoulder. 'Hey, Iris. What are you doing here?'

Archer should have figured they would know each other. Everyone in this town knew one another. It was unsettling.

'Hi, Noah. I'm uh…' She glanced at Archer and back up at Olive. She was probably calculating how difficult this job was going to be. He was sure a mute runaway was more than she'd bargained for. 'I'm interviewing for the position of nanny.'

'Wow, Olive. You hear that?' Noah tapped the little girl's leg where it dangled over his shoulder. 'Iris might be your nanny. That'd be cool. Iris is very cool.'

Iris smiled. 'Hey Olive.' She waved, but Olive continued her stare, tilting her head to the side as though she was considering the idea of Iris. Archer wondered what his daughter thought of her. That should matter, right? He shouldn't hire someone the little girl didn't like.

'What does a nanny do?' Olive asked, and the sound of her voice froze every muscle in Archer's body. He didn't blink. He didn't breathe for fear that she would remember he was there and clam up again.

Iris shrugged. 'I figure we'll just hang out together. Maybe go to some fun places. You can drive, right?'

Olive shook her head, the giggle he'd heard earlier returning. His heart was uncomfortable in his chest like it was too big to fit anymore.

'I'm too little to drive.'

39

Iris frowned like she didn't believe it and Archer had to bite down on his own smile. 'Are you sure? You have to be about six-foot five at least.' Iris gestured to her up on her perch and Olive laughed again.

'I'm on Noah's shoulders!' She patted the man on his head and Noah grinned.

'Oh! You're right. Sorry, my mistake. I guess I will drive us to the fun places.'

'What kind of places?'

'Do you like to swim?'

'I don't know how to swim.'

'Then I'll teach you.'

Archer was about to cut in that they'd hadn't agreed on swimming lessons, but Olive's face lit up at the suggestion and his heart just about gave out at the sight. Iris could teach her to sky dive if it made Olive look like that.

'You will?!'

'Sure. Oh. I mean, if your dad says it's okay.' Iris glanced back at him for the first time since this interaction began and it was like the fun went out of the party.

Olive's smile slipped.

Archer cleared his throat. 'I'm sure we can figure something out.'

Iris looked back up at Olive with a grin. 'That's dad talk for: if you ask enough times, I will totally give in and let you do it,' she said with a wink and Olive's eyes widened.

'Why don't we go back inside and discuss it, okay?' Archer asked and Olive nodded, which, frankly, felt like progress.

Noah lowered her to the ground and Archer decided not to feel jealous when she gave him a big squeeze of a hug goodbye.

'Come on, kid. Let's get to know each other.' Iris started back down the driveway and Olive followed. And just seeing them walking away together, side by side, so naturally, Archer knew she was hired. Hopefully, she still wanted to be.

'Thanks again, Noah. Sorry she keeps turning up here.'

'We don't mind at all,' he said with a grin. 'Sorry she keeps scaring the shit out of you.'

Archer blew out a long sigh and Noah patted his arm.

'You're doing the best you can. She'll get used to things soon.'

'Yeah. Thanks again.'

Noah disappeared back into the yard he shared with his girlfriend, Hazel. Archer hadn't known when he picked the house that Hazel had known Cate, but he was happy Olive had a familiar face next door. That is, until she kept disappearing to go find her.

He just prayed she never strayed farther than that.

One week into parenting and he didn't think his heart could take it.

Chapter Six

'So, you're just moving in with this guy and his kid?' Bex asked from where she was sprawled out on Iris's bed among half of her wardrobe—the other half being already stuffed in a duffle bag.

'Basically, yes.' Iris held up an old sweater to her chest. 'Keep, donate, or trash?'

'Trash,' Bex and Kira said in unison. Iris's gig at the Christmas-tree farm was over for the season, but she'd kept Kira as a friend.

'Don't subject the less fortunate to that,' Kira said with a laugh. She spun around in Iris's desk chair.

Iris tossed the sweater in the trash pile.

'Explain to me again, how you, the woman who finds children terrifying, got a job as a nanny?' Kira asked, still spinning.

'I'm not terrified of them.'

'That was your exact word! I believe you said they were "terrifying, unpredictable and perpetually sticky".'

'Ew.' Bex frowned. 'Perpetually sticky?'

'Well, they are,' Iris said, adding a holey tank top to the toss pile. 'Sticky, that is. But Olive is just one little girl. I'm sure I can handle it. She's not scary at all,' she lied. Iris was plenty worried about this new gig, but she wasn't about to let her friends know that. Then they'd only talk her out of it, and she *really* needed this job. And the free housing that came with it.

Kira had stopped spinning so she could pin Iris with a disbelieving stare.

'You don't think I can handle one child?' Iris asked, flicking her braid over her shoulder.

'Of course I do. But I told you, you're welcome to come stay with me if you can't make rent. We have space.'

Iris frowned. She appreciated her friend's offer. She really did. But staying with Kira and Bennett in their love nest just didn't sound appealing. Kira had been over the moon happy since he'd moved in, but Iris was not about to be a third wheel in their relationship. Or a witness to the constant sex they were probably having, judging by how much Kira smiled these days.

'It's not like we run around naked all the time or anything,' Kira said, reading Iris's mind.

Bex snorted.

'Naked or not, I'd feel weird. Although, I do appreciate the offer.'

'Hey, I offered, too.' Bex tossed her another sweater Iris didn't remember buying. Donate pile.

'And I appreciated that, too, but you know our … schedules don't match up.' That was the nicest way Iris could think to say that she couldn't tolerate listening to trumpet scales at 1am. She was weird like that.

'Look, I love you both and I am incredibly lucky to have so many options, but I think this is the best one.'

'Because he's hot?' Kira asked, one dark eyebrow raised mischievously.

'Is he?' Iris said, but her suddenly high voice gave her away. 'I hadn't noticed.'

Kira laughed. 'The entire female—and half the male—population of Dream Harbor has noticed.'

Iris shrugged casually, like she hadn't been thinking about Archer's unfortunate hotness ever since her interview two days ago. 'Well, I hadn't noticed. I guess he's not my type.'

'Mmm-hmm. I know exactly how that lie goes,' Kira said with a knowing smirk. She'd said the same thing about Bennett and look how that turned out. Now they were practically attached at the face.

'Don't you have flowers to plant or something?' Iris shot back.

'Not right now, no. But thanks for your concern.'

Bex laughed. 'Uh oh, Kira. I think you hit a nerve.' She sat up and started folding what was left of Iris's clothes. Iris had grown up with her cousin as practically a sibling. They'd lived next door to each other, each girl with just their mother. The foursome had done pretty much everything together. And so she had no qualms telling Bex to shut it.

But she was here helping her pack, so Iris decided to be nice.

'She didn't hit a nerve. I feel very good about my decision.'

Her friend and her cousin stared at her with matching incredulous expressions on their faces.

'I do! I told you, I can handle it.'

'But do you want to?' Kira's expression softened. 'Are you sure you want to *nanny*?'

Iris fought her urge to shrug and instead rolled back her shoulders in a stance of faux confidence. 'Yes, I do. I'm telling you, it's going to be easy. She's at school most of the day. And I get a free room! Think of all the money I will save. I figure, I do this until she's out of school for the summer and then I'll let Archer know he has to make other arrangements. It's a *good* plan.'

It was a good plan. She'd given it a lot of thought. She'd help out Archer and Olive for a few months until they got settled into their new life together, she'd save up some money, and then she'd move on. Like she always did. She'd even help Archer find a replacement for her when the time came.

Even she could handle dealing with one kid for a few months.

How hard could it be? Sure, Olive had a tendency to run off, and yes, she didn't speak to her father yet, but now Iris knew right where she ran off to and Olive spoke to *her* so that wouldn't be a problem.

And besides, plenty of people didn't love their jobs. This was something she had to do to make ends meet. Just for now. Just to catch up on a few bills, to save first and last month's rent for a better apartment, to fill the gaps her other jobs left in her bank account.

Iris could get one kid ready for school and pick her up each day. It's not like she had to be her parent, something Iris had zero interest in, in general. 'Mom' was not a job she ever planned on having. But nanny wasn't *mom*. She just had to keep Olive alive for a few hours a day.

It would be easy.

That was her new motto, and she was sticking to it.

'Okay, if you say so. I just want to make sure you're not making any rash decisions,' Kira said.

Iris laughed. 'Are you serious right now?'

Kira's straight face cracked, a giggle spilling out. 'I was trying to be!' She stood from her chair and gave Iris a hug. 'Just don't buy any real estate without looking at it.'

'We don't all have trust funds, babe.'

Kira grinned. 'Not anymore. That thing is long gone.'

Iris laughed. 'Thanks for helping with the packing.'

'No problem. I do have to go, though. Farm life calls!'

'Of course it does. See you at yoga tonight?'

'Wouldn't miss it!' Kira called as she made her way down the hall and out of Iris's apartment.

Iris turned her attention back to her cousin, expecting her to continue finding flaws in her plan, but Bex just put the last shirt in her bag.

'Be careful with this guy,' she said as she stood up from the bed.

'What does that mean?'

'It means, be careful. You're in a vulnerable position here, Iris. Don't let him take advantage of you.'

'Take advantage of me? Bex…'

'I'm serious,' she said, throwing up her hands. 'Mr. Fancy-Pants-Chef is used to being in charge, used to getting what he wants from his employees … things can go sideways quickly.'

Iris opened her mouth to argue but then shut it. She thought about Archer's disapproving looks, about the yells and crashes she heard coming from the kitchen at the diner, about his reminders to be *prompt*. Was Bex right? Was he the kind of guy who would also think he could take liberties with the nanny? Did he corner unsuspecting waitresses? Did he use his intimidating presence to get whatever he wanted from people?

And she would be living in his home.

There was no HR to report to if things got weird between them.

She shook herself. 'I googled him. Not a single complaint or rumor or whistle blower claiming he ever did anything untoward. His record is spotless, Bex. It's fine.'

'Hmm,' her cousin looked suspicious. 'He's spotless or he's very good at not getting caught being a dirtbag.'

'Bex…'

'Just take this. It will make me feel better.'

'What is this? Pepper spray?'

Bex grinned. 'Yep. In case he gets fresh.'

'Gets fresh? Bex, what are you, eighty-five?'

She shrugged. 'I should probably stop attending your classes for seniors.'

'Probably.'

'But I like them.'

'Me too. And don't worry, if Archer Baer tries anything with me, you can lead the mob of angry senior ladies that will be sure to hunt him down.'

Bex's smile grew. 'Perfect.'

Iris tossed the pepper spray onto the bed, a little afraid to be holding it, and gave Bex a hug. 'Thanks for looking out for me.'

'Someone has to, now that your mom ran off to Florida.'

'She didn't run off. She relocated to be with…'

'Gabriel,' Bex said, grimly.

'Right, Gabriel,' Iris echoed. She hadn't really bothered

committing his name to memory. Gabriel was the latest in her mother's long line of short-lived boyfriends, but he was the man currently making her mom happy, so who was she to judge? Her mother loved falling in love. She just wasn't very good at staying in it. Iris and Bex had a bet on how long this one would last. Iris figured he'd be gone by the end of the year.

'Do you think she'll come back after they split?' Bex asked, pulling away from their hug.

'I don't know. She likes the warm weather so I wouldn't be surprised if she stays. How's your mom?'

'Same as ever.' Bex's mom, Iris's Aunt Heather, had gone a completely different route, sworn off men and now lived in an ashram in Calabasas that Iris still wasn't fully convinced wasn't a cult.

'Tell her I said hi.'

'Will do.'

'Thanks, Bex.'

'Anything for my little cousin.'

'I'm two months younger than you.'

'Still counts.' She grabbed her raincoat off the back of the chair and headed for the door. 'Love you, bye!'

'Bye!'

Iris stood in her nearly empty apartment and couldn't help but smile. She had people who loved her and a new plan. And if there was one thing Iris loved, it was a new start. Maybe that was why she changed jobs so often. She loved a fresh start and spring was just the time to do it! Iris was ready to bloom like all the little buds on the trees still hiding from the chill.

Whatever the reason (certainly not the hotness of her new boss) Iris was excited for something new (or so she planned to keep telling herself).

49

Chapter Seven

Archer stood in the middle of the diner kitchen, assessing his staff. Maribel, Jess, and Cyrus stood to attention in front of him. Two waitresses and a cook. Maribel was probably in her mid-thirties, a mom with kids who Archer should probably pay attention to if he wanted to figure out this parenting thing, though so far, the woman had been unnervingly quiet, following his directions without complaint. Jess looked like she was just out of high school. Too chatty, too clumsy, but the customers seemed to like her. And Cyrus, well, Cyrus had worked here forever.

They'd closed the diner for the morning in order to get some much-needed cleaning and organizing done. The space still wasn't up to his standards and the trio looked exhausted. And the kitchen still looked like a mess.

Archer cursed under his breath and rubbed the back of his neck. How would he ever turn this diner into something resembling a place he'd have pride in? How could he ever call this *his* kitchen?

He couldn't.

And he wouldn't. This diner gig was just a temporary fix until he could find something better. Or until this whole custody thing was sorted and he could go back to his career in Paris. He pushed thoughts of the pristine kitchen in his old restaurant out of his mind. Crying in front of his staff wouldn't help anything.

It had been nearly two weeks since he'd moved here, and Olive had still only spoken about ten words to him. And all he could think was that she hated him and he was failing her.

But failing was not an option. It never had been for him.

When he hadn't made his middle-school soccer team in sixth grade, he'd practiced every night until it got too dark to see the ball in front of him, and he'd sure as hell made the team the following year. When he'd gotten a C in sophomore geometry, he'd convinced the teacher to give him enough extra credit to bring his grade up to an A by the end of the semester. And when he'd decided he wanted to be a chef, he'd attended four grueling years of culinary school, worked for years in kitchens doing every menial task available: washing dishes, preparing vegetables, working his way slowly up the entire brigade hierarchy. He had no time for anything else. He cooked and he slept.

But he sure as hell didn't fail.

When he'd taken this absurd diner job, the owner, Gladys, had promised him he could re-imagine the menu and have full run of the kitchen. The kitchen that was a complete disaster. Honestly, Archer didn't know how the place had passed its health inspections all these years.

But he was in charge now. He'd get the diner in good working order. He'd get his daughter to speak to him. And once he convinced the lawyers that he was a capable father and he gained full custody, he'd bring her to France with him and continue on the path he'd laid out for himself years ago.

'Tomorrow, we work on cleaning out the walk-in freezer,' he announced, and the three visibly slumped, but no one protested. 'And we need to get more food prepped before opening. It will make the breakfast rush go smoother.'

Cyrus nodded. The old man had been working here as a line cook since the place opened in the seventies. And with that level of seniority, he had pushed back against Archer's ideas all day.

'Hey boss?'

'Yes, Cyrus?' Archer wiped the sweat from his brow with his forearm.

'Gladys says we're changing the menu.'

'That's right.'

Cyrus shook his head with a laugh. 'The town ain't gonna like that.'

Archer frowned. 'The town will like it. Elevated comfort food. What's not to like about that?'

'The elevated part,' Cyrus said with a chuckle.

Jess started to laugh, too, but caught herself and clapped a hand over her mouth. It was possible Archer had raised his voice one too many times today.

'People will like it. Trust me. I know what I'm doing.' Maybe he didn't know anything about raising a child, but he sure as hell knew food. He knew the menu would be delicious. People would like it. 'I've worked in restaurants all over Europe. I think I can handle a new diner menu.'

Cyrus's bushy white brows rose. 'You might know what those European folks like, but I know Dream Harbor. If you take away people's favorite pancakes, especially the mayor's, well…' He let the threat trail off, just shaking his head in pity for the man that took away the town's pancakes.

Archer scoffed. They were diner pancakes. How could there be anything special about them? 'You leave the menu to me.'

The old man shrugged. 'It's your funeral.'

Jess giggled again and even Maribel cracked a smile.

'You're dismissed.'

Cyrus gave him a mock salute and the women wandered off to gather their things, chatting together quietly. Archer gave one last look around the kitchen before turning out the lights for the night.

***

'What do you mean, they sent the pancakes back?' Archer growled at Maribel even though he knew it wasn't her fault. Even though it made him an asshole. Even though Cyrus was right and he sure as hell wouldn't be admitting that anytime soon.

'The customer didn't like the pancakes,' she repeated her voice a little quieter than before.

Archer ran a hand angrily through his hair, hard enough to hurt. They were in the middle of the breakfast rush and this was the third time this morning that someone had complained about the pancakes. About his new pancakes. The ones he'd made with ricotta, sprinkled with confectioner's sugar and topped with a creamy lemon sauce. The ones that were objectively delicious. It was the one menu change he'd implemented so far, and they'd been sent back three times. *Three times.*

He avoided Cyrus's smug expression as he wiped his hands on a dish towel and tossed it on the counter.

'Who?' he demanded, already walking toward the dining room. Maribel scurried along behind him.

'Table two. The mayor, I did warn you…'

Archer pushed through the swinging doors and stormed toward table two. A man with glasses and a hideous tie smiled up at him.

'Was there a problem with the meal, sir?' Archer asked, swallowing down everything he wanted to yell at this mayor who was apparently some kind of pancake connoisseur.

'Oh, hello!' the mayor said, sticking out his hand. 'You must be the new chef. I'm the mayor of this fine town. Pete Kelly.'

'Archer Baer.' He shook the man's hand and attempted to organize his facial features into something other than a scowl.

'And this is my daughter, Hazel.'

'Hey, Archer.'

Archer blinked. His neighbor was the mayor's daughter? 'Uh … hello.'

'How's Olive doing? Noah mentioned she stopped by again.'

Stopped by, like his daughter was just paying a social visit and not continuously trying to escape him.

'Yeah, sorry about that.'

Hazel waved away his apology. 'Don't worry about it. We love Olive.'

His neighbors loved Olive. He should love Olive. She was his daughter for Christ's sake. He shook off the thought. The middle of his new restaurant (he refused to call it a diner even in his own mind or he would surely have a breakdown) was not the place to unpack every anxiety he was having about his inability to bond with his kid.

'Right. Okay, thank you.' He turned back to the mayor. 'The pancakes weren't to your liking?'

The mayor smiled up at him with pity. 'I'm a simple man, Archie. May I call you Archie?'

He went on before Archer could tell him absolutely not.

'I'm a simple man, Archie, and I think I just preferred the old pancakes. Do you still have those?'

Archer swallowed his frustrated sigh. It had been the same thing with the other complaints. They liked the old pancakes better. Could he make them those?

And the answer should be no. No, he could not make them sub-par pancakes because this was his kitchen now and he wasn't going to cook them pancakes that tasted like roofing tiles served with maple-flavored corn syrup.

But the actual reason he had to say no was that he didn't have the recipe for the old pancakes. And somehow no one else did either. Which was obviously bullshit, but Archer couldn't get the recipe from any member of his staff.

Cyrus swore up and down that the old cook, Martha, was always on pancake duty and that he was purely an omelet man. He'd pointed Archer to an ancient binder filled with the diner's old recipes, but Archer hadn't had time to go through it yet.

So, for the other complaints, he'd whipped up a simple pancake batter and served those. The customers hadn't dared complain again, but he'd noticed the plates came back with plenty of pancake left on them. Apparently, they weren't up to Dream Harbor standards either. Which was insane. They were just pancakes! Archer could make them a souffle with his eyes closed if they wanted, but somehow a simple recipe of flour, baking soda, eggs and milk wasn't good enough for them?

It was like he was caught in one of those nightmares where you're in school but can't remember how to open your locker or tie your shoes. The one thing he'd always been good at, always been able to do, somehow wasn't working anymore.

He cleared his throat.

'I can certainly make you a simpler pancake. I'll get it right out to you.'

'Thanks so much!' Pete clapped a hand on his shoulder before he could walk away. 'We are delighted to have such a talented chef in town. I'm sure you'll get your footing soon enough.'

Archer forced a smile before stalking back to the kitchen. Get his footing? He was a world-renowned chef, for fuck's sake. He had his footing. His footing was great. It was world-renowned.

'Cyrus,' he barked, storming back into the kitchen. The old cook looked up with a smirk. 'Make me another batch of simple pancake batter.'

Cyrus raised a gray brow but didn't argue. 'Yes, chef.'

'And Maribel, the mayor eats for free.'

'Yes, chef.'

Yes, chef. Those words used to mean something. They used to mean that he was the captain of the ship, that he was in charge, in control. And now the whole damn ship was sinking.

Chapter Eight

He'd completely forgotten the nanny was moving in today until he pulled into the driveway and found her hauling two garbage bags filled with her possessions in through his front door. He resisted the urge to throw the car into reverse and drive anywhere but here.

This was his life.

His house.

His kid.

He closed his eyes and rubbed his temples as though he could massage out the tension. He didn't live in Paris anymore. He literally didn't have a home there for the time being. He'd sublet his apartment to a friend of a friend for the rest of the year. This was all he had now. He didn't spend his time cooking and smoking and sleeping with waitresses anymore. Now he lived here, in the suburbs, and he got home at a reasonable time and used his paychecks from the diner to support his daughter and not to buy cigarettes and expensive wine.

It was the right thing to do.

For now. He just had to do it for now. In six months, if all went well then he and Olive could move back to France.

And with that helpful thought in mind, Archer got out of the car and made his way to the front door where Iris was currently wedged with her bags.

'Need some help?'

She turned abruptly. He'd startled her.

'Oh, hi.' She looked flustered, little wisps of hair escaping her braid. It was dry today and now he could see that it was somewhere between blonde and red, a rose-gold color he'd never seen before and … he was staring.

He cleared his throat and grabbed one of her bags.

'Thanks,' she said, shoving the other one through the door. 'You never really realize how much stuff you own until you have to move it.'

Actually, he'd had the opposite problem, needing to buy furniture and stuff to fill the house he'd rented, to make it feel like a home. Or a rough approximation of a home. But he didn't say any of that. He followed her into the house where a few more bags and boxes were now piled in the living room. Gladys was on the couch with Olive.

'Hello, there,' Gladys said. 'How's my diner?'

Honest answer? People hated his first new-menu addition, he couldn't find the magic pancake recipe that everyone loved so dearly, the staff hated him, and he still hadn't gotten the kitchen up to his level of clean and organized. He was failing, but Gladys didn't need to know all that.

'It's going well.'

'Wonderful!' Gladys beamed. 'I knew it would.'

'Hi, Olive,' he said. 'How was school?'

The silence that followed his question was only made worse by the two women shooting him pitying glances.

'That good, huh?' he said, trying to lighten the mood.

'Olive, why don't you tell your dad about the funny story you read in the library? Remember?' Gladys gave the girl a gentle nudge, but Olive just shook her head.

'That's okay,' he said. 'She can tell me later, if she wants to.' He swallowed the frustration and disappointment building in his chest. Failure after failure today.

'How about I show you to your room,' he said, turning back to Iris, but avoiding the pity in her eyes. He didn't need her pity even if that was what had convinced her to take the job in the first place. He just needed someone reliable to take care of Olive. Not that someone who moved their possessions in garbage bags really screamed *reliable*, but he couldn't keep piecing together childcare with local babysitters and retirees, and Iris was the best he had at the moment.

The therapist said Olive needed consistency. So that's what he was going to give her. Until she was feeling better, and then he would uproot her from everything she knew and get back to his real life abroad.

Christ.

He was so screwed. He was doomed to live here forever all because of some *accident*.

Accident? The word echoed through him and he immediately felt like shit for even thinking it. What was wrong with him? He could feel Olive's eyes on him from the couch, like she knew he'd just thought of her as an accident, like she knew fate had stuck her with the worst possible father.

'Follow me,' he said, gruffly, grabbing one of Iris's bags,

needing to get away from Olive's stare and Gladys's well-intentioned concern.

'This is Olive's room,' he gestured to the first door on the left off the narrow hallway that housed all three bedrooms.

'Very pink,' Iris said, sticking her head in and taking a peek.

'I didn't know what she would like,' he confessed, moving on quickly to the next room. 'The bathroom.'

Iris came up behind him and looked in. 'Only the one?' she asked, sounding concerned.

Why had it not occurred to him until right now that it would be awkward to only have one bathroom? Not until this very moment had he realized that he and Iris would be naked in the same shower every day. Goddamn it, now he was thinking about Iris naked.

'I'll get a lock for it. Right away.'

He did not look back but continued charging down the hall, suddenly needing this tour to be over. 'This is your room.' He pointed into the last room on the left.

'And that one is yours?' She gestured to the room across the hall.

Right across the damn hall! Why was this house so small? And why had he not noticed until right now?!

'Uh … yes.' He blew out a defeated sigh. There was no way this was going to work. 'Look, Iris, I'm sorry. I get it if you can't take the job. This is … I didn't … this wasn't very well thought through.'

They were standing on opposite sides of the hall now, but the hallway was so narrow and they were still uncomfortably close. Like they would be. All. The. Time. If she moved in here. Crammed together in this little house. Sleeping across from each other. Bathing in the same damn room.

Iris was watching him, studying him. Thinking.

Could she tell what he was thinking? That he was already being the worst kind of lecherous boss? He would be her *boss*. He could never touch her. He'd never get permanent custody of his kid if he was caught fucking the nanny. Instinctively, his fingers balled into fists at his side, like they were mourning the loss of something they'd never had.

This was the worst idea he'd ever had.

Luckily, Iris was sure to be about two seconds away from calling the whole thing off. There was no way she would still want the job after seeing the living conditions...

'I still want the job.'

Wait. What? 'You do?'

She shrugged. 'I need a job, and this one pays well and comes with a place to stay. So, yeah. I still want the job.'

Shit. Could he fire her? He should fire her right now. He could not have her living under his roof, looking like that.

Looking soft and lovely, with her hair curling around her ears and her wide eyes staring at him. She was actually wearing real clothes today, jeans and a sweater but he could still remember how she'd looked in those leggings, how he'd seen every delicate curve of her.

Oh, no, no, no ... abort plan! Archer had slept with enough co-workers to know it was a very bad idea and that was when they'd had their own homes to retreat to. And it had still always blown up in his face. He hadn't done it since he became head chef. He'd been very purposeful in not abusing his power. And this dynamic? Nanny and employer? Was there a working relationship more ripe for misunderstandings?

'I can still have the job, right?' Iris asked, her question breaking through his spiraling thoughts. 'Because I kinda already gave up my apartment and I don't really have the cash at the moment to get another one. I mean there's my cousin's place, but she plays the trumpet all night and there's Kira's, but I really don't want to have to hear her and Bennett doing it all the time because that makes a friendship awkward, you know?'

He didn't know. He didn't know anything anymore. He didn't know how to make pancakes, or raise a child, and he certainly didn't know how to say no to Iris Fraser.

'Of course.' He ran a hand through his hair and leaned back against the wall. 'Yes, of course you can still have the job.'

Iris beamed. 'Thanks!' Her expression turned serious. 'But just so you know, I have pepper spray.'

'Pepper spray?'

'In case you get fresh,' she said, grabbing her bag and heading into her new room.

In case he gets fresh? Christ. What had he gotten himself into?

Chapter Nine

I ris bolted upright in bed. An unfamiliar bed, in an unfamiliar room. She rubbed her eyes and pushed her hair out of her face. The room was only partially dark, thanks to the streetlight shining in from the road. The walls were bare, the bedspread was a generic navy blue. There was a single nightstand with a single lamp. And nothing else.

If Iris didn't know better, she'd think she was in some sort of monastery situation. Or nunnery? Cloister? She didn't really know the right word and considering it was … she glanced at her phone … 1am, her brain wasn't really working, but the room definitely looked like it belonged to someone who'd taken a vow of chastity, or a vow of really sad decorating.

Eventually, she remembered that she was in her new room at her new job and that she had to wake up in five hours and take care of a small child that she barely knew. But that was fine.

The crash she heard seemed less fine, though.

She swung her legs out of bed, avoiding the pile of bags she hadn't had time to unpack yet, and crept toward the door. She didn't know if this nannying gig included protecting Olive from night-time intruders, but she figured she should go investigate anyway. For safety's sake.

The hallway was dark when she stepped out of her room, but a night light glowed from the bathroom. She paused, hearing more noise coming from the kitchen. Was someone cooking in the middle of the night? Considering Archer's bedroom door was open, she had a pretty good idea of who it was, but she was curious and nosy and maybe wanted to get a peek of this famous chef in action, so she tiptoed the rest of the way down the hall and peered around the corner.

Archer was in the open kitchen furiously whisking something in a metal bowl. His brow was furrowed in concentration and his forearms flexed with the motion. Iris's mouth went dry. The man was dressed in a tight white undershirt and a pair of gray sweatpants, which, as far as Iris was concerned, was the same as a woman cooking in lingerie. She should go back to bed. It was not her business what the eccentric chef man did in the middle of the night.

Spying on him cooking with all his sexy chef muscles on display was not in her job description. Or in her best interest for that matter. He was obviously off limits. He was her boss for one thing, and for another she was living with him and taking care of his daughter. Bex wasn't totally wrong, this was a bit of a sticky situation, and she couldn't make things stickier by thinking she could have anything to do with this man.

Right. So. Back to bed.

She had every intention of leaving, she really did, but right as she went to turn around, Archer lifted his head.

The bowl clattered to the counter, spraying some kind of batter all over his shirt.

'Jesus!' he hissed, clapping a hand to his chest. 'What the hell are you doing?'

'Sorry! Oh God, I'm so sorry!' Iris hurried out of her hiding place, scanning the kitchen for paper towels. 'I heard a noise and I thought I should come and check, you know just in case someone was trying to kidnap Olive, and I didn't know you were … you were…' She gestured to Archer and his chest and his arms and damn it she was staring at him again! Where were those stupid paper towels?

'Kidnap Olive?'

Iris heard the incredulousness in his voice, but she was no longer looking at him and instead stooping down to the shelves below the island in her search for towels.

'Here they are!' She stood, holding the roll in her hands to find Archer staring at her like she was a crazy person. Which she clearly was. 'Uh … here you go.'

He took the offered paper towels and swiped at the mess on his clothes. So much for not making things stickier. Iris bit down on an ill-timed laugh.

Do not think about making your boss sticky!

'Is there a reason you think Olive is in danger of being kidnapped?' he asked, with a raised eyebrow when he met her gaze again.

'No, not particularly, but you know, you listen to enough true-crime podcasts and you start to get a little paranoid.' She grimaced at that admission. Maybe he didn't want a paranoid person watching his kid. She really needed to be more careful with her tendency to tell people everything about her. Now was not the time or the place.

Not with Archer dressed like that, with the batter seeping through his shirt and making it nearly transparent in places and her in her PJs. Oh God, she just remembered what she was wearing. Or more importantly not wearing.

Iris was currently dressed in nothing but an oversized T-shirt and a pair of panties. And that was it. Iris WAS NOT WEARING PANTS in front of her boss. Dear God, why? She tugged at the hem of the shirt like that would somehow help the situation when all it did was draw Archer's gaze down to her bare legs.

One second and then two. Heat flooded every one of Iris's limbs. Archer, her new boss and sexy chef extraordinaire, was staring at her legs, in his kitchen, in the middle of the night. Was this a pepper-spray situation? Was it a pepper-spray situation if she *liked* that her new boss was staring at her legs?

Maybe she should pepper spray herself.

Archer cleared his throat, tearing his eyes away from her bottom half. A new expression was on his face. Gone was the composed chef, the man in charge. And in his place was a man undone, if only for a second, only a breath before he schooled his features again, before his mouth flattened out again, before disappointment replaced … lust?

Iris swallowed hard.

'You should probably put some clothes on,' he said, voice rough but stern. 'Or go back to bed.'

Her cheeks went up in flames, but she didn't know if it was embarrassment or desire that heated them.

'Right, sorry. I'll get out of your way.' She pulled her shirt down over her ass and hightailed it out of there. But it was a long time before she fell back to sleep.

Archer was gone by the time Iris had to wake Olive up for school, so it was just the two of them for breakfast. And thank goodness for that because Iris didn't feel up to facing Archer after her pant-less performance last night. The look on his face as he'd stared at her, like he wanted her to be his next meal, had haunted her for hours. It still was actually and if she didn't have a small child to tend to, she might have let herself luxuriate in it for a bit longer. But there was no time for that today.

Olive sat at the island, her short legs swinging under the tall stool, the lack of confidence in Iris's ability to take care of her clear as day on her face.

'So,' Iris said, attempting her best I'm-a-professional-nanny-and-I-love-spending-time-with-small-children smile, 'what would you like for breakfast?'

The little girl frowned. 'I'm not hungry.'

Hmm. Her first hour on the job and already a conundrum. Was she supposed to force her to eat?

'Well, you need energy for school, right? You don't want to fall asleep in the middle of math class.'

This seemed to give Olive pause. She wrinkled her little nose as she thought about it. And Iris had to admit, she was pretty cute. Objectively speaking. Like a puppy. Small things were always cute.

'I don't like what he has.'

It took Iris a minute to parse what Olive was saying. 'You don't like what your dad buys for breakfast?'

Olive nodded.

'You probably could have told him that,' Iris pointed out before heading back down the hall to her room. 'Hold on.'

She returned a minute later with a box of strawberry Pop-Tarts in hand. She never moved places without them. They were the perfect emergency breakfast.

'How about one of these?'

Olive's eyes widened. 'I've never had one.'

'You've never had one? Man, what were your parents feeding you?'

Olive froze. Iris froze. What the hell was wrong with her? How had she forgotten why she was here?!

'I shouldn't have said that. I'm sorry, Olive. I know your mom was the best. I'm sure she fed you all kinds of good things.'

Olive sat fiddling with the silver wrapping of the Pop-Tarts, a small frown on her face. Iris honestly didn't know how a five-year-old processed grief or how much she understood about what had happened to her mom and why she was stuck living with people she didn't even know.

All of a sudden, Iris's heart hurt.

'Hey, I'm going to heat one up for you, okay? And then you can try it and we can talk about your mom, if you want, or we don't have to. Okay, Olive?'

Olive nodded but didn't speak, her dark brown gaze following Iris around the kitchen. Iris didn't know how to help a child process the recent death of their mother, but she was pretty good at distraction.

'First, we unwrap the pastry,' she trilled in her best Julia Child impression. 'And then we simply place it in the toaster for two minutes, not a moment more!' She dropped the Pop-

Tart in the toaster with a flourish and was rewarded with a giggle.

'Now,' she went on with a smile, spinning toward the fridge, 'some juice!' She continued on this way, narrating the breakfast making process like she was on a cooking show, delighting in Olive's laughter at the spectacle.

Maybe she was good at this nanny thing after all.

Feeling pretty cocky led them to be ten minutes late for kindergarten drop-off, and with Olive wearing a pair of unicorn slippers to school, but Iris was counting it as a win.

She'd made Olive laugh. Not bad for her first day as a nanny.

Chapter Ten

A nother shit day at work. Another morning of rejected dishes, of customer complaints, of Cyrus's know-it-all smirk. Archer hadn't been this bad at his job since he was a line cook in college, getting constantly screamed at for his uneven vegetable cutting.

And it sucked.

Archer had lost his sanctuary. He'd lost the one place he felt totally in control. And now he was in control of nothing. He stood on his own stoop, staring at his front door, and raked his hands through his hair, working up the courage to go inside. If any of the neighbors witnessed this daily ritual, they probably thought he was insane.

He opened the door and was greeted with … nothing. No sullen child on the couch, no TV blaring a baking competition, no new nanny parading around without pants.

Archer sucked in a sharp breath at the memory. The memory he'd been doing a pretty good job of repressing since it happened three days ago. Iris in nothing but a T-shirt, her

LAURIE GILMORE

hair tousled from sleep, her eyes bright as she rambled on about murder podcasts. They were only a few nights into this situation, and between his need to perfect his pancake recipe and his half-naked nanny, he'd slept for maybe two hours each.

He dropped his bag by the door and peeled off his chef's coat. It was absurd that he still wore the damn thing. No one that ate at a diner gave a shit that the guy flipping their pancakes went to four years of culinary school, apprenticed under some of the best chefs in Europe, and ran his own kitchen for the last several years. People came to a diner for consistency, for comfort. For the same damn food they'd been eating for the past twenty years. And it was for that reason that Archer's new recipes were going up in flames.

Giggling from down the hallway momentarily distracted him from his depressing thoughts. He found Iris and Olive in Olive's bedroom sitting cross-legged on the floor. A circle of stuffed animals sat with them.

'Pinkies up!' Iris said in the worst British accent he'd ever heard. She held a tiny teacup with her pinky stuck out. Olive did the same, a big smile on her face.

'Why do we have to put our pinkies up?' she asked, still not noticing Archer standing in the doorway.

Iris shrugged in that way that she did, like life was a game she was playing. 'It's fancier that way,' she said. 'It's the same reason we're wearing these lovely hats.' She tipped back the hat she was wearing, something made of straw that had been covered in big tissue paper flowers, and caught Archer's eye.

'Oh look, Olive!' she said, her voice overly bright. 'Your dad's home! We should invite him to our tea party.'

As usual when he entered the room, he felt the joy flee

74

Olive's body. Smile gone. Laughter gone. Ability to speak, gone.

'Uh, that's all right. I don't want to interrupt your fun,' he said.

Iris unfolded herself from her seat and came to where he stood, grabbing him by the hand. 'Oh no, I insist. You simply must join us. The tea is top notch.' She slipped back into that terrible accent, but it seemed to be working. Olive was having a hard time keeping the smile from creeping back onto her lips.

Iris dragged him down to the floor and before he could really register what was happening, he was seated beside a rainbow striped narwhal and a bear with one eye. Olive peered at him from under her hat.

'Well, thank you for the invite,' he said, offering Olive a tentative smile. She didn't return it, but she didn't look away. 'I could really go for a cup of tea.'

Iris grinned at him as she poured him an imaginary cup. 'There you are, dear,' she said. 'Olive here was just telling me about her day. Do go on, Olive.'

And maybe Iris was a genius or maybe she was a crazy person, but between her insane accent and the fake tea and the stuffed guests and the homemade hats, Olive was loosened up enough to actually speak in his presence. He wanted to cry into his imaginary tea.

'We have assigned seats in the cafeteria now because we were being too loud,' she said. 'But it's not fair because I'm not loud.'

'Of course you're not loud,' Archer burst out, irrationally angry about this injustice. 'What kind of school is this? Why would they punish you if you didn't do anything wrong? I should go down there.'

Iris was looking at him with a strange sort of smile on her face as though maybe she thought he was being crazy but also maybe as if she was proud of him or something.

'Settle down, Papa Bear,' she said, patting his knee. 'Let's not storm the elementary school quite yet.'

'Well, it's not fair,' he grumbled and a small smile curved Olive's mouth.

Iris laughed. 'Lots of things aren't fair. You may have noticed.'

Like a girl losing her mother at five years old and being forced to live with the father she'd never met? Yeah, he'd noticed, but neither of them said it out loud.

Iris turned back to Olive. 'Look kid, sometimes crappy...' She paused and leaned toward Archer. 'Can I say crappy?' she whispered.

'I don't know.' He hadn't exactly had time to formulate his parental stance on cursing.

Iris shrugged. 'Sometimes crappy things happen to you even if you've done nothing wrong.'

Olive looked at him pointedly, like he was the crappy thing, and he just nodded because he kinda was.

'But,' Iris went on, lifting her tea cup, 'we just have to keep going and find the good things. Like tea parties with friends. Isn't that right Mr. Higgenbottom,' she said, patting the bespectacled frog sitting next to her.

Olive giggled. 'That's not his name.'

'Of course it is. He told me.'

More giggles. 'No! His name is Hoppy.'

Iris frowned. 'Hoppy? That is an objectively terrible name for a frog!'

'I think it's a good name,' Archer chimed in, and Iris sent him a bemused smile.

'Oh, really?'

'Sure. He hops, doesn't he?'

'Yeah!' Olive chimed in. 'He's a frog. He hops.' And maybe she wasn't talking directly to him and maybe this wasn't quite the bonding moment he was making it out to be, but she was talking *with* him, *near* him, and goddamn if that wasn't something.

'Okay, okay.' Iris held her hands up in surrender. 'You guys win. But then what are we going to call this guy?' She pointed to the blue bunny. 'Also Hoppy?'

Olive's brow furrowed in thought and Archer had to bite down on a smile.

'How about Mr. Blue?' he suggested, and Olive's face lit up. In his direction!

'Yeah. Mr. Blue.'

Iris rolled her eyes, but she was also having trouble keeping the smile off her face. 'You guys are the worst at this.'

Olive was on her feet now, too excited to sit anymore. 'No, we're the best at it.'

We, as though they were a team.

Iris stuck out her tongue and Olive returned the gesture. 'Well, this little lady here is obviously Prunella,' Iris said, holding up a pig wearing an apron.

Olive squealed in delight. 'No! Not Prunella.'

'Maybe Pinky?' Archer suggested.

'I think her name is…' Olive tapped a finger on her nose as she thought. 'I think her name is Polly! Polly Pig.'

'Good one,' Archer said, and his daughter beamed. *Beamed at him.*

And Iris looked smug as hell that her little tea party had worked. Between the accent and the hat, Archer was wondering if maybe she was a bit more *Mary Poppins* than he'd originally thought.

But then he remembered her ass under that T-shirt and he thought maybe not.

Chapter Eleven

He heard Iris's footsteps this time, so he was prepared for her appearance in the kitchen and didn't make a fool of himself by pouring pancake batter down his front.

'Did I wake you?' he asked as she settled herself at the stool across from him on the island. She was wearing a pair of shorts under her T-shirt tonight, thank God.

'No, I was just having trouble falling asleep.'

'Is your room not comfortable? Because I could…'

'No, no, the room is fine. Very comfortable.' She shrugged. 'I don't know, just couldn't sleep.'

'Hmm.' He went back to sifting the flour into his bowl. Maybe the pancakes weren't fluffy enough.

'What are you making?'

'Pancakes.'

'You're making pancakes at midnight?'

'Yep.'

'Why?'

He let out an exasperated sigh, but only found Iris smiling at him when he looked up. She was beautiful when she smiled.

No. Not allowed.

'The diner patrons aren't happy with my changes to the menu.'

'Oh, yeah that doesn't surprise me. This town can be very stuck in its ways.'

'Hmm.'

'So why don't you just go back to the old recipe?'

'Because I don't know it,' he ground out, getting more frustrated the more they talked about it.

'But you're a chef.'

'Yes.'

'And you can't figure out how to make pancakes?'

He dropped the whisk he was using into the bowl with a clatter. Iris flinched.

'I can make pancakes just fine.'

'So, the problem is…'

'The problem is that the people in this town want them to taste exactly how they used to taste, and I don't have the recipe and the old cook is gone and the rest of the staff won't cooperate, and I just need to figure it out…'

He pressed his hands flat onto the counter, his head hanging between his shoulders. Iris laid her hand over his and stopped his spiraling thoughts. Her fingers were cool and comforting. She gave him a little squeeze before pulling her hand back again.

'I'm sure you'll figure it out.'

'Why would you be sure about that?' he asked, and he really wanted to know. Why on earth would Iris be sure about him doing anything? He'd done nothing but fail spectacularly since he got here.

She shrugged, her long braid sliding over her shoulder. 'You seem like a guy who figures things out. You know,' she gestured toward him, waving her hand in his general direction like she had when she'd been wondering about his tattoos. He felt his body light up, like she'd actually touched him. 'Very competent and all that.'

He huffed a laugh. 'Yep, super competent. A chef who can't make pancakes and a dad who can't get his kid to talk to him.'

'She talked to you today.'

He frowned. 'Only because you tricked her into it.'

'I'm pretty sure half of dealing with kids is just tricking them into doing stuff.'

He couldn't help his gruff laugh. Maybe he should be more concerned about his nanny talking about tricking his kid, but at this point he was just so grateful that he and Olive had had a positive interaction that he wasn't going to question Iris's techniques.

'I think she's a little afraid of you,' she said.

'Afraid of me? Why would she be afraid of me?' Was that true? He'd tried so hard to be gentle around Olive, soft. He'd offered to color with her for Christ's sake. What else did he have to do, sing nursery rhymes?

It was Iris's turn to sigh in frustration. 'Because Olive spent her whole life with her mom and now you're like this big, intimidating man in her life.'

'I'm not intimidating.'

Iris rolled her eyes. 'Yeah, okay.'

'I didn't ... I mean, I'm trying ... I don't yell at her or anything.'

'You don't have to yell, it's your whole vibe.'

'My vibe?'

She sighed again. 'Yes, your very intense vibe. Like the way you're staring at me right now it's as if you can see through to my bones or something. It's unnerving.'

He blinked and looked away. He hadn't realized he was staring at her.

'I have a hard time believing you didn't know any of this. You spend your day bossing around people in your kitchen, right? I mean, aren't you intimidating on purpose?'

'Not here. Not at home. I just…' He sighed. 'I don't know how to do this.'

'I'm sure you'll figure it out.'

'Like the pancakes?'

She gave him a soft smile that permeated through all the shit he was feeling at the moment, leaving him warm. 'Like the pancakes.'

He looked away again, busying himself with adding the wet ingredients to the dry. 'Do you want to be my taste tester?' he asked when the batter was done, and Iris was still sitting at the island watching him.

'Do I want to eat pancakes in the middle of the night? Uh, yes please.'

He couldn't help his smile. There was something contagious about Iris's easy comfort. He shouldn't have encouraged her being here with him in the middle of the night. He should have sent her back to bed, drawn a line, set a boundary between them. They weren't lovers or even friends. She worked for him. He shouldn't be pouring out his problems to her and he certainly shouldn't be letting her comfort him.

But as disciplined as Archer was in the kitchen, he'd always been reckless with women. He could never seem to help himself. He liked women. He liked their softness. Too many times he'd fallen into bed with the wrong woman just because he'd needed a soft place to land.

Archer made bad choices with women. And so, he melted butter in the pan and poured in enough batter for one big pancake.

'Will you do the fancy-flip thing?'

'Fancy-flip thing?' he asked with a raised eyebrow, trying and failing to not be thrilled that Iris wanted to watch him cook. For the first time in two weeks, he felt like he knew what he was doing, that he was in control. Like his real self was clicking back into place.

'The thing where you flick the pan and flip the pancake without using a spatula.'

Archer flashed her a cocky smirk and flipped the pancake with just a flick of his wrist. Iris clapped and he felt like he could do anything.

He slid the pancake onto a plate on the counter between them and handed Iris a fork. Her gaze drifted to his before taking a bite. Archer might be failing at a lot of things at the moment, but he still knew when a woman was into him and the heat in Iris's eyes was irrefutable.

She chewed slowly, a little sigh of happiness leaving her lips. Archer watched intently, waiting for the verdict.

'It's delicious,' she said, taking another piece. 'But it's not the same.'

Archer was leaning on the counter now, elbows on the smooth surface. He took his own forkful of pancakes. 'What's wrong with it?'

Iris shrugged. 'Is it weird if I say it's too good?'

'Too good?'

'It tastes too good. Too fluffy. I think maybe the old diner pancakes were denser.'

Okay, so sifting the flour was out.

'Did you try a mix?' she asked, popping in another bite. 'Aunt Jemima or something?'

'You want me to make pancakes using a mix?'

Iris laughed. 'Jeez, you sound like you're about to have a stroke. It was just a suggestion.'

He tried to calm down whatever horrified expression was on his face, but seriously, a mix? There was no way he was serving people food made from a mix. That was unacceptable.

'I'll tweak the recipe again, but I'm not using a mix.'

Iris smiled at him as she finished off the pancake. 'So, you're really good at this, huh?'

'Cooking? Yeah, I hope so at this point.' He smirked and made more bad decisions. 'Stay home for dinner tomorrow and I'll make you some real food.' She'd been out to eat with her cousin her first few nights here, but suddenly he wanted to see her face when he fed her more than this disappointing pancake.

Dangerous thoughts, Archer. She's not yours to cook for.

But when everything else felt like failure, Iris's smile felt like success. He wanted more of it.

Iris's smile grew. 'Okay, I'll let you make me dinner.' She hopped down from the stool. 'Goodnight, Archer.'

It wasn't until she was out of sight that he realized he was staring again.

Chapter Twelve

'He's making you dinner? What the hell is going on over there, Iris?'

'Bex, calm down.' Iris was driving to her ten o'clock aerobics class while Olive was at school. They'd actually made it on time today and she was feeling pretty good about that until her cousin called to rain on her parade. Maybe she shouldn't have mentioned the late-night chat and pancake testing as well as the subsequent dinner invite, but it wasn't like it was a date or something.

'He's making dinner for Olive and himself and just offered for me to join them. It makes sense. We live in the same house, I can't just not be home whenever he is.'

Her cousin's long-suffering sigh came clearly through the speaker. 'You need to keep the line between you very clear, Iris. He's your *boss*.'

'I am aware of that, thank you. And nothing even happened!' Besides some light ogling while he cooked, she was only human. And it was impossible to avoid noticing how sexy her new boss was. But despite what Bex thought, she could practice restraint. Just because she found a man sexy did not mean she had to immediately jump his bones. She understood the boundaries here, but she wasn't about to turn down a delicious (and free) meal.

'Anyway, are you coming to class today?'

'No, can't today. I picked up a few more lessons.'

'Okay, I'll text you later.'

'Just be careful, Iris. If things go sideways with this guy, you're out of a job and a place to live. Unless you want to reconsider my offer…'

'I love you, Bex! Gotta go!' Iris hung up before she could get lectured anymore. Growing up, the girls had seen plenty of men come and go in their mothers' lives and it had left Bex wary of all men. Iris on the other hand, may have been more like her mother than she cared to admit. Much like her employment record, Iris's relationship record didn't exactly reflect longevity. She liked relationships like she liked her chicken wings, hot and fast.

If she'd learned one thing from her mother, it was that romantic love was fleeting but sex was fun while it lasted. And while her mother never seemed overly distraught when things ended, it was young Iris who was left missing the latest casualty of her mother's wandering attention. Eventually, she learned to stop hoping that her mother's latest boyfriend would maybe one day become her new stepdad, but clearly some damage had been done because grown-up Iris didn't bother getting too close to any man.

Things just seemed safer that way.

And besides, she wasn't reckless enough to sleep with her boss.

She pulled into the parking lot of the Y, grabbed her gym bag and headed in. The ladies were already congregating around the pool by the time she got in. The room was hot and humid and chlorine-scented. It felt like home.

Teaching her seniors exercise classes had been the one job that had stuck with Iris over the years. She would never abandon her students.

'Good morning, girls!' she said, getting everyone's attention.

'Good morning, Iris!' the ladies trilled. Iris smiled. These were her people. Fully formed people who could tell her exactly what they wanted and needed. She didn't have to guess what they were thinking or worry that they were starving to death. All the ladies looked fully fed and happy this morning.

'How's the new job?' Carol, one of her most loyal students asked as Iris checked them off one by one on her clipboard.

'It's going well.'

'Oh? How's Olive doing?'

Iris nearly laughed. As if these women didn't know how Olive was doing. As if they weren't on a constant rotation of 'just stopping by' or 'we were in the neighborhood'. Archer's freezer was overflowing with 'how's Olive' casseroles.

'As well as can be expected, I guess.'

'Of course, the poor dear.'

The women were dying to ask more, Iris could feel it. They were vibrating with curiosity. But she wasn't about to air Archer's life out for the whole town to examine.

'And the living situation...' Janet ventured... 'Is that going well, too?'

Estelle scoffed. 'You all just want to know what it's like living with that handsome chef.'

Janet turned scarlet, nearly matching the giant tropical flowers on her bathing suit. 'I did not say that.'

'But you meant it.'

'Ladies, we should really start class,' Iris said, trying to steer the women back to business. Maybe knowing exactly what they wanted wasn't always a blessing. These women wanted the details.

'Now you're going to hold out on us, Iris? You told us all about that fella you met at that music festival last summer.'

'And the one from the yoga retreat.'

'And the guy you met in the produce department at the grocery store.'

'Yes, well,' Iris cut in quickly before Marissa could elaborate on Iris's sweaty weekend fling with Pablo. She really did need to learn to keep her mouth shut. 'That was different. This is just a job, and Archer is my boss, and so far things are going well.'

Disappointment filtered through the group.

'Now, let's get in the pool and get started,' Iris said brightly, leading the way to the water.

'He *is* very attractive,' she heard Carol whisper to Janet.

'He sure is, but have you been to the diner lately? He's turning the place upside down.'

'With that body, he can cook me whatever he likes.' The women burst into giggles and Iris jumped in the pool, wishing she could stay underwater long enough to miss out on her class of seventy- and eighty-year-olds waxing poetic about Archer's muscular arms and broad chest. But unfortunately, her lung capacity just wasn't that good. Instead, she cranked her workout playlist and started shouting commands.

Eventually, everyone fell into line. Everyone except Iris's brain, which was happily playing, on a loop, its own playlist of the way Archer's arms looked when he cooked.

Not helpful, brain. Not helpful at all.

Olive had come home grumpy from kindergarten, so they were watching baking shows when Archer arrived back later that evening. Iris had been skeptical of the appeal of this one, but she was now fully invested in whether that designer purse was actually made out of cake.

'Hey, welcome home,' she said when Archer entered, but neither she nor Olive took their eyes from the screen.

'Hey,' Archer said, shedding his chef's coat and tossing it on the chair.

'It *is* cake! I can't believe that.' Iris slapped a hand on her knee. She would have sworn that cake purse was the real deal.

'I told you so,' Olive mumbled, though her victory still wasn't doing much for her mood.

'What is she eating?' Archer asked, his eyes on Olive.

'A Pop-Tart,' Iris said, facing his intense disappointment. God, and this guy wondered why his kid was silent around him. With that face how could she not be? He looked chiseled from a very disappointed stone.

'Do you know how processed those things are?'

'I know that they taste good, and that they are one of the two things I've gotten her to eat.'

He frowned. 'What's the other?'

Ah ha! Mr. High and Mighty Food Snob didn't know what Olive liked to eat either.

'Strawberries.'

'Hmm.' He stalked off to the kitchen.

'Just eat your Pop-Tart,' she whispered to Olive. 'I'll handle your grumpy dad.'

Olive took another defiant bite.

'Good girl.' Iris patted her head. She still had the braided pigtails Iris had put in this morning, although they'd gotten a little fuzzy throughout the day. She looked rumpled and sleepy and Iris had to admit, the little creature was growing on her.

She followed Archer into the kitchen. 'Bad day?'

He scowled, pouring himself a drink. 'It was fine.'

'You never specified what you wanted me to feed her. If there's an approved menu, I'm gonna need it.'

He sighed, his shoulders sagging. 'No, sorry. I just…'

'You just want her to eat and she's eating. You can teach her to like all your fancy French food later, okay? One step at a time.'

His stare was unreadable until he gave a short nod. 'You're right. As long as she's eating something.'

'Exactly. I on the other hand am totally on board to eat something other than Pop-Tarts.' She noticed the bags Archer had set out on the counter and she started to unpack them. 'What are you making?' She didn't really know if it was appropriate for her to be chatting in the kitchen with him, but Olive didn't exactly need supervision in her TV watching. Especially since Archer put child locks on the doors so she couldn't sneak out of the house anymore.

'Steak frites,' he said, pulling potatoes out of one of the bags as well as a bottle of wine. 'Glass of wine?'

Drinking with the boss? The lines were getting blurrier. But what was she supposed to do? Hide in her room until dinner was ready? She'd spent her first few evenings here going out for dinner just to avoid this situation but that was untenable. She lived here. Surely, she could have a glass of wine with dinner.

'Sure, thanks.'

'Red, okay? This one pairs really nicely with the steak.'

'Sounds good.' She watched him pour the wine and pull the rest of the ingredients from the bag and she could imagine what he must have been like before coming here. Competent, talented. A man who was confident in his abilities. And he'd given it all up.

He was peeling potatoes faster than she'd ever seen anyone peel before when she blurted out, 'It's really amazing that you gave this up.'

His hands stopped. A slight frown crossed his face, making her regret her words.

'I mean, not that you gave it up forever, but it's amazing that you left your old life to come here, to Dream Harbor and the diner and all … it must be … different.'

He made that amused huffing sound she supposed passed for a laugh and went back to the potatoes, chopping them into precise slices. Like a machine. She'd been right about those hands. Capable of all sorts of tricks.

'Different is an understatement.' His attention shifted to where Olive sat on the couch, and he somehow didn't chop his own fingers off. 'But it's not like I could just leave her.'

'Plenty of people do.'

He paused his chopping, his intense gaze landing on her again and suddenly it was too warm in the kitchen.

She cleared her throat. 'My dad didn't have too much trouble taking off and he knew about me. So…' She shrugged.

'It's kind of a big deal that you came back for her.' Iris refused to identify as someone with daddy issues, she absolutely did not let the man who knocked up her mother have that type of control over her life, but it *was* a big deal that Archer had come back. He could have looked the other way and continued on with a life he'd already established. But he didn't. He was here. And he was trying.

He was still looking at her, but less like he was disappointed and more like he maybe didn't regret hiring her.

'Hey, Olive,' Iris called into the living room, needing to break the tension. 'You should come in here. Your dad is like a real-life cooking show.' She watched Archer as she said it and she relished the smile that lit up his face for one brief moment before he bit it back and continued chopping.

Olive appeared by her side before she could try and coax another smile from him. Later. She would try again later because now that she'd seen one she wanted more.

'What's he making?' Olive asked, climbing up onto the stool next to her.

'French fries.'

'I like French fries.'

Archer was still concentrating on the meal, but his lips twitched up.

'Me too,' Iris said. 'I hope he doesn't mess them up,' she whispered loudly, and Olive giggled.

'I can make steak frites in my sleep. I won't mess them up,' Archer said, with that confident smirk he'd given her the night before when he was cooking pancakes. And she knew she was seeing the real Archer.

'Sleep cooking! Wow, that would put an interesting spin on cooking shows, huh, Olive!'

The little girl's forehead crinkled. 'Sounds dangerous.'

Archer chuckled. 'I promise to stay awake.' He dumped the cut potatoes into a bowl of cold water and then started unwrapping the steak from its brown paper package.

'I don't want that,' Olive said, immediately recoiling in horror at the slab of raw beef.

'Have you tried it before?' Archer asked, his voice gentle and calm, like he was trying not to scare her, like he had listened to Iris. 'You might like it if you try it.'

She shook her head.

'Okay,' he shrugged. 'More for me and Iris, then.'

'Iris is eating it?' Olive asked, looking up at her.

'Damn right I am. I'd be happy to eat your piece.'

Olive frowned.

'I'm going to cook it first,' Archer told her. 'With butter and rosemary.'

'What's rosemary?'

'It's an herb. Here, smell.' He held out a sprig to Olive and she took it between her tiny fingers. She brought it to her nose and took a tentative sniff. Archer's lips had curved into a small smile again and Iris didn't know who was cuter: Olive with the rosemary under her little nose, or Archer watching her.

'Smells good,' she said.

'So, there you go. Maybe you'll try a tiny bite.'

'A teeny tiny bite,' she countered.

Archer grinned. 'The teeny-tiniest bite. A little mouse bite.'

Oh, she liked that. Her face lit up. 'A little cutie, little mouse bite,' she sang.

'Hey, wait a minute! Does this mean I don't get your piece anymore?' Iris said in mock outrage and Olive giggled.

'You get your own piece,' Olive said, leaning her elbows on

the counter. 'What are you doing now?' she asked Archer, ignoring Iris's huff of outrage over her decreased portion.

'I'm going to season the steak. Do you want to help?'

Olive's eyes widened. 'Yeah!'

Archer looked like he might float away from shock and happiness, but he held it together and slid the salt dish across to Olive. 'We need a big pinch of salt. Can you do a big pinch?'

Olive made a little pinching motion with her fingers. 'Like this?'

'Bigger.' Archer took a liberal pinch of salt and sprinkled it over the steak. 'Like that. Now you.'

'Like this?'

'That's perfect! Very good.'

Olive beamed at her father and their matching dimples nearly killed Iris. She took another sip of wine and watched the twosome make dinner together, with Archer explaining everything along the way and Olive soaking in the attention. By the time they ate, Iris was amazed the food could fit past the lump of emotion in her throat.

She was glad she'd trusted her gut. These two needed her and they needed each other, and she was helping bring them together. And just like Mary Poppins, once they didn't need her anymore, she would just put up her umbrella and float right on out of here.

But after tonight's cooking demonstration, she wasn't so sure it would be as easy as she'd originally thought.

Chapter Thirteen

A few nights later, Iris was heading back to her room from the bathroom when she nearly collided with Olive in the dark hallway.

'Olive! What are you doing up?'

The little girl didn't answer; she just kept walking down the hall, her blankie trailing behind her. She had a vacant look on her face that reminded Iris way too much of a horror movie. Was her head about to start spinning on her neck?

'Olive, where are you going?' Iris followed her back out to the main living space. Archer was cleaning up the kitchen and he looked up when they entered.

'What's going on?'

Iris shrugged. 'I'm not sure. Hoping it's not a poltergeist situation.' God, she was totally right. Children were scary. Just when she thought she had this one figured out, she'd got possessed by the devil. Or something like that.

'A what?' Archer shook his head. 'Olive, you should be in bed.'

The girl didn't respond or even look at him, just made her way to the front door and started fiddling with the knob. Iris and Archer looked at each other in confusion.

'What the hell is she doing?' Archer whispered.

'Trying to escape? In her sleep?' Iris suggested.

'You think she's sleepwalking?'

'Honestly, I think that is the least horrifying scenario right now.'

Archer crept up behind her and Iris followed him. He was Olive's dad. He could get murdered first.

'Hey, Olive,' he said softly. 'Let's go back to bed.' He put his hands on her shoulders and tried to steer her away from the door.

'Be careful,' Iris hissed. 'Aren't you not supposed to wake a sleepwalker?'

'I don't know,' he hissed back. 'What happens if I do?'

'I don't know!' Iris had goosebumps up and down her arms. Something about the dark house and Olive's unseeing eyes were really freaking her out.

'It's fine,' Archer whispered, his voice firm and steady. It was a comforting sound in the dark. 'Come on, sweetie, back to bed,' he coaxed, gently moving Olive back to her room, and thankfully, she let her sleepy shuffle take her back to her bedroom. Archer went with her, tucking her into bed while Iris waited in the hall. Just in case.

'Is she okay?' she asked when he emerged, closing the door softly behind him.

'I think so. Scared the crap out of me, though.' He slouched against the wall behind him.

'Me too. That was creepy.'

He smirked. 'Creepy?'

'She looked like a horror-movie kid!'

'I'm really starting to question the media you're consuming. Murder podcasts and horror movies?'

Was he teasing her?

'I was ready to call a young priest and an old priest.'

Archer laughed. The sound was low and rich in the silent house. Iris leaned against the wall behind her and slid down to the floor. Archer looked at her like he might return to the kitchen and leave her there alone, but instead he slid down his wall as well, mirroring her position.

'I don't know how I'm going to sleep now, wondering if she's going to get out of the house.' The teasing smirk was gone and now he just looked tired and worried. Again, it struck Iris how much he'd given up to be here, how much he'd sacrificed already for his daughter.

'You put those locks on. I don't think she can get out.'

He nodded but still looked doubtful, like he knew intellectually that she couldn't get hurt, but some part of him would always worry that she would.

Parenthood, man, what a mindfuck.

'I guess this is what it's gonna be like,' he said quietly, as though he wasn't talking to her anymore. His foot brushed against hers seeking the comfort of contact. 'One thing after another. We just figured out the eating thing, and now she tries to escape in her sleep.'

It was a serious moment. He was worried about his kid, but something about the insanity of the whole thing struck Iris as funny.

Giggles escaped from her and she clapped a hand over her mouth. Archer's head snapped up in surprise.

'Are you laughing?'

Her shoulders shook with the effort to hold it in. 'Yes?' she squeaked. 'I'm sorry, but it's kinda funny. She had us both totally freaked out.'

Archer shook his head, but that smile was creeping back on his face.

'I think this is an "if you don't laugh you'll cry" moment,' she said between giggles. 'We are both in way over our heads here.' Probably not something she should admit to her boss, but it felt better this way, that they were in this together, that they were going to figure out how to deal with Olive together.

For now.

They would be in it together until Iris was sure Archer could handle things on his own and then she would leave because this … this level of worry and exhaustion and … and total helplessness was not something she planned to sign on for the long term.

Parenthood was not for her.

'So, you really didn't know about her?' Iris asked the question she'd been dying to ask since she took the job.

'I had no idea.'

'You and her mom weren't…'

'We worked at the same restaurant, slept together a few times, and then I left for Europe. I didn't hear from her after that.'

'Wow.'

'Yeah,' he sighed.

Iris couldn't imagine having news like that dropped in her lap.

'Do you want kids?' he asked.

'God, no,' she blurted out and then immediately felt awful for her reaction. 'Sorry,' she winced. 'I mean, kids are wonderful, I just never really pictured myself as a mom... What about you?' she went on, feeling braver in the dark. 'Did you always want to be a dad?'

'God, no,' he echoed her, with a wry smile, meeting Iris's eye across the hall. 'But here I am.'

She smiled at him. 'I guess your old life wasn't very conducive to having a kid.'

'Definitely not. A lot of late nights, long hours. I'm not sure how people fit kids into that lifestyle.'

'But here you are,' she whispered.

She wasn't sure he'd admitted it to himself yet, but Iris knew he was all in now. Archer was Olive's dad, and he wasn't going anywhere. He was going to do what was best for Olive. Iris could see that, even in the dark, even with Archer looking like he needed about a week of solid sleep. Whether he knew it or not, Archer was a good dad.

Archer's foot pushed against hers again. 'Thanks,' he said.

'For what? Believing your child was possessed?'

His laughter washed over her like a caress in the dark. 'No, just for ... cheering me up, I guess.'

He was looking at her, his gaze tracing over her face, slipping down to her bare shoulder and back again. Iris knew she'd been flirting with him since she moved in, and she also knew that she shouldn't be flirting with him at all...

Nothing could happen between them.

Obviously.

He was her boss, and she needed this job, and she certainly didn't need to get caught up with a guy with a kid. And he couldn't be seen as the type of guy who has a fling with the nanny. That would definitely conflict with the whole *doing what was right for Olive thing* he was working on.

Iris could leave at any time if she was just his nanny, but if she was anything else…

She shook her head.

Nothing else was on the table anyway, but what was the harm of a little flirtation? It was hard for Iris to resist. She'd always been a flirt. She liked the banter, the teasing, the small touches. Was that so wrong? It didn't always have to lead anywhere.

It was harmless, really.

Except when she met Archer's gaze again, even in this dark hallway, even though it was only their feet pressed together, Iris already knew nothing about this was going to be harmless.

He looked dangerous in the dark. His hair was disheveled again because he'd been messing with it in that way that made Iris want to substitute her fingers for his, and a dark stubble covered his jaw. It would burn. If he kissed her that stubble would burn her skin. A shiver ran through her at the thought.

She thought about the dedication and sacrifices he'd made to achieve what he had. About how he was so damn good at what he did. Iris had never really dedicated herself to anything. She flitted from job to job, man to man.

She was a flake.

Archer clearly found her attractive. And she him. But they would never mesh well together. She would drive him crazy with her inattention, her inability to stick with anything.

And she knew she was in trouble when even this imagined rejection hurt her feelings.

'I should get to bed,' she said. 'For real this time.'

'Right. Of course.'

She got up, but Archer stayed where he was, like a sentry outside of Olive's door.

'You going to stay there all night?'

He shook his head. 'Nah. Just for a bit longer.'

Iris stood looking down at him for another moment, at the worry still etched onto his face, at the exhaustion in his eyes and she wanted to help. To do something to make that smile come back.

But, like she told him, she was in way over her head. Unqualified to be a nanny. Unqualified to be anything other than an employee to this man.

So she gave him a small nod and went to bed.

It took a long time to fall asleep, wondering if he was still out there keeping watch.

Chapter Fourteen

'Hey, Arch! How are things going?'

'Hey, Dad.' His father's face filled the screen, the big smile on his face almost able to cheer Archer up. He wasn't sure exactly when it had happened, but at some point his dad had become his best friend. That fact alone said a lot about what Archer had been focused on for the last decade. His dad was the last man standing in the friend department, and that was probably only because he was legally obligated to care about Archer's problems.

And today felt like a day he needed his dad's no-nonsense approach to life, to put those problems into perspective.

Archer was sitting out behind the diner on an ancient bench he imagined had been used for smoke breaks throughout the last century. The sun was shining and the air was still chilly, but Archer had needed a break. And a cigarette. Unfortunately, he wasn't allowed one of those anymore, so he had to settle for the fresh air.

He'd given up on the classic pancake recipe for the

moment. Instead, he'd put a lemon poppy-seed pancake topped with creme fraiche on the menu today, and he nearly had an early-morning riot on his hands.

Eventually, he'd managed to convince a few patrons to try them, and Tim and Tammy had even cleared their plates. He was trying to take that as a win, but after his long night of sleeping propped up in the hallway, he had a headache and desperately needed a nap.

'You look like hell.'

'Thanks, Dad. That's nice of you to say.'

His father chuckled. 'How are things going with Olive?'

They hadn't wanted to overwhelm Olive all at once with a bunch of new family members, so his father hadn't met her yet, even over the phone, but Archer had been updating him nearly every day.

'She was sleepwalking last night.'

'Sleepwalking? Wow, that's a new one.'

Archer ran a hand down his face. His stubble was nearly a beard now and he really needed to shave. And probably get a haircut. But grooming himself really hadn't seemed important today when he'd been terrified all night that his daughter was going to sleepwalk into the street.

'Yeah. I put childproof locks on the door already, but it still freaked me out. I slept in the hallway,' he admitted with a wince.

'The hallway? You sound like me when you were a baby.' His dad had that fond smile on his face that people always got when they reminisced about their children, even as they told the most heinous stories of sleepless nights and diaper blowouts, like it had all been as magical as it was horrendous. The smile had never made sense to Archer before, but now he could almost imagine telling this sleepwalking story someday with that smile. But not today. Today, he just felt miserable and exhausted about it.

'Really?'

'Oh, yes. I was so worried about you when we brought you home. You were so small! And I was responsible for you. It felt very heavy.'

Heavy. Exactly. Everything had felt heavy since he found out about Olive, suddenly his life had this weight when before he'd moved through the world unencumbered. He wasn't sure he could carry it all.

A flash of Iris, her smile in the dark, her foot resting against his, appeared in his mind. She'd made everything feel lighter. Just for a moment.

But helping to carry his burdens was way above Iris's paygrade.

'So how did you manage it?' he asked.

His father's smile grew. 'I'm not sure I did.' He chuckled. 'I still worry about you all the time.'

'You don't have to worry about me, Dad.'

He scoffed. 'Oh, okay. I'll just stop now after all this time.'

'So, I'm just doomed, then? To worry all the time?'

'Pretty much.'

'Thanks, this has been a wonderful pep talk.'

His dad laughed again. 'It'll get better, Arch. You won't sleep every night in the hallway. I can promise you that much.'

'Well, that's comforting,' he said, the sarcasm intensified by how tired he was.

His father ignored it. 'How's the nanny working out? What's her name? Lilly? Rose?'

'Iris.'

'Right, I knew it was a flower name. How are things working out with Iris?'

Archer had never been particularly good at lying to his father, which had made for an interesting relationship when he was a teenager and very often ended up confessing to whatever he and his friends had gotten up to on Friday nights.

But he'd somehow managed to omit the fact that Iris wasn't actually a sweet old lady but a gorgeous yoga instructor with a wardrobe of too tight, too tiny clothing and how he'd found himself sniffing her shampoo in the shower this morning like some kind of lovesick teenager.

'Fine,' he choked out. 'Things are going fine.'

'Fine?' His father's eyes narrowed behind his glasses like he wasn't buying it. 'Yep. Fine. Olive likes her, so that's really all that matters.'

'Hmm. How's the living arrangement working out?'

The living arrangement in which Iris wanders the house at all hours of the night in the T-shirt that slips off her shoulder, and smiles at him in the dark, and makes him laugh even when he doesn't want to? That living arrangement?

Archer swallowed. 'Fine.'

'Hmm.' His dad was studying him, but luckily Archer was saved by his stepmom, Cathi.

'Is that Archer?' she cooed, her face eclipsing his father's on the screen. 'Hi Arch! How's Olive? When do we get to meet her?'

Archer's parents had split when he was in high school, and when his father remarried, he'd picked a wife who was opposite from Archer's mother in nearly every way. Where Archer had never seen his mother wear more make-up than an occasional swipe of chapstick, Cathi was never without a full face, her bleached blonde hair done up like she was heading somewhere much fancier than golf with his dad. Archer's mother was a scientist, always traveling somewhere in the world to study the effects of climate change on bird migration, while Cathi did nails at the local spa and was always home to spend time with his dad, the two nearly inseparable since the day they'd got married at the courthouse with Archer as their witness.

Archer loved his mother, but he understood why his dad loved Cathi. And she'd always been kind to Archer, never trying to become his new mom, but there for him when his mom couldn't be.

'Hi, Cathi. Soon. I just want her to get a bit more settled.'

'Of course, that makes perfect sense. You're such a good dad already, Arch. We're so proud of you.' She beamed at him through the phone, and maybe it was the sleep deprivation, but he almost wished he was there with them, even though he hated golf and his stepmother's too-tight hugs.

'Thanks.' He wasn't sure Cathi knew what the hell she was talking about on that front, but it was nice to hear anyway.

'All right, Arch, we gotta go.' His father's voice came from somewhere behind Cathi's hair.

'Oh, that's right! We got a one o'clock tee time today,' Cathi said, blowing Archer a kiss before disappearing from the screen. 'Bye, honey!' she called.

'Bye.'

'Hang in there, kid.'

'Thanks, Dad.'

'And next time I want to hear about the nanny.' His dad's face was the same, stern no-nonsense face that had gotten

Archer to spill his guts about the time he and his friends skipped class to go smoke in the woods behind the school.

Archer swallowed his guilt. 'Uh, yeah. Sure. Not much to tell.'

His father frowned.

Archer frowned back.

'I'll talk to you tomorrow,' his dad said. 'Love you, Arch.'

Archer sighed. 'Love you, too.'

He ended the call and sat staring at the phone. He just couldn't imagine how he would ever live up to his father's example. It was like the guy had been born knowing what to do. Although Archer was too young to remember if or when his father had ever been uncertain or screwed up stuff. Was five still too young? Or would Olive remember every single one of his fuck-ups to relay to her future therapist?

Oh, God, he could only imagine what she was telling her current therapist!

He groaned, cradling his head in his hands.

'Uh, chef?' Maribel was leaning out the back door with a concerned look on her face.

'Yes?' He straightened against the brick wall behind him, attempting to look at least somewhat competent.

'Cyrus says we're out of zucchini for the sandwiches.'

'How can that be?'

Maribel gave him a small smile. 'A lot of lunch orders for that veggie sandwich.'

'Oh.' Something like pride filled his chest. He remembered what that felt like. 'Tell him to sub in summer squash for today.'

'Got it.' She was about to turn to go back in, but gave him another once over. 'Something wrong?'

He almost shook his head and denied anything being wrong, but Maribel had kids and it took a village, right?

'Olive was sleepwalking last night. I'm worried she'll get out in the middle of the night.'

'Oh, I had a sleepwalker.'

'You did? Please tell me you didn't have to sleep outside their door until they turned thirteen.'

She laughed. 'No, no. Just put bells on the door.'

'Bells?'

'Yeah, we pulled some out of the Christmas decorations and tied them around the doorknob. That way, if he tried to open the door we heard him.'

'That's brilliant.'

'Parenthood makes you resourceful.'

'Something to look forward to, I guess.'

She gave him another sympathetic smile, but not like she felt bad for him, just that she understood what he was going through.

'If it makes you feel any better,' she said, 'my kid never tried to go anywhere. We'd just find him on the couch or sometimes in his sister's room. Once he curled up in the dog's bed and went back to sleep.'

He chuckled. 'That does make me feel better, actually. Thanks.'

'Of course, chef. I'm here if you need anything.' She ducked her head with another small smile and went back into the diner.

And just like last night with Iris, things felt a little lighter.

Chapter Fifteen

Two days later, Archer had the day off—as enforced by Gladys, who insisted he needed to balance work with his new family life. After watching him pace around the house for the first half of the day, Iris suggested they go to the spring farmers' market, mostly because he was making her crazy. Archer had perked up at that, and even though he was clearly planning to get things for the diner, Iris figured it still counted as a day off. Especially since Olive was along for the trip.

Iris had her tight by the hand as they made their way through the stalls. If she'd had a leash, she totally would have used it. She didn't trust this kid for a second. Not after her little sleepwalking episode.

'Can we get strawberries?' Olive asked.

'Not in season yet,' Archer said, and Olive frowned.

'We'll get something else that's just as good,' Iris assured her, even though looking around she saw mostly lettuce and other greenery she was sure Olive would immediately reject.

'Pretty good selection,' Archer said, perusing each table as they walked.

'We might not be Paris, but we do know how to have a farmers' market,' Iris said dryly and Archer rolled his eyes.

'So, what are you going to get?' she asked.

'I like to take a lap first and just see what everyone is offering.'

'Sure, makes sense,' Iris said, spotting and waving to a few of her students.

'Arugula looks good,' Archer said, his forehead creased in thought. It was similar to watching him cook. He was in chef mode. Iris bit down on a smile. Way too many neighbors out here today, and the last thing she needed was to set off the rumor mill by gazing at her boss with a goofy grin on her face.

'PUPPIES!!' Olive's screech stopped Iris in her tracks and nearly gave her a heart attack. She looked up to see Kira, Bennett and half of their pack in tow. 'Let's go see them!!' Olive tugged Iris along behind her through the crowd.

'You brought Elizabeth and Benny to the farmer's market?' Iris asked Kira as they approached.

Kira smiled, patting the big dogs on their heads. 'They're very well behaved.'

Bennett laughed. 'Yeah, Benny only snatched one peanut-butter cookie from Annie's booth.'

'That was a misunderstanding,' Kira said. 'And we paid for it.'

'Can I pet the puppies?' Olive asked, eyes wide. Elizabeth, Bennett's biggest dog, was nearly her height, and she gazed at Olive, her tongue lolling out of her mouth.

'Sure,' Kira said, squatting down to Olive's level. 'She likes it when you scratch right here.' She demonstrated by scratching between the dog's ears, and Olive followed suit, her face lighting up when the dog nudged closer to her.

Iris smiled and looked up to glance at Archer, but apparently they'd lost him.

'I was going to introduce you to Archer,' she said. 'But he's wandered off.'

Bennett laughed. 'How are things going with the new gig?'

Iris shrugged. 'It's fine.'

'Oh, and how's life with the chef?' Kira asked, standing back up with a knowing smirk on her face.

'Also fine.'

Fine, as in she spent way too much time thinking about how *fine* he was.

Kira's smirk grew.

But luckily, Olive had moved on to petting Benny and was now getting full-face licks and her delighted giggles attracted Kira's attention.

'Oh, he likes you!' she said, and Olive beamed.

'She probably tastes like maple syrup,' Iris said with a laugh.

'Well, that is the way to Benny's heart.'

'Iris, can we get a dog?'

'That's a question for your dad.'

'Where is he?' Olive asked. 'I need to ask him right now.'

Kira laughed. 'I like your spirit, kid.'

'Why don't we stay here with Olive, and you can go track him down,' Bennett said with a not-so innocent smile, like he knew the last thing Iris should do was spend time alone with her sexy boss. He was starting to fit in with this town a little *too* well. Him and Kira both.

'Yeah!' Olive cut off any response Iris was about to give. 'I'll

113

stay with the dogs and you go find my dad and then we'll ask him.'

Iris glanced back and forth between Bennett and Kira's conniving smiles and then sighed in defeat. 'Fine. I'll go find him. Won't be long.'

'Have fun!' Kira said with a wink.

'Don't take your eyes off of her,' Iris said, ignoring that comment. 'She wanders.'

'If you think this child is going to willingly leave these dogs, then you're crazy, but we'll keep a very close watch. I promise.' Kira raised a hand to her heart in a solemn vow and Iris just glared at her before traipsing off to find Archer.

It wasn't hard. He was surrounded by half a dozen septuagenarians and most of the book club.

'I had a sleepwalker!' Marissa was telling him as Iris approached. 'The little guy was always ending up in the strangest places. Found him one morning up in his tree house in the backyard.' She laughed like that was hilarious, but Archer looked horrified.

'Outside?' he croaked.

'Don't worry, they outgrow it eventually.'

'Right. That's very … comforting.'

'Did you try the baked ziti I dropped off last week?' Carol asked, nudging her friend aside to get closer to Archer. Iris bit down on a laugh. 'I would love to get a chef's opinion on it.'

'It's always a bit dry, if you ask me,' Estelle muttered, and the laugh escaped Iris's mouth.

'I … uh…' Archer stalled.

Iris knew for a fact most of the meals the town had dropped off were still frozen solid. Relief flooded Archer's face when he caught sight of her, as though he knew she would save him from having to explain that they were only three people and couldn't possibly consume that much food. And also, that he was a food snob.

'Okay, ladies, harassing-the-new-guy time is over now. Off you go.'

'Oh, Iris, you're no fun.' Marissa giggled.

'See you in class, girls.'

'Bye, sweetie.' Carol gave her a quick peck on the cheek, followed by more hugs and shoulder pats and goodbyes from all the other ladies.

'Your adoring fans?' he asked as the ladies wandered off.

'Some of the many,' Iris said with a smile.

'Where's Olive?'

'She's with Kira and Bennett and their dogs. Oh, and you should brace yourself because now she wants one.'

'Oh, God. Am I supposed to get her a dog?' The panic was clear in his voice.

Iris shook her head with a laugh. 'You don't have to get her a dog.'

'Okay, good. I don't think we can manage a dog.'

Iris ignored that *we*, the one she was not at all sure she wanted to be a part of, and started rifling through the canvas bag slung over Archer's arm. 'Whaddya get?'

'Mostly some fresh herbs, some lettuce, arugula…'

'Everything's green.'

'It's early in the season.'

Iris frowned. 'Come with me.' She linked her arm through his and tugged him through the crowd.

'Hi, Annie, hi, George,' she said when they arrived at the bakery table. 'This,' she said, turning to Archer, 'is the best table at the market. And baked goods are always in season.'

He smiled, that dimple popping in his cheek, and Iris had to look away lest she do something inappropriate here in the middle of town like lick her boss's face.

'Hi, Iris, hi, Archer, what can I get you?' Annie asked.

Iris shook the inappropriate thoughts from her head and turned her attention to the table spread with delights. Shortbread cookies, cardamom twists, sugar cookies in the shapes of little bunnies and chicks, chocolate donuts, and iced lemon pound cake were laid out in front of them. Annie had outdone herself this week.

'We'll take two slices of the pound cake and…' she turned to Archer, 'what do you think Olive would like?'

His brow furrowed in concentration as he considered what Olive might want and it was that consideration that nearly did Iris in. He was so damn thoughtful when it came to his kid.

'The bunny cookie.'

'Excellent choices,' Annie said, putting their treats in a bag and taking Iris's card for payment. 'Enjoying the market?' she asked Archer.

'I am, actually.'

Annie laughed. 'Don't look so surprised.'

He smiled. 'Sorry. I don't mean to be an asshole.'

'It just happens sometimes,' Iris finished for him with a pat on the arm. 'Thanks Annie!' she called, pulling Archer to their next stop. 'One more thing before we circle back to Olive.'

She kept her arm linked through his, her hand resting on the curve of his bicep. It was nice, walking side by side with him. It was nice to be out of the house together.

Not that it could be anything other than a friendly trip to the farmers' market, but she was allowed to enjoy the feel of

Archer's arm beneath her hand and the occasional brush of his hip against hers. Wasn't she? Of course she was.

The only dangerous part was that this nice day out together might make her want more of them.

'Here we are.' They stopped at the florist's table. 'Plenty of colors,' she grinned up at him and his returning smile had her stomach flipping and her cheeks warming.

'Beautiful,' he said, his eyes still on her face and, damn, he was handsome out here in the light of day. All this fresh air was making her lightheaded.

Lupita, who was manning the booth today, cleared her throat and Iris tore her gaze away from Archer's.

'Hey, Lu.'

'Hi Iris.' Lupita glanced from Iris to Archer, a knowing look on her face but Iris could not deal with another busybody Dreamer today.

'A bunch of the yellow tulips and a bunch of the pink, please,' Iris said before the woman could ask any questions about Archer or Olive or their living arrangement or Archer's family history.

'Here you are.' Lupita handed Iris two bundles of flowers wrapped in brown paper and Archer handed his card over before Iris could get to hers.

'Thanks, Lu. See you Tuesday for my spring wreath-making class,' Iris said before they walked away. 'I wasn't trying to make you buy me flowers,' she said to Archer, jokingly, but finding him looking at her intently again.

'I don't mind buying you flowers.'

'In a professional way, of course,' she said, not able to help the teasing smile on her face.

'Of course,' he said with a slight smile of his own. He'd

dipped his head closer to her ear and his words were warm on her cheek. His hand slid to the small of her back, guiding her through the crowd. The press of his fingers into her body sent sparks skittering down her spine.

But stronger than the feeling of Archer's big, warm hand was the feeling of the town watching them. And Iris knew this town. She knew how they thought and how they talked. And if they thought anything untoward was going on between her and Archer, what would that mean for his custody agreement?

The town would probably be delighted if they were officially together, but Archer couldn't be seen as someone who had casual flings left and right. What kind of environment would that be for a little girl? Never mind that it was the exact environment that Iris had grown up in, and she'd turned out just fine, except for maybe a bit of an issue with commitment.

But that didn't matter. Archer needed to be seen as the responsible dad that he was.

And she could not get in the way of that.

'We should probably find Olive,' she said, taking a hard right past the last booth and onto the grassy lawn where she'd last seen Olive and Kira. Archer's hand dropped from her back and she refused to feel sad about its absence. It was one thing to flirt with Archer in the privacy of his own home, but out here they needed to be careful.

She had to be careful with this considerate man and his little girl. The last thing she wanted was to cause problems for either of them.

Chapter Sixteen

'I have a great idea,' Iris announced as she swept into the kitchen. She'd had a yoga class to teach this evening, so Archer hadn't seen her for dinner with Olive. It had been a silent and awkward meal, but his daughter had eaten two servings of pasta with copious amounts of butter and parmesan on it, so he wasn't going to push her to speak, too. One thing at a time.

'Oh?' he asked.

'A town meeting,' she said triumphantly like this should make sense to him.

'What about it?'

'Oh, right, I forgot you're an outsider,' she said with a teasing smile. 'Dream Harbor has biweekly town meetings where people can bring up any issues pertinent to the community.'

'Okay…'

She let out a frustrated breath and he tried not to notice how cute she was when she was excited. But it was impossible.

She was adorable. It had been impossible not to notice as she led him through the farmers' market yesterday and it was impossible now as she hopped up onto her usual stool, eyes bright with her great idea.

'I thought we could go and ask if anyone had thoughts on the pancake recipe.'

He wiped his hands on the towel hanging over his shoulder and crossed his arms over his chest. He did not stand like that to make Iris's gaze flick over his biceps, he just happened to be comfortable this way. And if Iris noticed his arms, well, that was not his fault.

'Let me get this straight,' he said. 'You want me to try and get some kind of town consensus on this pancake recipe?'

'I heard you put poppy seeds in the pancakes last week, Archer.' She raised a brow in accusation.

'I did.'

'People did not like it.'

'I know.'

'Okay, so I think this might be a good way to get some more ideas on things to try.'

'I don't think so.'

Her face fell and he wanted to kick himself, but pleasing Iris was not something that should be on his list of priorities. Keeping the diner afloat and Olive alive were his priorities. Not seeing the nanny smile.

'It's my diner now and I'm in charge of the menu. I'm going with what I think is best.'

There was something new in her eyes when she looked at him again, something he hadn't seen from her. She looked … pissed.

'What's it like?' she asked with a little scoff.

'What's what like?'

'To be so damn confident in yourself, to think you know what's best about everything?'

'I don't—'

'No, I'm really curious, because I've never felt that about anything, really. I've never just known what I wanted to be or what I wanted to do and I've just kinda drifted around, but you,' again that little scoff, 'you know exactly what you want to do. You're a big important chef and you're the expert, so—'

'I'm not,' he said, his voice sharp, cutting through her little speech. 'Not anymore. I'm barely fucking holding on here, Iris.'

She held his gaze, those green eyes zeroing in on his every insecurity. She lifted her chin. 'I've lived here my whole life,' she said. 'And a lot of things have changed because things always do, but those pancakes have been the same for my whole life. There's comfort in that, Archer. People like that. They need it. I need it.'

'You do?'

She shrugged, like she'd let him see more than she'd intended when she'd started this conversation. 'The diner is one of the few places left in town that the old folks remember going to when they were kids. It's important to them, so it's important to me.'

'I don't think it's true.'

'What?'

'That you don't know what you want to do with your life, that you're not confident. Iris you're amazing at what you do. At everything you do.' He had yet to see her struggle with anything. From where he stood, Iris didn't drift, she floated. She floated and she danced and she laughed and she just made everyone's life *better*. She made his life better. Even when he felt like everything was falling apart.

'Nah.' She shook off his compliment. 'You know what they say—"Jack of all trades, master of none"—or something like that.'

'Nobody's a master of anything. Look at me. I can't even make pancakes.' He gestured to the mess on the counter, wanting her to forgive him, wanting her to see the truth of him.

She relented, giving him a small smile, the soft light of the kitchen catching the gold in her hair. And she was just so…

Tempting.

'What's that from?' she asked. Her eyes had flicked down and she was pointing to one of the scars on his arm, a long one that ran across the top of his forearm, right above the wrist.

'Oven.' He'd been moving too fast, desperate to prove himself to his professor, and his arm had hit the hot oven rack as he was pulling out a fresh batch of croissants. They came out terribly, just to add insult to injury, and his professor had actually spit a bit of one out in front of the whole pastry class. Archer hadn't slept the rest of the week. He ate and breathed croissants, baking batch after batch until they were perfect. Because he didn't fail.

Or at least he didn't in his old life.

He felt exhausted just thinking about it.

'And this one?' Her finger hovered over his arm, pointing to another scar.

'Cast-iron skillet.'

'And this one?' She trailed a single finger over the scar on the underside of his wrist and her touch sparked along his skin. She was looking at him again, her head tilted, eyes curious.

And suddenly his old life didn't exist.

The only real thing was this kitchen. This kitchen and Iris's fingertip leaving a trail of raised hairs along his arm.

He wanted to take her to bed.

He wanted to tuck her in.

He wanted to…

'Broken glass,' he said, his voice rough with everything he wanted to do to her. That he *couldn't* do to her.

There were too many things he couldn't do right now. He wanted to growl in frustration.

'I didn't know cooking was such a dangerous job.' Her finger was still on him, tracing back and forth over that scar.

'Restaurant kitchens can get intense,' he ground out, struggling for control. 'A lot of fast-moving parts. Add heat and sharp objects, and it can get dangerous sometimes.'

She took her hand away and Archer had to bite back the shuddering sigh he felt building in his chest. He'd known it was a bad idea to hire Iris as his nanny. He knew he was attracted to her. He knew how precarious a situation it was to have a single woman living under his roof, for both of them.

But this was so much worse than he'd thought.

If Iris was going to look at him like that and touch him like that…

What was he going to do?

He hadn't smoked since moving here, but suddenly he wished he hadn't given it up.

'What kind are you trying tonight?'

Archer blinked. Pancakes. She was talking about pancakes while he was thinking about taking her to bed.

'Buttermilk.'

'Yum.' She wiped her finger around the edge of the bowl where the batter had dribbled over and lifted it to her mouth. Archer grabbed her wrist.

'Hey!'

'What are you doing?' he asked, leaning closer. What was *he* doing? Why was he touching her? Why was he leaning across the counter toward her? Why was his entire focus fixed on her luscious mouth? He'd clearly lost his mind, but she was reeling him in with those damn eyes and that mischievous smile. It was back and he wanted it to stay. He didn't like that he'd upset her, that he'd slipped into his cocky-bastard tendencies. He found that he didn't want to be that guy anymore. At least not around Iris.

'Licking the batter.' The word *licking* sent fire through his veins and a million inappropriate thoughts through his head.

'You shouldn't eat raw batter.' He was still holding her wrist and her pulse fluttered beneath his fingers. Her tongue swiped along her bottom lip and Archer nearly groaned.

'I was just going to have a little.' The batter was dripping down her finger.

'I should probably taste it first. Make sure it's good.' His voice was low and rough, and they were far too close and her pulse had sped up and this was a bad idea and ... his mind blanked as he took Iris's finger in his mouth and licked it clean. He ran his tongue over the length of it, that finger that had just teased along his skin, nipping the tip before he released it with a quiet *pop*.

Her eyes widened but she didn't pull away. Instead, a small whimper escaped her lips. Oh God, he wanted to pull her onto the counter and lick the rest of her. The thought slammed into him. It was a visceral need, a demand from every inch of his body.

Never mind that his mind was screaming at him to stop! To turn back and find the line he wasn't supposed to cross!

He couldn't hear that voice anymore.

All he could hear was Iris's breath, mingling with his own, like they'd both run to get here. He tugged her closer, his hand still wrapped around her wrist, the taste of pancake batter still on his tongue.

Her gaze flicked down to his mouth and lingered there. She licked her own lips like she was thinking about what she wanted to do to his.

'Archer.' His name sounded like a plea.

'Tell me to stop,' he nearly begged. If she told him to stop, he would. He would step away and they could pretend he'd never done that, he'd never tasted her skin. 'Tell me to stop, Iris and go back to your room.'

Another little whimper.

He was close enough now to run his nose along the soft skin of her cheek. He was going to kiss her. He was going to kiss his nanny and ruin absolutely everything, but he couldn't stop himself, he couldn't pull away. He didn't want to.

Until he heard the distant ringing of … Christmas bells?

'What…' Iris's voice sounded far away and dreamy. She'd turned from him and he wanted her back, but she was tugging her wrist away and hopping down from her stool and moving toward the door.

The front door where Olive once again was trying to get out in her sleep, the Christmas bells on the door ringing with every attempt.

Christ.

He let the air rush out of his lungs, let the kitchen and living room rush back into his consciousness, let his body shake off the feel of Iris in his hand.

He'd almost kissed her.

He'd almost ruined everything.

'Come on, kid,' Iris whispered, ushering Olive past him and back down the hall. 'Time for bed.'

He let her tuck Olive in. He waited in the kitchen.

She didn't come back.

Chapter Seventeen

A few days later, Iris was sitting at Hazel's tiny dining room table sipping a cup of tea.

'So, she doesn't remember it?' Hazel asked, her gaze turning to where Olive and Noah were playing checkers on the coffee table. His nieces, Cece and Ivy, were sprawled out on the carpet next to them coloring in their coloring books. Hazel had had the bright idea of creating Pumpkin Spice coloring books to sell to tourists, but the locals loved them, too. Iris personally owned one and had sent one to her mom for Christmas. They'd sold out twice this month already. The girls were currently working on a very creative interpretation of The Pumpkin Spice Café, complete with purple pumpkins and a pink Casper in the window.

The layout of Hazel's cottage was similar to Archer's, except for the kitchen having walls and being closed off from the living room, but Hazel had co-opted a corner of the living area for a dining room table. From her vantage point, Iris could see Olive jump three of Noah's checkers. The little girl smiled triumphantly as he groaned.

'Nope. I asked her and she just looked at me like I was nutty.'

'Hmm.' Hazel's brow furrowed as she took another sip of tea.

'Anyway, I thought maybe if we came for a daytime visit, she'd stop trying to get over here at night.'

'It's worth a try,' Hazel said. 'And this was the perfect time, with Ivy and Cece here for the weekend.'

'Yeah, we like Olive!' Ivy shouted from her position in the living room, and Olive gave her a shy smile. The girls had just met an hour ago, but the cousins were happy to let Olive join them in playing with their favorite uncle. The foursome had already made matching friendship bracelets.

'Yes, we like Olive, too,' Hazel said.

'Were you and Cate close?' Iris asked.

'Not very. But she used to bring Olive into the bookstore all the time.'

Iris found herself wishing she'd known Cate better. Maybe that would have helped Olive get through this whole thing. While Dr. Bloomfield, Olive's therapist, had assured her that children were resilient, Iris still couldn't imagine losing her mother at such a young age. Or now, for that matter.

'Noah, please tell me you're letting her win,' Iris said, shaking off her melancholy for Olive. If the little girl could still find it in her to laugh at Noah's horrible checkers skills, then so could she.

'I really wish I could,' he said. 'But she's a killer.'

'Olive's the best at checkers,' Cece said, coming to stand beside the coffee table.

'Yep, the *best* best at checkers,' Ivy repeated, and her cousin shot her a look that said she didn't like to be mimicked but would allow it for the sake of complimenting their new friend.

'Good girl, Olive,' Hazel said. 'Show him no mercy.'

'Thanks, babe.'

Hazel grinned at him, and he winked back.

'How's that trip you guys are planning?' Iris asked.

'I'm still worried about leaving the store, but Noah almost has me convinced we should go.'

'We're definitely going,' he called, and Hazel rolled her eyes.

'We'll see.'

Iris smiled. She understood why Olive kept trying to sneak over here. It was nice here. It felt like a home, like people that loved each other lived here. You could feel it. Archer's house still smelled like fresh paint and Ikea furniture.

'Hey, Olive,' Iris said, an idea striking her. 'What's your favorite color?'

'Yellow,' she answered, without hesitation. If Iris could have the confidence of a kindergartener declaring their favorite color, she'd be all set.

'We should repaint your room.'

Olive's head spun so fast to face her, Iris's poltergeist fears almost reignited.

'Really?! Paint it yellow?'

Iris shrugged. 'Sure.'

'Yay!' Olive was up and dancing and the girls joined her chanting, 'Yellow! Yellow!' And the checkers game was forgotten.

'Shouldn't you check with Archer?' Hazel asked, a bemused expression on her face as Noah joined in the dancing.

'Probably. But I don't think he'll mind.' She didn't actually know that at all, but after Archer had licked her finger two nights ago, she'd been avoiding him. She didn't really feel up for a chat about redecorating. Not when she'd been about to pour that entire bowl of batter over her head just so he would lick her everywhere else.

It seemed best to steer clear.

'What do you think about sleeping with your boss?' she blurted out, and Noah froze mid-dance move.

'Hey, girls!' he said, too loudly. 'How about we move this dance party outside?'

'Yeah!' they all shouted.

He followed the girls racing out the side door, flashing Iris an amused smile on his way out.

Hazel spun to face her, eyebrow arched in question. 'What's going on over there, Iris?'

Iris sighed with all the drama she was currently feeling, which was a lot.

'He almost kissed me.'

'He what?!' Hazel looked murderous. 'That is unacceptable. Totally inappropriate.'

'Hazel...'

'How dare he? Doesn't he realize he holds all the power here?'

'Hazel...'

'I mean, really, taking advantage of the situation like that.'

'Hazel!'

Her friend blinked in surprise. 'What?'

'I one-thousand percent wanted him to.'

'Oh.' Her eyes widened behind her glasses. 'Huh.'

'Yeah, I know.'

'So, what are you going to do?'

Iris groaned. 'I don't know! I mean, objectively, I know it's a very bad idea. I need this job and I even kinda like Olive now and I don't want to mess with her ... with her healing process. Plus, a free place to live has been great. I actually have some money in my bank account for the first time in ... maybe ever.'

Hazel nodded. 'Okay, good. So I think that's your answer.'

But Iris hated that answer.

'On the other hand,' she started, and Hazel closed her eyes and sighed. 'Just hear me out! On the other hand, he's really hot!' Okay, that didn't sound like the best reasoning.

'Iris, plenty of people are hot. Go find a different hot person.'

Iris groaned again. She didn't want a different hot person and maybe that should alarm her more than anything, but now she was on a mission to convince Hazel this was a good idea. As though Hazel was the one in charge, and with her permission, Iris could have sex with the hot chef guilt-free.

'It's not just that!' He was also dedicated and persistent and sexy and those forearms haunted her dreams, and ... she was getting off track. He'd come back for his daughter. He was honorable and sweet, when he wanted to be—and talented, so freaking talented. Hadn't Hazel ever heard of competence porn? Watching this man chop veggies had made Iris hornier than anything in a long time.

'There's this tension between us,' she said, instead of listing all of Archer's best attributes. 'Maybe we need to just get it out of our systems?' And no one needed to know. Except apparently, Hazel.

Hazel looked at her over the rim of her mug like Iris was

the dumbest person to ever live. It was very possible that she was.

'Do you really think that has worked for anyone in the history of the world?' Hazel asked. 'When has sex ever made things easier to walk away from?'

'When it's really bad?' Iris suggested.

'So, you want to have sex with Archer because you think it will be really bad and you'll be able to move on and work for him with no problem after that?'

Damn, Hazel and her damn reasoning. Iris should have tried this with someone else. What was Kira up to today? She made questionable choices all the time.

'No,' Iris confessed. 'I don't think it would be bad at all.' The feel of Archer's tongue on her finger, lapping up the batter, echoed through her body, the memory of it nearly as strong as the real thing. No, it wouldn't be bad at all. If that tongue could make her feel like that from just licking her finger, just imagine what he could do if he licked—

'Okay, so I think you need to take sex off the table.'

Or do it on the table…

Iris shook her head. 'Right. Of course. You're one hundred percent right.' She wasn't stupid. She knew what she was doing every time she snuck out of her room to talk to him in the dim light of the kitchen, to ogle his arms, to flirt with him, letting her shirt slip down her arm, flaunting her shorts that were barely shorts. She'd broken down his defenses.

And all he was trying to do was to prove to himself, his daughter and the entire town that he was dad material. Being seduced by the nanny probably wasn't going to help his case.

God, she was the worst.

Noah and the girls raced back into the house.

'Is it safe?' he asked, shaking water from his hair. 'It started to rain.' He grabbed a towel from the hall closet and tossed it onto Olive's head. She giggled from underneath it.

'It's safe,' Iris said, and Hazel raised a brow. 'It is! You're right. I will be keeping things strictly professional from here on out.'

Hazel still looked skeptical, and Iris was still *feeling* skeptical, but she was determined now. No more flirting with the boss. No more sexy eyes and suggestive smiles. Nope. She was all business.

Ha! 'All business' was never something Iris had been called, but she could do it. She got up and went over to help Olive dry off. She rubbed the towel over her head, savoring the giggles still coming from underneath. If she screwed things up with Archer, she would definitely have to leave. And oddly enough, she didn't want to leave this kid. She didn't want to think about how Olive would feel if she did leave.

Not that she thought Olive liked her all that much, but she tolerated her. She talked to her and even occasionally ate the food Iris gave her, and frankly, that seemed like a lot at the moment. She didn't want to think about Olive having to get readjusted to a new grown-up in her life. Not yet.

'All dry?' she asked, pulling the towel off. Olive's hair was a wild mess around her head. Cece and Ivy were walking around with towels still over them pretending to be ghosts or zombies. It was unclear. Olive laughed at them before turning back to Iris.

'Can we have ice cream for dinner?' she asked.

'Don't push it, kid. We still have to break the news to your dad that we're repainting that pink nightmare of a room.'

Olive frowned.

'Oh, stop. Your dad is a good cook. Maybe he'll let you help again tonight.'

That got Olive to brighten slightly.

'Here, take an umbrella,' Hazel said, joining them at the door. 'It's really pouring now.'

'Thanks. And thanks for the pep talk.'

'Anytime.'

'And thanks for the checkers game, Noah.'

'I still want a rematch,' he said, shooting a fake glare at Olive.

Olive grinned.

'I'll see if we can arrange that,' Iris said with a laugh. 'But during the daytime and with permission, right Olive?'

Iris earned herself a scowl for that, but she ignored it and steered Olive out the door.

'Bye, Olive!' Ivy and Cece called from the doorway.

'Bye, girls!' Iris tugged Olive back under the umbrella from where she'd scooted out into the rain to wave to her new friends.

Time to go home and face Archer.

And act like he was nothing but her boss.

Chapter Eighteen

'Why does it smell like wet paint in here—' Archer stopped dead in the doorway of Olive's room, a scowl etched on his face.

Oh, right, Iris had forgotten to mention the whole room-painting idea. She winced. 'We're just doing a little makeover.'

'A makeover?'

'Yeah! And I'm going to have a sleepover in Iris's room tonight while it dries,' Olive told him over her shoulder while moving her little roller up and down the wall. Iris had gotten the room prepped while Olive was at school and the two had been painting all afternoon, although Olive hadn't really been pulling her weight with that tiny roller, and Iris's arms were tired. She brushed a stray hair from her face with her forearm, not wanting to use her painty fingers. She was not a neat painter. Most of her overalls and seventy-five percent of her skin was splattered in buttercup yellow.

'I hope that's okay,' she said with an apologetic smile.

Archer glowered from his position in the doorway. 'Can I speak with you for a minute?'

Iris glanced at Olive, and the little girl just shrugged as if to say Iris was on her own with this one. 'Thanks a lot, kid,' Iris muttered as she shuffled after Archer, down the hall and out into the kitchen, fully prepared to be scolded for not checking with him first about the paint. She should have. She knew that. But it was hard to check in when she was avoiding him like the plague. A very sexy plague.

'I think I owe you an apology,' he said.

Iris blinked. 'You do?' Well, that was not what she was expecting.

'Yes, I do. About the other night…'

Oh, that. That thing Iris was very purposefully not thinking about. About Archer's tongue on her skin and all his intense energy focused directly on her, like he wanted to put her on the counter and use that tongue in so many more interesting ways. She definitely hadn't gotten off in the shower this morning thinking about it.

That would have been inappropriate.

'I shouldn't have done that. It was … I was … I don't know what I was thinking. I apologize.'

'Oh.'

He ran a hand roughly through his hair like he was frustrated with himself. 'Maybe this isn't working out. I don't want to make you uncomfortable, and I obviously did…'

'I'm comfortable! Very comfortable. Really, no need to apologize.'

'Iris.'

'I'm fine.'

'Iris, I licked you.'

Oh, God, why did he say that out loud?! The word *lick* sounded absolutely filthy from his stern mouth.

'It really wasn't that big of a deal. Or it doesn't have to be. We can just forget it.' She blew the hair from her face, really wishing she wasn't mostly yellow for this conversation.

His frown had only intensified with her protests.

'Look, Archer. It wasn't all you.' She felt the flush rise to her cheeks. She hadn't ever planned to meet this head-on, but here she was. 'I was flirting with you, too. It was mutual.'

A muscle twitched in his jaw like he was grinding his back teeth.

'But you were right,' she went on. 'We need to keep this professional. Which I fully intend to do. From now on. Okay?' She really didn't want to get fired. Not now. Not when things were going well with Olive and she had some extra cash, and she really didn't want to find a new place to live.

He relaxed slightly, his gaze still holding her in its grasp. Finally, he relented. 'Okay, fine.'

Iris blew out a sigh of relief. 'Great.'

'But, Iris…'

'Yeah?'

'You need to ask me before redecorating my house.'

'Right. Sorry.'

He softened a little more, his brow smoothing out. 'But I am glad you're making Olive's room more homey for her.'

Iris smiled. 'You're welcome.'

He nodded. 'Right. Okay, I'm going to shower before dinner, but you're welcome to stay.'

Her smile grew. 'What are you making?'

'Nothing fancy tonight. Salad Nicoise with fresh sourdough.'

'Not fancy? Sir, before I moved in I ate cereal for dinner five out of seven days a week.'

He looked truly horrified by that statement and Iris couldn't help but laugh.

'Dinner's at seven.' He stalked off to the bathroom and Iris definitely didn't imagine him stripping down for the shower. She didn't have time for that. She had a bedroom to paint.

'You didn't finish while I was gone?' she yelled in mock dismay as she came back into Olive's room. 'What did I even hire you for?'

Olive laughed. 'I can't reach the top!'

'Oh, right. You're short.' Iris frowned at her and Olive giggled some more. 'I forgot.'

'I'm a kid!'

'That explains a lot.' She ruffled Olive's hair. 'Come on, let's finish up before dinner. Your dad's making something good.'

Olive wrinkled her nose. 'Good for you or good for me?'

'You can't survive on Pop-Tarts alone, kid. Trust me. I've tried.'

'Hmph.'

Olive wasn't painting anymore. In fact, she wasn't even standing anymore.

'You're getting paint in your hair,' Iris said.

'I don't care.'

Iris stepped over her prone body. 'Suit yourself.'

'Iris?'

'Yeah?'

'Can my mom see me still?'

Oof. Alarm bells immediately started ringing. She was not qualified for this conversation. But Olive was staring up at her with big, round eyes and so much sadness. Sadness a five-year-old should never have to carry. It made Iris want to scoop her up and wrap her in something soft and keep her safe.

She sighed. 'I don't really know.'

'Grandma says she can.'

'Grandmas are pretty wise, so she's probably right.' Iris sat down on the plastic drop cloth next to Olive. 'I don't think people we love ever really leave us.'

'So, she *can* see me?'

This did not feel like the time for abstract, philosophical thoughts on what happened after death. This baby missed her mother. And at this point, Iris would say literally anything to make her feel better.

'Yeah, she can see you.'

Olive smiled. 'Do you think she'll like my new room?'

Iris swallowed all the uncomfortable feelings that were rising in her throat. 'I think she'll love it.'

Olive was running one hand up and down Iris's leg and Iris wondered if she even knew she was doing it. It was the first time Olive had ever reached out to touch her.

'I had a neighbor who died when I was young,' Iris told her, thinking of Josie and their quiet afternoons together. It hadn't made sense to her that Josie could simply stop existing. She was still there in her favorite soap operas and her special Sunday sauce. Iris refused to think of her as *gone*. 'But I know she's with me when I eat certain foods or see a hummingbird in the garden. She loved hummingbirds.'

Olive was quiet for a long time, her little hand still moving, tracing the seam of Iris's overalls.

'We used to have a garden,' she said after a while.

'Do you want to plant a new one? I bet your mom would like it if you had one again.'

LAURIE GILMORE

Olive nodded, her gaze solemn when it met Iris's.

'Okay, deal,' Iris said, still trying to steer this conversation in a direction that didn't make her want to cry.

'I never had a dad before,' Olive said, ping-ponging between topics in a way Iris had learned was common for her age.

'Me neither.'

A shuffling sound in the hallway caught Iris's attention. Archer had paused at Olive's room after his shower. He raised an eyebrow in question at the two on the ground, but Iris smiled to let him know everything was fine. Or mostly fine.

'But now I have one,' Olive said, not noticing her father.

'Yes, you do. You're lucky.'

'I am?'

'Sure. Your dad came right away when you needed him. That's what makes a good dad.' Her gaze snagged on Archer, on his face, on the smile tugging at his mouth.

'Really?'

'Of course! You don't want one of those dads that doesn't show up. Trust me.'

Olive was thinking this over, her nose scrunched up and her mouth twisted to the side.

'But where was he before?'

'He was …' Iris didn't really know what Archer wanted Olive to think about why he hadn't been with her from the start.

'You were a surprise,' he said, startling them both.

Olive sat up. 'A surprise?'

'Yeah, your mom was doing such a great job that you didn't need a dad right away. But then when your mom … uh…' He

140

glanced at Iris, panic clear on his face, like he wished he hadn't waded into this conversation.

'Your mom knew your dad would take such good care of you when she was gone,' Iris jumped in.

Olive frowned.

'You were a great surprise, Olive,' he said, his voice rough. 'The best one, really.'

Iris didn't know how much of that he meant, but he was definitely selling it.

Olive brightened. 'I was?'

'Yep.'

'And what about Iris?' she asked, turning her attention back to Iris. 'Did I surprise you, too?'

'Big time.'

'Really?' Olive was clearly thrilled to be surprising people left and right.

'Sure. I didn't expect to actually like you.'

'Iris, jeez,' Archer huffed but Olive just threw her head back and laughed.

'I thought you'd be terrible, actually,' Iris went on. 'I thought you'd be sticky and weird.'

'I'm not weird!'

'Oh, you definitely are, but so am I, so I like it.'

Olive was up now, hopping from foot to foot. 'I surprised everyone.'

'You sure did,' Archer said with a grin, that dimple popping in his cheek. Iris looked away.

'All right, kid, quit stalling. We need to finish the job.'

'I'll help,' Archer said.

'You just showered.'

'Not everyone paints themselves when they paint a room,'

he said with a teasing smirk, his eyes roving over her paint splattered body.

Iris huffed. 'Then they aren't having nearly enough fun.' She stuck her tongue out at him and he grinned.

And that conversation they'd just had in the kitchen felt like it was a million years ago and not at all relevant anymore.

Chapter Nineteen

Somehow, in between haunting his dreams and painting his daughter's room, Iris had convinced Archer to attend a Dream Harbor town meeting. He didn't believe it would help, but he'd been the head chef at the diner for three weeks now, and he was still getting complaints about the pancakes. And even though some of his other menu options, like the veggie sandwich and the French onion soup, had taken off, he couldn't get what Iris had said out of his head. The people came to the diner for comfort. Not elevated comfort food, just the comfort of a familiar place with familiar food. And maybe that was something worth giving them.

'No, no, no. We can't sit there.' Iris tugged on his arm and led him away from where he was about to take a seat.

'Why not?'

'That's where the book club sits.'

'So?'

Iris looked at him with an exasperated sigh. 'We can't just steal their seats.'

'But they're not even here.'

'Oh, they'll be here, and I'm not about to be the one to take their seats.'

'Are they assigned or something?'

Another sigh and an added eyeroll. 'No. It's just ... it's just how it is. That's where they sit.'

Of course. That was just the way it was. Same seats. Same pancakes. Archer was suddenly feeling less positive about this plan. He had a feeling the residents of Dream Harbor were about to eat him alive.

'Hey!' A dark-haired woman who Archer recognized from the farmers' market rushed up to Iris and gave her a quick kiss on the cheek. They hadn't really had time to meet that day; Iris had suddenly been in a rush to get home. 'I didn't know you were coming,' she said to Iris.

'We decided at the last minute.'

'Oh.' The woman turned her shrewd gaze to Archer's face. 'Hello, there.'

'Kira, this is Archer. Archer, this is my friend, Kira.'

'I remember. You're the reason my kid wants a dog now.'

A slow smile spread across Kira's face. 'Sorry about that, but it's nice to *officially* meet you. I've heard a lot about you.'

'No, she hasn't,' Iris hastily cut in. 'What are you doing here, anyway? Is Bennett here, too?'

'He's over there saving our seats. Come on.'

Iris followed Kira through the crowd, and Archer followed behind. He'd never imagined a small-town biweekly meeting would have a turn out like this, but maybe he should have known. If they cared that much about their diner offerings, they must care about everything else, too. Again, he questioned the sanity of throwing himself at the mercy of this crowd.

It was his kitchen, his menu, his reputation on the line. And if his old dreams were dead, he wasn't about to fail at this new one. He'd never once crowd-sourced a recipe before. But ever since Iris had called him out for being a cocky bastard, he'd been trying to adjust. He thought Cyrus was going to tip over when he asked for his opinion on the new egg dishes he was working on. Thanks to Maribel's recommendation, they'd hired a culinary student to help prep in the mornings, and their breakfast service had gone much smoother because of it.

The women stopped in front of a row of folding chairs on the side of the meeting space. A dark-haired man with a striking resemblance to Superman stood up to greet them.

'Hey, Iris.'

'Hi, Bennett. This is Archer.' She gestured to where he loomed behind her.

'Hey, man, nice to meet you.' Bennett stuck out his hand and Archer shook it. 'Welcome to the town meeting.'

'Yeah, thanks. I didn't realize it would be this … well-attended,' Archer said, glancing around as people started taking their seats.

Bennett chuckled. 'Oh, it's a whole thing.'

'So why are you here?' Kira asked as they slid down the row into their seats.

'Archer is going to ask for pancake suggestions,' said Iris.

Kira's brows rose until they were hidden under her bangs. 'Yikes.'

'Yikes?' Archer queried, and she smiled at him in a rather ominous way.

'Just, I'm sure they'll have a lot of suggestions for you.'

Iris shot her a glare. 'Exactly. That's the point. It'll be good.' She patted his knee in a way he guessed was supposed to be comforting, but all that registered in his brain was that Iris was touching his leg. 'You'll get lots of new ideas to try and I'm sure one of them will be the right one.'

'The old one,' he muttered.

'The one everyone wants,' she shot back with a little smirk when he looked at her. She had her hair in her usual braid, cinnamon-laced with ginger that somehow looked beautiful even under the garish lights of the meeting hall. Little wisps of hair had escaped it and framed her face, her eyes twinkling and mischievous, her lips tipped into a playful smile. Like she was always teasing him about something.

The past few days had been awkward between them, neither knowing how to behave. The easy comfort they'd been starting to fall into had been broken by his actions and his subpar apology, and now they spent most of their time keeping Olive as a barrier between them.

But right now, Olive was home with Kimmy reading in the blanket fort she'd set up with Iris earlier in the day. And there was nothing between him and Iris. Nothing between her hand and his knee.

'Let's get started.' A man spoke into the microphone behind the podium and the feedback squealed through the room. 'Sorry about that,' he said with a wince. 'But at least I got your attention.'

He smiled through the groans in the room.

Archer recognized him as the mayor. He'd been back into the diner several times since Archer started, always tried the latest pancake iteration, and always found it lacking.

'We have something exciting on the docket this evening,' the mayor went on.

'Is it about no-mow May?' someone shouted from the audience. 'Because I don't understand it.'

'Well, no...'

'It's for the pollinators!' someone else shouted back, ignoring the mayor's protests.

'I have to have a mess of a lawn for a month for the bees?' The first voice did not seem pleased with this idea.

'Yes, for the bees! No pollinators, no food,' an older lady in a floral top countered.

'That's a bit of an exaggeration,' a gruff old man added.

'If we could just get back on track...' The mayor attempted to get the meeting in order, but the room had descended into an argument about, from what Archer could gather, whether or not dandelions were weeds or flowers and if not mowing your lawn for a month really did anything helpful for the earth.

Iris leaned into his side. 'This is pretty typical. Don't worry, they'll tire themselves out in a minute or two.'

'Hmm.' He frowned, and to his shock, Iris reached up and pressed two fingers between his eyebrows. 'What are you doing?'

'I'm smoothing out these aggressive forehead lines.'

'Why?'

'I think this will go better if you look less like you're going to murder everyone.' She took her fingers away and he wanted them back. He wanted them tugging on his hair, he wanted them digging into his back.

'This is just my face.'

She shook her head. 'No, I've seen you with different faces. Like when you look at Olive and you get all soft and gooey.'

'I don't get gooey.'

'Oh, you definitely do. You may not know it yet, but that kid's totally got you wrapped around her little finger.'

'Me? You're the one repainting her room and building forts all day.'

'It's all just part of my job.'

'Okay, sure.' Who were they kidding? Olive had them both wrapped around her finger. How could she not? She needed them. And Archer had never been needed before. Not like that.

The commotion around them had died down, bringing Archer's thoughts back to the meeting.

'What I was actually going to say,' Mayor Kelly said, with a pointed look to the crowd, 'is that we need to discuss the brand new, upcoming Strawberry Festival. We don't even have a name for it yet.'

'Isn't the "Strawberry Festival" a name for it?' Archer whispered to Iris.

She rolled her eyes at him like that was an absurd thing to say. 'Not here it's not. Dream Harbor likes a more … elaborate name.'

'But,' the mayor went on, 'before we get to that, we have our very own world-renowned chef here tonight and he has something to say.'

'Is it an apology for that travesty of a short stack he served me the other day?' A man down front called out.

'Less of the murder face,' Iris whispered and Archer tried his best to decrease the level of his scowl.

'Archer, why don't you come up here?' The mayor gestured enthusiastically to the podium.

'Good luck,' Kira whispered as Archer shuffled out of their row.

Judging by the disapproving faces he passed on his way to the front, he was going to need it.

'Welcome, chef,' the mayor said with a smile and a handshake. 'The floor is yours.'

Archer looked out at the eclectic crowd. It seemed that representatives from every age bracket and cultural community were present this evening, and they were all staring at him in expectation. He rolled his shoulders back. He could do this. He'd handled the dinner rush at more restaurants than he could remember at this point. Surely, a little town meeting wouldn't be too bad.

If he was stuck here in this town, at this diner, he was going to give it everything he had, just like he always did.

'Right,' he said. 'I'm aware of people's feelings about the pancakes.'

'They stink!' a little old lady yelled from the back. Probably a friend of Iris's.

Archer cleared his throat and went on. 'I'm aware they are not what you are accustomed to and I'm working on the recipe.' Here's where he needed to swallow every urge in his body to say 'fuck it' and do what he thought was best. 'I thought I would check in and see if you had any input on what the original pancakes tasted like. Anything that might help me get the recipe right.'

Kaori Kim stood up. 'Hello, chef. Kaori, book-club president.'

A few people groaned but Kaori just shushed them.

'We already know each other,' Archer reminded her, waiting for her suggestion.

'Has anyone tried calling Martha?' she asked, ignoring Archer's comment. 'Wouldn't she have the recipe?'

'I—'

'She's off the grid,' Noah chimed in, with a nod of acknowledgement to Archer. 'And I think the pancakes should have blueberries.'

'Don't listen to him,' a grizzled old man said. 'He's not even from around here. And we're trying to get the old pancakes back, not add new ones with fruit in them!'

Noah laughed. 'Thanks for clearing that up for me, Norm.'

The old man scowled in his direction.

'If we're adding new ideas, I want chocolate chips,' a woman in the third row added. Archer recognized her as the woman who'd found him his house. Barbara something.

Archer ran a frustrated hand through his hair. He didn't need people to tell him that blueberries and chocolate chips were popular add-ins for pancakes! What part of *chef* were these people confused about? He knew how to cook, for Christ's sake. He just needed to figure out what the hell was in the elusive original diner pancakes.

'I think cinnamon would be nice,' another woman, Jeanie, whom he knew from the cafe, added in.

'The originals definitely had more vanilla,' Annie argued.

'Wait, can we circle back to Martha?' the woman seated next to Kaori asked. 'What do you mean "off the grid"?'

'Oh, hey, Isabel,' Noah said. 'She ran off with a Brazilian helicopter pilot. Most of the time she's completely out of cell reach.'

'How do you know that?' Kaori asked.

Noah shrugged. 'Gladys told me.'

Gladys stood up from the back of the room. 'It's true. And he's only forty-five. Can you imagine? Martha's nearly seventy.'

'Good for her!' someone shouted, and Archer lost the room again. The debate this time ranged in topic from what was an appropriate age gap in a relationship to the safety of helicopter travel to whether or not fruit had any place in a pancake.

Archer was helpless to intervene.

He found Iris in the crowd. She was laughing, her face lit up in amusement. He felt his own lips tip up. It was all just too absurd not to laugh at. And compared to the pressure of plating the perfect dish, of impressing the critics, of keeping the kitchen running night after night, it was kinda nice for things to be … silly … for a while. It was like the lid had been lifted off the pressure cooker that was his life and the steam was slowly seeping out. He felt the tension leaving his body with every absurd comment and joke from the audience.

Eventually, the chatter about Martha's love life and cell reception died down and Archer did get some suggestions for the recipe. Most residents agreed that the pancakes should be more dense than fluffy, probably cooked in butter not oil, and definitely didn't contain Greek yogurt, ricotta cheese, or anything fancier (not his word) than buttermilk. Apparently, the closest he'd come was the batch he'd made last Tuesday, so he'd have to check his notes on what he'd done that day.

By the time he'd walked back to his seat, the crowd was mostly filled with smiles and nods in his direction. Even if he never found the recipe, maybe this wasn't a bad idea. At least everyone had gotten a chance to have their pancake-related feelings heard. Something Archer had never thought he would care about.

But here he was. In his new life, in his new town. And for the first time since arriving, he didn't feel totally devastated about that. As a chef, it was his job to feed people and these people wanted pancakes.

He slid into his seat next to Iris and she gave him a big smile.

'Good job,' she whispered. 'You've appeased the mob. They'll probably be nicer to you now.'

'Probably?' he whispered back, taking the opportunity to lean closer to her.

'I can't make any promises. If you serve those buckwheat pancakes again, they'll string you up in the town square.'

He laughed louder than he meant to, but luckily he was drowned out by whatever the crowd was debating now, something about a Strawberry Queen and whether or not beauty pageants were empowering or a relic from a highly patriarchal past and if they needed one for the Strawberry Festival. Iris smiled at him, her eyes dancing.

'You should come out for drinks with us,' she said, still holding his gaze.

'I don't think that's a good idea.'

'I won't tell HR, I promise.' Her smile was all teasing mischief and he wanted to kiss it. How did she do that? How did she make everything a game?

'Iris…'

'Archer, come on. You've been living the dad life for three whole weeks now.'

'Four, actually. Since I moved here.'

'Four! That's a whole month. See, you deserve a night out.'

'We can't go out together, Iris. That's just going to confuse things even more.'

She shook her head, her braid slipping over her shoulder. He wanted to pull out the elastic and run his fingers through the rose-gold waves, wrap them around his hands and tug her close. Which was exactly why he should go straight home and take a cold shower.

'No, this is fine,' she insisted. 'There will be a bunch of us going. It's just a night out with some friends. Don't you want friends here, Archer?'

Did he want friends here? Did he have friends in Paris? He'd worked such long hours, the only people he ever saw were staff from the restaurant. Sure, plenty of nights they'd go out for drinks after work and that was why so many of them ended up sleeping together, but that was what made it all a bit toxic, too.

What would it be like to have regular friends? Friends he just hung out with when he wanted to, not people he was forced to be in a hot kitchen with for fourteen hours a day and then drank with because there was literally no one else in his life?

Might be nice.

'Fine,' he agreed and Iris whisper-squealed.

Kira craned her neck around Iris and grinned at him. 'This is going to be fun,' Kira said and Bennett just shook his head.

It was possible he'd made a mistake.

Chapter Twenty

Mac's was slammed. Which was typical for a town meeting night. After those things, everyone needed a drink.

Iris stood in the doorway with Archer, scanning the crowded pub for Kira and Bennett, who'd promised they'd get a table. Instead, she spotted Noah first, his height and his hair making him stand out in the crowd. He waved and Iris waved back.

'They're over there. Come on.' She grabbed Archer's hand and started pulling him through the crowd. It was what she would have done with whoever she was with, grab their hand, but now that Archer's fingers were tangled with hers, she couldn't think about much of anything else. They were big and rough, calloused on the palms. Strong. Capable. *Talented* hands.

Thankfully, they arrived at the corner booth her friends had snagged before Iris could let her mind wander to all the places she would like those hands to travel. She dropped his hand before Kira could comment on any of the things Iris could tell

LAURIE GILMORE

she was thinking. Iris shot her a 'don't you dare' glare that just made Kira's smile grow.

'You made it!' Annie was standing beside the booth with Kira and she greeted them with hugs. Archer's startled face from inside of Annie's embrace made Iris giggle.

'Of course we did,' Iris said. 'The after-meeting drinks are the best part of the town meeting.'

'Cheers to that,' Logan said from his seat in the booth, raising his pint in Iris's direction. She was pretty sure he hadn't even made it to the meeting in the first place.

'That was another bizarre example of Dream Harbor's quirkiness,' Kira said.

'Oh, you love it.' Annie bumped her with her hip and Iris smiled at her friends. Already crowded in the booth with Logan were Hazel, Jeanie, and George. Noah was taking their drink orders to bring up to the bar, so she ordered a hard cider and Archer ordered a local ale.

The book club was taking up most of the stools at the bar, the PTA parents were getting rowdy in the back corner, and several of Iris's favorite aerobics students were sipping their wine and working on an enormous basket of fries at two of the high-top tables in the center of the pub. The whole place was dark and homey as all good pubs should be. Dark wood, dark furniture, dim lighting. The perfect place to be on a rainy April evening.

Behind the bar, Amber and Isaac were scrambling to fill drink orders and Noah ended up waiting on more than just their own table. Iris saw him making the rounds around the dining room.

'So, you brought the chef,' Annie said, letting her gaze

wander to where Archer was still hovering somewhere over Iris's shoulder.

'Yep. He needed a night out.'

'I hope it's all right that I crashed your night,' he said, his voice a deep rumble that Iris could feel vibrate down her spine. The crowd had forced him to stand closer, his breath tickled her ear when he spoke.

'Honey, half the town is here!' Kira yelled to be heard over the din of the crowd and the music streaming in over the speakers. 'You didn't crash anything!' She leaned a little tipsily into Iris.

'Have you been drinking already?' Iris asked her and Kira winked.

'We had to get here early to get the booth,' she said. 'And then we may have done a couple of shots to pass the time.'

'Okay, where's Bennett?' Iris asked, scanning the bar. The first thing to go when Kira got tipsy was her filter. And Iris really needed her to keep that thing on tight right now.

'Bathroom. He'll be right back.' Kira refocused her attention on Archer. 'So,' she said, tipping her head as she examined him. Oh lord, here we go. 'Archie,' Kira went on and Iris expected Archer to correct her but his laugh caressed the back of her neck instead.

'Settle an argument for me.'

'Okay…'

'Grits and polenta are different, right?'

Iris blew out a sigh of relief. A food question? That was fine. Demanding what business Archer had licking his employee was another matter altogether, and of course Iris had already told Kira about that. She required zero drinks to lose her filter.

'For sure. They're both made from ground corn, but the texture is totally different. Polenta is usually coarser. And prepared differently.'

'Thank you! That's what I said!' Kira shouted. 'Where the hell is Bennett? I told him they were different.' With that argument won, she stormed off in the direction of the bathrooms.

'I want to introduce you to someone,' Annie said, breaking the weird silence Kira left in her wake and tugging Archer by the sleeve.

He looked back at Iris with a shrug as Annie led him toward the bar, so she followed close behind. She didn't trust any of these people not to make things even more weird between her and her boss.

'Archer, this is Mac. Mac, Archer,' Annie said, gesturing between the two men. 'Mac's basically your only real competition in this town.'

'Oh?' Archer said. 'Competition for what?'

'Food,' Annie replied, leaning against the bar. Mac hadn't stopped staring at her since they came over.

'Are you saying my food is good, Annie?' he asked.

Annie flicked her gaze toward him with a sigh. 'I would never say that and you know it.'

He shook his head, his mouth tipping into a cocky smirk.

'Mac is a cook,' she said, clearly leaving out any evaluation of said cooking. 'So I thought you two should meet.'

'Are you sure you didn't just want an excuse to come over here and talk to me?' Mac asked, leaning closer to Annie across the bar. Their eyes met, and even Iris could feel the heat.

'I was just trying to be neighborly,' Annie ground out.

'I'm sure you were, darling.'

'Don't. Call. Me. Darling.'

Mac grinned.

They held each other's stare for so long, Iris was considering slipping away with Archer before Annie and Mac either started kissing or someone got stabbed, but finally Annie broke first and looked away.

'Do you two need a minute to…' Make out? Murder each other? 'Talk?' Iris asked.

'Of course not,' Annie said briskly, like they hadn't all just witnessed some sort of staring-contest foreplay situation. 'I just thought these two would have something in common.'

Mac stood back to his full height and nodded to Archer.

'Yeah, of course. I'm no world-renowned chef,' he said, meeting Archer's hand for a shake above the bar top. 'But it's nice to meet you.'

'Hey, good food is good food,' Archer said. 'And right now, I'm not sure this town thinks my food is any good.'

Mac scoffed. 'Don't worry about it. This place loves to fuck with people. They'll calm down, eventually.'

'They don't like to fuck with people,' Annie said. 'They just like to protect what makes Dream Harbor special.'

'And crappy diner pancakes make Dream Harbor special?' Mac asked.

'Don't speak ill of the pancakes!' Iris hissed. 'They'll hear you!' She glanced around at the crowded bar and Mac laughed.

'Sorry, Iris. And no offense, man.'

'None taken,' said Archer. 'I can't even get them right anyway.'

'You will,' Iris said, running a hand down his arm, only realizing when she reached his wrist that she was tracing the muscles she was so fond of staring at. She yanked her hand back. 'I'm sure you'll figure it out.'

Archer's dark gaze was on her and she felt her cheeks heat from the attention.

Annie cleared her throat. 'Do you two need a minute to...' She raised an eyebrow in question with a knowing smirk on her face.

'Nope. We don't need a minute for anything,' Iris said.

Mac just shook his head. 'I gotta get back to work. It was nice to meet you, chef.'

'Yeah, you too.'

'Oh, is that Jacob and Darius? I have a bone to pick with them. Jacob!' Annie called, starting to head across to him and leaving Archer and Iris alone. Or as alone as one can be in a crowded bar next to a table full of friends. But still.

At least Noah had brought over their drinks. She took a sip of her cider.

'So,' she said, flicking her gaze up to Archer's face. He looked his usual handsome self tonight, a little bit disheveled, with his five o'clock shadow and his hair in messy waves that flopped over his forehead. For someone who ran an immaculate kitchen (from what Maribel had told her at yoga, Iris was right. Archer demanded perfection from his staff and the diner was spotless these days), his physical appearance was always a little bit messy. As though he spent all his effort on his work and that left little effort for himself.

The way she ran his house must make him crazy. It was rarely—if ever—clean when he got home from work. Olive was always alive but not always tidy or cute or happy. Most days, Iris still didn't really know what her job entailed, but Olive hadn't missed a day of school on her watch, and Iris had only forgotten to pack her lunch twice (she'd dropped it off for her, of course). But none of what she did for Archer and Olive was perfect or spotless or immaculate.

It was all messy.

But Archer hadn't said a word about it.

'I think that went well,' she continued. 'The meeting, I mean.' Not whatever weird energy they'd just witnessed between Annie and Mac. Iris had her own chef that looked at her like he wanted to devour her, she couldn't deal with Annie's problems too.

'As well as it could have, I guess.' He gestured to an open high-top table and they moved over to it. The stools had been borrowed by another table, but they at least had a place to put their drinks and lean their elbows.

'I'm glad you came out.'

He took another swig of his beer. 'Yeah, me too. It's been a while. Actually, I don't think I've been out at 9pm in a long time.'

For a second, Iris thought he meant he liked to tuck in early but then she realized he was usually working at this time of night.

'You were basically nocturnal?'

A small tip of his lips sent a thrill through her body. 'Basically.'

'Isn't it nice to be able to see the sun now?'

'I wouldn't know. It's been raining since I got here.'

Iris shrugged. 'It'll clear up eventually.'

He was studying her over the rim of his glass and Iris fidgeted with the pull tab on her can of cider. The coziness of the pub was suddenly too hot, too close. She wished this tiny table between them was bigger.

How on earth was she supposed to maintain friendly professionalism when the man looked at her like that? All that dark intensity aimed directly at her? It made her want to say 'Yes, chef!' and do anything he asked.

Uh, oh. Danger, Iris! Danger!

It was exactly that type of attitude that had led to those sweaty two-night stands in a stranger's tent at a musical festival, and to her mother changing boyfriends every other year. In that way, she and her mother were the same, chasing that spark, falling for men that burned hot and then burned out.

Would Archer burn out?

'How do you do that?' he asked.

Iris blinked. Do what? Turn a glance into an entire relationship in her head? Easy. A very active imagination. Probably not what he was asking though.

'Do what?'

'You're always so … positive about things.'

'Oh, that.' She shrugged. 'It's a double-edged sword. It's also why I'm always late. Optimistic people are overly optimistic about their ability to get somewhere on time. And they're usually wrong.'

Archer's smile grew and there was that damn dimple.

'Are you not a positive person?' she asked.

Archer's smile morphed into a frown. 'I'm not really sure. For so long, I just set my mind to something and then I did it. I didn't really think about whether it would work out or not.' His laugh was a little harsh, a little bitter. 'For a while, I actually thought I was in control of how things would go.'

He shook his head.

'You told Olive she was the best surprise. Did you mean it?'

He was quiet for a beat and Iris was sure she'd overstepped, but things felt different here at the pub. They were just two people out for a drink. Not a boss and employee, a father and a nanny. And besides, they were surrounded by people instead of being alone in the kitchen. How much trouble could they possibly get into? Right?

'I meant it. She's… I…' He huffed a frustrated sigh. 'It's hard to explain. At first, I felt bad I didn't have this instant love for her, like this immediate fatherly reaction, but now, I don't know, when she looks at me with those big eyes…'

'I feel ya. Those eyes are killer.'

Archer laughed like he was relieved that Iris had jumped in and agreed with his confusing and messy and beautiful feelings about Olive.

'Yeah. They are. And she's so … vulnerable, she really needs us, Iris.'

Iris swallowed hard. The way he'd just lumped them together did incredibly concerning things to her insides. Did she like it? Did she want Archer to think of them as a little family or was that thought insane and terrifying?

She internally shook herself. That wasn't what he said anyway. He was just stating the facts. Olive, a minor who was literally incapable of feeding herself, needed both her father and the woman employed to take care of her during the day. Right. That was all. No need to get tummy-swooping feelings over that.

'And she's funny, too,' Archer went on. 'And, oh my God, when she wants to cook with me? That melts my heart.'

Iris grinned. 'See, soft and gooey.'

He laughed. 'I guess you're right.' He shrugged. 'Anyway, yeah, I guess I did mean it. She was the best surprise. Even though I still miss my old life. A lot. And that diner is making me insane. And this town…'

Iris waved away his list. 'Yes, yes. I get it. The kid is growing on you. The rest, not so much.'

He smirked. 'Other things are growing on me, too.'

Aha! She was right. Flirting was back on the table when they were out here in the world. It was safe out here.

'Oh, yeah? Like what?'

'Like, long red hair clogging my shower drain.'

Iris's laugh surprised her so much she almost spit her cider out. 'Hey!'

'There's so much of it!' He said it like it was a problem, but the way he was eyeing her braid made her think that maybe it wasn't a problem at all.

Iris smiled. 'It's not red, anyway. It's strawberry blonde.'

'Oh, excuse me for not knowing the exact color of the hair causing plumbing issues.'

'You're exaggerating!'

He laughed. 'Maybe a little.' His eyes roved over her before landing back on her face.

'Nice to know you're thinking about me while you're in the shower, though,' she teased.

'Oh, Iris, you have no idea.' The words were a low rumble, muttered under his breath as though maybe she wasn't meant to hear them. But she had. And the idea of Archer thinking about her in the shower zipped through her body, hot and dangerous.

She leaned across the table, like a really stupid moth to a really sexy flame.

'You think about me in the shower, Archer?'

He held her stare and she was trapped. 'Iris,' he growled in warning. She was pushing it. This was wildly inappropriate. But didn't that just make it hotter?

'Tell me about it,' she said and watched the muscle in his jaw flex and his eyes darken. Oh yeah, definitely hotter. But they were safe here in the middle of the bar. This was just harmless flirting.

Just keep telling yourself that, Iris.

'Those nights when you come out to the kitchen…'

'Yeah?'

'I can't get you out of my head afterwards. Your mouth and your hair and that damn shoulder that's always bare. I want to rake my teeth across it.'

Iris's breath caught, forgetting where they were, forgetting that they were surrounded by half the town. She pressed her thighs together. If they were at home, she would have already climbed across this table and attacked him. But they weren't at home.

'And then what?' Her voice was quiet, breathless and nearly lost in the noise of the pub, but Archer's gaze was trained on her lips.

'So, I get in that shower that smells like you, like your shampoo, and lotion and just like … you. And I think about how you were naked in that same spot earlier that day. And I think about what would happen if I had joined you.'

Iris let out an involuntary groan, and the place was loud enough that no one heard. In fact, everyone else was going about their evening with no regard to the fact that they'd escalated to full-on foreplay over here.

Archer smirked, that dimple mocking her.

'What would you do if you joined me?' she asked, not

willing to be the one who blinked first in this game of sexy chicken they were playing.

He shrugged and took another swig of beer. 'It depends on the night,' he said. 'Sometimes just thinking about you naked and soapy is enough to get the job done.'

Heat shot to Iris's face and between her legs simultaneously.

'Other nights…' He shrugged again and Iris wanted to scream. *Other nights, what?! What do you think about on the other nights?* 'Other nights, I think of wrapping all that strawberry-blonde hair around my fist and, well…'

And what?! Paint me a picture, chef.

But her surroundings were slowly seeping back in. What the hell were they doing in the middle of the bar?

Archer had apparently realized it a second before her. This had gotten wildly out of hand.

'We need to stop talking about this, Iris, or it's going to be very awkward for me to walk away from this table.'

She giggled like a maniac. 'Right. You're right. Sorry, I don't know what came over me.' Yes, you do! It was him, he came over you. Don't think about coming!

'It was my fault. That was way out of line,' he said.

'It wasn't. I egged you on.'

He huffed a laugh. 'We are not good at this, Iris.'

'At what? Being super professional around each other?'

'Yeah, that.'

'I know. I'm sorry, but in my defense, you're really hot.'

Archer's smile grew. 'Oh, really?'

'Don't pretend you don't know. That makes it even worse.'

'Well, in my defense, you're really hot, too.'

'Thank you,' she said with a grin.

Archer laughed again and she loved it. She wanted to eat that laugh with a spoon.

'But I really don't want to mess this up for Olive,' he said, suddenly more serious than he'd been all night. 'She's been through so much and she likes you and I don't want anything to ruin that. I've slept with enough co-workers to know it never ends well.'

'Of course. You're right.' She finished off her drink, desperately needing another. 'Don't worry, I'll keep it in my pants.'

'I appreciate everything you've done for her. She's already made so much progress.'

Iris still didn't feel like letting the kid eat processed snacks and throwing some sheets over the dining-room chairs to make a fort was really doing all that much, but if Archer wanted to praise her, who was she to stop him?

'Thanks. I'm glad you're happy with how things are going.'

As much as Iris agreed that a fling with Archer definitely did not mesh with her keeping this job, the fact that this conversation had gone from scorching hot dirty talk to a job-performance meeting was pretty lame.

'I'm going to grab another drink,' she said. 'Want me to get you one?'

Before Archer could answer, Kira, Annie, and Noah landed at their table with a tray of shots.

'You two looked way too serious over here,' Annie said with a devious grin. 'But we have the antidote!'

'Shots, really?' Iris asked. Post-meeting drinks did not usually include shots, but apparently, they were going big tonight.

'Iris, we are on the fourteenth consecutive month of winter,' Kira said. 'We need to drink.'

'Makes sense to me,' Archer said, grabbing a shot and tossing it back.

Kira and Annie cheered.

Iris took a shot.

And at that point the night got a bit fuzzy.

'You can cook when you're drunk?' Iris asked, delighted by this prospect. They were back home, and pancakes seemed like the perfect thing to cap off this night. She was starving after her dance-off with the aerobics ladies.

'Of course I can,' Archer said, still cocky even in his inebriated state. He looked even messier than usual, his hair flopping over his forehead, his eyes sleepy. But he was quicker to smile now, and Iris liked that a whole lot.

'You have a dimple,' she told him as he mixed the batter.

'I know.'

'It's cute.'

He smiled bigger. 'I know.'

'God! You are so cocky!'

He laughed, too loud for the time of night. Iris shushed him. 'Don't wake Olive! Isn't one of us supposed to stay sober? For like emergencies?'

Archer paused in his mixing, considering this. 'I might be a really bad dad.'

For some reason, probably tequila-related, Iris found this hilarious. Archer stared at her in surprise but then started laughing again, too.

'Sorry,' Iris said between giggles. 'I don't think you're a bad dad at all! I'm definitely a shit nanny, though. You should probably fire me.'

'Maybe. Then I could finally fuck you.'

Iris froze.

Archer froze.

They stared at each other until Iris started laughing again. 'Oh my God, Archer. Did you really just say that?'

A flush had worked its way up his neck. 'No. Let's pretend I didn't.'

'Okay, we'll pretend that you don't have the hots for me.'

'You have the hots for me, too,' he said, pouring pancake batter into the pan.

'So maybe I should quit so *I* can fuck *you*.'

'Jesus, Iris. Don't say things like that!' He looked like he was in physical pain now and Iris couldn't stop giggling.

'I'm sorry! But this is getting ridiculous!'

He did the pan-flip thing and Iris gasped. 'You can do that drunk, too!'

Archer winked at her, and she nearly tipped off her stool in a fit of laughter.

'Breakfast is served,' he said, sliding two pancakes onto her plate with a flourish.

Iris dug right in. 'These might be the best pancakes ever,' she said with her mouth full.

Archer grinned and Iris reached out and stuck her pinky finger into his dimple. He turned toward her hand and pressed a kiss into her palm. Heat shot through Iris's body.

'Are you going to lick my finger again?' she tried to tease, but her voice came out all breathy and low.

He shook his head before he ran his lips from her palm

down to her wrist. He kissed the sensitive skin there and then worked his way toward her elbow, kissing and licking his way across her arm.

'You're so soft,' he murmured. 'Salty and sweet. Perfect.'

Iris sat perfectly still, except for the rapid beat of her heart. She was afraid that if she moved or spoke or blinked, he would stop. And she didn't want him to ever stop.

'Iris,' he groaned. He was leaning across the island now, pulling her toward him. His lips were on her biceps, tracing the curves of her muscle.

'Yes,' she whispered.

He pressed his lips into her shoulder. His breath was warm on her neck. Iris was dizzy with the proximity, far drunker than she was at the bar. Drunk with wanting. Drunk with anticipation.

'We should stop,' he said, his teeth grazing the bare skin of her throat.

'Or…' she breathed. 'We could keep going.'

He groaned. 'We're both drunk.'

'Some people would argue that makes things easier.'

'Iris.' Her name was a rasp pulled from the back of his throat. He was still kissing her neck, soft and urgent at the same time. Iris felt it down to her toes.

'Okay, I know. You're right.'

Archer lifted his head and his lips were swollen, pupils blown wide. Oh God, Iris had never been one for resisting temptation and now there was a beautiful man right in front of her! Hers for the taking, if she wanted him. And normally, she would totally take him.

But he would regret it.

The thought crashed into her. Archer would regret this. He

would just take it as further evidence that he was a bad father. And Iris couldn't do that to him.

'Let's just go to sleep, okay?' she said even as the entire rest of her body screamed in agony, *Let us have him!*

Archer blinked. 'Right. Good idea.'

Iris got down from her seat and took his hand. 'Make sure the stove's off,' she said, before she led him down the hall to bed.

In the morning, she would blame the tequila for guiding her into his room instead of her own. But if she was honest, it was what sober-Iris had been wanting to do all along.

Chapter Twenty-One

When Archer's alarm went off at 4am, he had a raging headache, an incredibly dry mouth, and an arm draped over his bare chest. It was not his arm. It was a very feminine arm, slender and smooth. He also had a semi-erection and the vague sense that he had tasted this skin. That he'd run his lips over Iris's delicate wrist, that he'd kissed her inner arm, that he'd nibbled on her neck.

Oh, fuck.

He peered over to the space beside him and found Iris face down in his pillows fast asleep.

No, no, no.

This was not happening. He did *not* take his nanny to bed. He very specifically had been fighting against this outcome since day freaking one. How did this happen?! And *what* exactly did happen?

He was comforted to realize that he still had his pants on and from what he could tell, Iris was at least wearing a shirt.

That had to be a good sign, right? Or at least a sign that things hadn't gone too far.

Who was he kidding? Having Iris in his bedroom under any circumstances was too far. Damn it. He squeezed his eyes shut and tried to replay the night back. The meeting had gone relatively well. Then Iris had convinced him to come out to the bar. He nearly groaned out loud remembering what he'd said about his shower fantasies. And that was *before* he was drunk. What the hell did he do after he'd had too many of those shots Iris's friends kept buying?

Little bits and pieces of the rest of the night flashed through his head. Iris grinning at him over her drinks, Iris in a dance-off with a group of older ladies, Iris giggling in the back seat of the Uber on the way home. Okay, so the memories were essentially a slide show of Iris being irresistible.

He remembered paying a bemused looking Kimmy when they got home and then... Christ, did he make Iris pancakes? She stirred next to him, and he could feel the exact moment when she woke up. Her entire body stiffened.

'Uh oh,' she muttered into the pillow, not bothering to lift her head.

'Yeah, uh oh.'

'Shit.'

'Double shit.'

'Archer, what did we do last night?'

Her arm was still draped across his body, her strawberry scent still warm and inviting. God, he wished she could stay. He wished he could roll her over and do everything he was apparently too drunk, thank God, to do last night.

But he couldn't. They couldn't.

Olive was doing well. Her therapist said the steady environment he was providing at home was a big help to her healing process. So what would happen if he slept with Iris and things inevitably got messy between them? What would happen to Olive? She would lose another person close to her. He couldn't do that to her just to satisfy his own misguided lust.

He ran a hand down his face. 'I'm pretty sure we didn't do anything but eat late-night pancakes and fall asleep next to each other.'

And I may have licked the sweat from your neck…

Iris rolled over, taking her arm and her warmth with her.

'Okay,' she said almost to herself. 'Okay, that's good.'

'Look, Iris…'

'Please don't apologize. I promise you it was equally my fault. Again.'

She sat up and leaned against the headboard with a groan. When he looked up at her she was rumpled from sleep. Her hair had come loose from her braid and was in a tangle around her face. Crease marks from the pillow covered one cheek. She looked like a hot mess. Like an adorable hot mess he wanted to tuck back into his bed and bring a glass of water and some Advil to.

And for a split second he had a vision of Iris that wasn't just as a quick fling, but as someone who stayed. Someone who could be there for him and for his daughter. Someone he could take care of.

Which was not something he'd ever wanted or had time for in his life. But his life was different now. Maybe now he had time to care for a partner? He had a house and a kid and he worked totally reasonable hours and maybe that meant he could want other things, too? Maybe the untimely death of his old life was the opportunity for the birth of a new one?

One with Iris in it.

And he realized it was the first time he'd thought about staying here with Olive that hadn't sent him into a spiral of disappointment and panic at his aborted goals.

'Town meetings do not usually end that way,' she said, interrupting his thoughts. 'Last night was a bit of an anomaly. I blame cabin fever. April is always a little nutty around here.'

'Well, thank God for that. I don't know how this town would survive if everyone always drank that much.'

Iris gave him a weak smile. 'Sorry, I wormed my way into your bed.'

'I don't think that's how it happened.'

'Oh, it definitely was.'

He remembered his hand in Iris's, her tugging him down the hall, leading him into his bedroom. Did they kiss? Did he touch her beyond that ill-advised moment in the kitchen?

This was why he never drank tequila.

'Don't worry,' she went on. 'I didn't take any liberties.'

'Liberties? With me?' He couldn't help his smile. At the moment, he was feeling like she could take whatever she wanted from him. 'I thought you didn't remember what happened.'

'It's coming back to me.'

He waited for her to elaborate, but she just added, 'I get snuggly when I'm drunk.'

'I think you might be the only person on earth with that drunken trait.'

'Probably.'

'Are you wearing my T-shirt?'

Iris smiled sheepishly. 'I got syrup on mine.'

There was no reason to point out that she had a room full of clothes right across the hall. They obviously had not been thinking clearly last night. And besides, she looked so damn good in his T-shirt, his resolve to not kiss her was weakening. Would it really affect Olive all that much if he did? Would she even need to know about it? Parents kept stuff from their children all the time.

Iris yawned dramatically. 'You wake up so early.'

'I know. This used to be when I went to bed.'

Her face was tender when she looked down at where he was still lying in the pillows. His life was upside down, but he was feeling less and less bad about it.

'Iris?'

'Yeah?'

'I had a fun night.'

Her smile grew, lighting up the dim room. 'Me too.'

And then she leaned down and kissed him, soft and sweet on the cheek. It took all of his strength, every ounce of 'trying so hard to be a good dad and not fuck up his kid's life' to not pull her down on top of him.

She was right *there*…

'Dad!' At the sound of Olive's voice outside his bedroom door, Archer had three immediate thoughts: One: she'd called him *Dad*! Two: was she hurt/sick/scared or some combination of the three? Three: what the hell would happen if she found Iris in here?

Iris for her part was frozen halfway between kissing him and sitting up, her eyes wide and terrified like they were about to get busted by the feds or something.

'What do we do?' she hissed.

'I don't know,' he whispered back.

'Dad?' Olive called again.

'Be right there!' he croaked.

'Where's Iris?' she asked through the door.

Iris winced. 'Oh God. She knows! She knows! What do we do?!' she whispered, and jumped off the bed, looking around the room frantically for a place to hide.

Archer got up and grabbed her by the shoulders. 'Calm down. She doesn't know anything,' he whispered back.

Iris nodded, but still looked like she was ready to jump out the window. So apparently, her head was not in the same place as his. Iris did not wake up this morning picturing a cozy life together. Of course she hadn't.

This was just a job.

He was just her boss. A boss she flirted with. But nothing more.

He'd let this whole thing get away from him and he'd risked Olive's mental health for it.

'Just stand over there,' he whispered to Iris before opening up the door and peeking out.

'What's the matter?' he asked Olive.

'Is Iris in there with you?'

'Uh...'

'Here it is!' Iris called loudly, pulling something off his dresser as she walked by him. 'I was just looking for this ... uh...' she looked down at what she'd grabbed. 'This men's deodorant. The ladies one just doesn't cut it for me. Oh, Olive, what are you doing up?'

Olive glanced between the two of them, him in just his sweatpants and Iris in nothing but a T-shirt, and Archer held his breath.

'I'm thirsty,' she said. Thankfully, her five years of life hadn't provided her with any reasons why it would be weird for her dad and her nanny to be caught in the same bedroom together half naked.

'Let me get you some water,' he said, sighing in relief as he ushered her down the hall. He glanced over his shoulder in time to see Iris sneaking back into her room.

Her little walk of shame down their hallway made him feel far worse than his tequila headache.

―――――――

Archer was not the only Dream Harbor resident with a hangover. By nine o'clock, every booth was full, and everyone wanted hot coffee and greasy food. Archer's new breakfast sandwich of eggs, country sausage, gruyere cheese in a croissant was a huge hit.

'Another sandwich and two orders of the buttermilk pancakes,' Maribel called out on her way into the kitchen. Archer had left several of his more successful pancake options on the menu and people were actually ordering them.

Cyrus poured four puddles of batter on the griddle and Archer assembled the sandwich. Despite his rough start to the day, the diner was running smoothly. Maribel and Jess were carrying out orders as fast as Cyrus and Archer could cook them up and for once, the customers seemed relatively pleased.

He'd only been beckoned out of the kitchen once and that was so the mayor could thank him for his input at the meeting last night and report that the townsfolk felt very pleased to have a say in what happened at their beloved diner.

More and more, Archer was becoming convinced that these people didn't actually care all that much about the pancakes and instead were torturing him as some sort of hazing ritual. But if he was passing the test then all the better. Especially if it helped when it came time to reassess the custody agreement. Olive had called him *Dad* this morning. There was no way he was giving her up now.

At least one part of his life was going smoother, because the more he thought about Iris today, about how she'd felt lying next to him, the more confused he got. They'd nearly been caught and the look of terror on Iris's face was enough to tell him she wasn't at all interested in something serious with him.

Luckily, the breakfast rush flowed directly into the lunch rush and Archer didn't have much time to think.

'Two veggie sandwiches, one French onion soup, and one side salad, chef.'

'One BLT on sourdough, one order of sweet-potato fries, and a hot coffee, chef.'

'One stack of pancakes with blueberries, one veggie sandwich, and one tomato soup with grilled cheese.'

The orders kept rolling in and Archer and Cyrus's rhythm picked up. Cyrus manned the griddle while Archer assembled sandwiches and salads, dishing up soups and making sure the plates looked presentable before being sent out. It was different from his previous kitchens, smaller and more intimate. With so few employees, they really needed to work together well and Archer had to admit, it was nice to work in a kitchen with so little drama. They just got it done.

By the end of the day, Archer was sweaty and covered in splashes of soup and salad dressing. Cyrus grinned at him.

'Another good day, chef,' the old man said, much more chipper since Archer had started taking more of his input.

'It sure was, chef.' Archer wiped the sweat from his brow with his forearm. Cyrus beamed. He loved it when Archer called him chef. As far as Archer was concerned Cyrus was one. The man had been cooking for people for forty years. If that didn't make you a chef, then Archer didn't know what did.

'Nice job today,' Archer said to Maribel and Jess, and Holden, the new waiter they'd hired.

'Thanks, chef,' Jess said, grabbing her coat and heading out the back door.

'Have a good night!' Maribel called, following her out.

Holden was chatting with the dish-washer, Meg, and the way she was giggling made Archer hope he wasn't about to lose his drama-free kitchen.

By the time the kitchen was cleaned up and he was heading home, it was after five. He ignored the excitement he felt at the thought of seeing Iris again and gave his dad a call. If anyone could talk some sense into Archer, it would be him.

He dialed and put his dad on speakerphone.

'Hey, Arch!'

'Hi, Dad.'

'How are you? How's the weather up there?'

Archer frowned through the windshield. It had finally stopped raining but today was windy enough to still warrant a jacket. Archer was wondering if warmer weather was ever going to get here. 'Not great.'

His dad chuckled. 'It's beautiful down here. Played eighteen beautiful holes today.'

Archer had grown up outside of Boston but his dad and

stepmom had retired down in South Carolina, and they never tired of telling Archer about how nice the weather was.

'That's great, Dad.'

'What? You didn't call to hear me brag about the weather?' he asked with a chuckle.

'Not really.'

'So, what is it, then? How's little Olive? I've got a good story all picked out for next time.'

Archer had started doing video chats between Olive and his dad, and his dad had taken to reading her stories to break the ice. When Olive asked him if he was her new grandpa, Archer was sure his dad was going to cry. He'd be lying if he said there wasn't a tear in his eye, too.

'That's great, Dad. Olive's fine. She's doing really well, actually.'

'Okay, so what's the problem?'

Archer cleared his throat. 'Uh, it's the nanny.'

'Not working out?'

'No, she's working out great. Olive loves her. Iris seems to know how to get her out of her shell and to make her feel better when she's down.'

'That sounds perfect. So, what's the problem?'

'Uh … we…'

'Archie, please don't tell me you slept with the nanny.'

It stung a little bit that his father would assume he would do that, but he wasn't totally wrong.

'No, not really. I mean, no. We haven't *slept together*, slept together.'

'Get to the point, son.'

Archer sighed. This was why he'd called, right? His father's no-nonsense approach to problems.

'We got drunk and slept in the same bed, but nothing happened.'

'Archer.'

'I know. It's bad, but I can't seem to—'

'Can't seem to what? Act like a gentleman? Behave like the man I raised you to be?'

'That's not it. It's not like that.' Archer ran a frustrated hand down his face. It wasn't like that, was it? He knew his feelings weren't one-sided, but that didn't make any of this a good idea.

'Then what's it like, Arch? Because I'm as happy as can be about that little girl, but you got one woman pregnant and now you can't keep your hands off the nanny?'

Jesus, when he said it like that it made Archer sound like a real piece of shit.

His father's tone softened. 'Look, I know you're doing right by your daughter, and I'm proud of you for that. But I don't see how getting involved with the nanny is a good idea. No matter how cute she is.'

Cute did not begin to explain how he felt about Iris. She was gorgeous and bright and funny and … this was not helpful.

'You're right, Dad. Of course.'

'Of course I am. Sleeping with the nanny? That would make things very complicated. Then what?'

What would happen next? If he slept with Iris, what would *she* want to happen? Would she want it to be a one-time thing?

Or *could* she want more? It confused the hell out of him that that idea didn't scare him. More with Iris could actually be great. They were already living together. His kid already loved her. Maybe this all made sense.

Well, it made sense to him. Maybe it would horrify Iris.

Iris who claimed she never actually wanted children and had only signed onto this job because she was about to be evicted, and now he was what? Planning their wedding?

This wasn't him.

Archer didn't have dreams of a wife and a family. He had dreams of being the best chef he could be, of perfecting his skills, of someday earning that Michelin star. And now everything was muddled and he was clearly losing his grip on what he really wanted. On what he'd *always* wanted.

'Yeah, I don't know. It would be awkward, I guess. And I really don't want to have to find someone new for Olive.'

'So, there's your answer.'

'Right. Thanks.'

There was his answer. His perfectly reasonable, obviously correct answer.

And he hated it.

Chapter Twenty-Two

The next day, Iris was in the middle of leading the class in savasana and avoiding thoughts about waking up in Archer's bed when her phone started vibrating.

'Let your arms lay at your side,' she said in her calm, yogi voice while she glanced at the screen. 'Feel the floor rise up to meet you.'

It was Olive's school. That couldn't be good, right? Schools don't call to just let you know everything was going great.

Iris grabbed her phone and tiptoed toward the door of the yoga studio. She'd been teaching here for nearly a year, one of her longer-held jobs, actually, and she knew where all the creaky floorboards were. She avoided them as she spoke softly to her students.

'Acknowledge thoughts as they come and let them drift by like clouds in the sky…' she trailed off as she stepped out into the hallway, pausing next to the giant gold buddha statue.

'Hello?'

'Hello, is this Ms. Fraser?'

'Yes, that's me.'

'Ms. Fraser, Olive is sick. She has a fever of one-hundred and one. You'll have to come pick her up.'

'Oh … uh…' Iris glanced back in the little window in the door. Her class was still lying obediently in the dark with their eyes closed. Luckily, this class was nearly over but she was supposed to teach one more this morning.

'I have to come pick her up like right now?'

The nurse made a noise that Iris was sure was judgmental. 'Yes, Ms. Fraser. Unless I should call her father instead?' They'd listed Iris first on the emergency contact forms, since taking care of Olive was her day job and all.

'No, no. That won't be necessary. I'll be right there.'

'Very good. Thank you.'

Iris opened her mouth to thank her back, but she'd already hung up. It occurred to her that being a school nurse was up there with school bus driver as possibly one of the hardest jobs in the world, so she decided not to be insulted by the hasty hang up.

She glanced at the buddha. 'Well, I guess I have to go figure out how to take care of a sick kid. Wish me luck.' She snuck back into the class and brought her students out of their relaxed state as quickly and gently as she could.

'Okay, and bring your senses back to the room. Blink your eyes open and go live your life. See you next week!' Okay, so maybe not that gently, but she had to get out of here. That school nurse sounded serious, and Iris was worried she'd get in trouble if she was late. In trouble with whom, she wasn't really sure, but she didn't really want to find out.

Half the class was still blearily sitting up as she skipped out of the room. On her way out to the car she sent a quick message to one of the other teachers from the studio, Tara, to see if she could pick up her next class. She got a quick 'Sure!' in response so that was one issue taken care of.

Iris dialed Bex and put her on speaker as she got into her car.

'Hey, what's up. Shouldn't you be teaching?'

'I was,' Iris responded as she pulled out of the small parking lot behind the yoga studio. 'But Olive got sick. I need to pick her up at school.'

'Oh, so why are you calling me?'

'I don't know! I thought you might have some ideas on what I'm supposed to do with a sick child.'

Bex snorted. 'Why on earth would you think that?'

'I don't know! Because I'm panicking a little bit.'

'Just put on *The Price is Right* and make her drink juice. That's what my mom used to do.'

'Okay, yeah. That makes sense. Thanks.'

'Are you regretting this nannying gig now?'

Iris pulled into a parking spot in the front of the school. 'Not yet, but ask me in twenty four hours.'

'Good luck.'

'Thanks.'

Iris had to ring the bell and get carded by the office assistant before she was allowed through the locked doors. She pushed all the reasons why this was the state of American elementary schools out of her mind. One crisis at a time, and a kid with a fever felt slightly more manageable than the gun lobby.

She walked down the colorful hallway to the nurse's office. Elementary schools still smelled the same, at least. Some combination of peanut butter and crayons. A teacher with a

LAURIE GILMORE

line of twenty, sweaty kids filed out of the gym and walked past her. Iris waved to the little girl at the back of the line who kept falling behind because she was too busy trying not to step on the cracks between the floor tiles. She smiled at Iris with a gap-toothed grin.

The nurse, as expected, was a frazzled older woman who looked very relieved that Iris had shown up. Three other kids sat lined up on chairs waiting for their ride out of there.

'Ready to blow this pop stand, Olive?'

Olive just looked at her with a glassy-eyed expression that did nothing to ease the worry in Iris's gut.

'Come on, kid.' Iris took her backpack for her and led Olive out the door.

'She can't come back until she's twenty-four hours fever-free!' The nurse called after her.

'Hear that, Olive? Twenty-four hours with no school! Lucky you.'

Olive just looked at her and coughed pitifully. Yikes. Okay, time to get her home and cozy on the couch. That was what Iris would want if she was sick. To be in her jammies in front of the television with a cup of tea. Can kids drink tea? Hmm, she should google that. She was going to have to google a lot of things.

Archer's phone started blowing up right as the lunch rush started.

'Chef, your phone is ringing.'

'Yes, I hear it, Cyrus.'

'Maybe you should answer it.'

Archer sighed, wiping the sweat from his brow with the back of his forearm. 'And then who is going to plate all this food.'

Cyrus shrugged. 'Might be something about your daughter.'

Shit. Jesus, why hadn't that even occurred to him? The phone stopped and then started again and now Archer was convinced something was very wrong with his daughter. His daughter who he'd momentarily forgotten existed. He sucked.

He strode over to where his coat was hanging in the back office and grabbed the phone from his pocket.

'What's wrong?' he asked as soon as he saw Iris's number and hit answer call.

'Olive's sick.'

Sweat dripped down his back, dread dropping like a stone in his gut.

'What do you mean sick? How sick? Is she okay?' With each question he felt his anxiety increasing. He didn't know how to have a sick child. He barely knew how to have a *well* child.

'I don't know, the nurse called, and I had to pick her up from school and I thought we would just get in our jammies and rest and drink juice, but she's really hot and listless and the internet says we need kids Tylenol but we don't have any and I don't know what to do and I'm sorry and I know this is my job and...'

'Iris, breathe.' Somehow her panic forced him out of his own. At least one grown-up should not be freaking out at a time, right? That seemed integral to the process of raising a kid.

'I'm sure she's going to be fine,' he went on. 'Kids, get sick all the time.' That was true, wasn't it? Kids were gross and filled with germs. He was pretty sure this was all completely normal, even though it felt like the fire alarm was going off in his head.

'I guess.' Iris's voice was small and scared and another jolt of worry shot through him.

'I'm coming home. I'll stop at the store and get the fever reducer, okay?'

'Okay, thank you. I'm really sorry.'

'Stop apologizing. It's my fault. I should have stocked the house with all this stuff. I'll be there as quickly as I can, okay?'

'Okay.'

As soon as he'd disconnected with Iris, he strode back out into the kitchen. The new guy, Holden, had already stepped up to Cyrus's position at the grill and Cyrus was plating the dishes.

'Don't worry, chef,' Jess said, patting his arm before loading her tray with the meals. 'We got this. Go take care of Olive.'

Good to know that they could hear everything he said in the office, but he didn't have time to worry about that now. He was just happy he could leave and be certain the diner would be fine without him. It had been existing without him for years, after all. And what a liberating thought that was.

'Thanks, everyone. See you tomorrow.'

By the time Archer made it home, with bags filled with canned soup, kids Tylenol, saline nasal spray, all-natural honey lollipops, a thermometer you apparently put under the kid's armpit and one for her mouth because he didn't trust armpit temperatures, a new Pumpkin Spice coloring book in case she was bored, a tub of Vicks VapoRub, and bubble-gum flavored cough syrup, he was a tangled knot of worry.

But he was a dad now and if his own amazing father had taught him one thing, it was that dads kept their shit together in times of crisis.

He opened the door quietly, in case Olive had fallen asleep, but Iris was there to meet him before he was even over the threshold.

'You're here,' she said, and her whole body sagged in relief. And it did something to him, this relief, this idea that he was here and now things would be better, that he would help. Olive needed him and Iris needed him, and it was different than being needed at work. It was different than being the boss, than running a tight ship, than making sure everything went perfectly. Here, they just needed *him*.

'I'm here. How's Olive?'

Iris glanced back toward the couch where Olive's face was barely peeking out from a pile of blankets. 'She says she feels cold, but her skin is burning hot and the internet is filled with a lot of strong opinions about what we should do.' Iris's usual playfulness was gone. There was no mischief in her eyes, no smile playing around her lips. She was worried. Worried about his kid. And that did something to him, too, but he didn't have time to explore that right now.

Instead, he grabbed her chin and tilted her face up to his.

'It's going to be fine, okay? We'll figure this out. Together.'

'Together,' Iris echoed and the little crease of worry between her brows softened. And he knew they were talking about getting Olive healthy again, but he found himself wishing the together applied to *more*.

He cleared his throat, realizing he still had his hand on Iris's face. He dropped it and they both snapped out of the moment.

'Okay, right. First things first.' He walked over to the couch and sat gingerly on the edge. He put the back of his hand on Olive's forehead. She was alarmingly hot. No wonder Iris was freaking out. 'Hey Olive, I'm going to take your temperature, okay?'

'My eyeballs hurt,' she said.

He glanced up at where Iris was hovering nearby. 'Her eyeballs hurt?'

Iris shrugged. 'She keeps saying that. I thought maybe she meant like a headache behind her eyes?'

'Anything else hurt, bud?'

'My neck feels scratchy.'

'Your neck? You mean your throat?'

Olive just looked at him with glassy eyes. Jesus, how were you supposed to help a person who didn't even know their own body parts?

'Let's just take your temp.' He pulled out the armpit thermometer and tucked it under her arm while Iris washed the oral thermometer. They tried both and both declared Olive had a fever.

'One-oh-three point eight! That's really bad, right?' Iris hissed as they stared at the tiny digital screen.

'Google says high temperatures are more common in children than adults,' he said, glancing back at his phone. 'Let's give her the Tylenol. We can also do a cool compress on her forehead. Has she been drinking fluids?' he asked as Iris hurried to the kitchen to wet a washcloth.

'Sort of. She didn't really want anything.'

'Hey, Olive,' Archer said, sitting down beside her again. 'You need to have some medicine to help you feel better. And some juice, too, okay?' He managed to get her upright enough to drink down the meds and a mouthful of orange juice. 'You'll feel better soon, kid,' he told her, brushing her hair from her face. She looked so small and pitiful, and it physically hurt to see her like that. He hated it. And he hated that he couldn't just make this go away for her.

He never knew that so much of being a parent was just feeling helpless in the face of your kid's struggles.

'Sit with me?' Olive asked.

'Yeah, of course I will.' He moved some pillows around and Olive curled up with her head in his lap. He rubbed slow circles on her back, hoping he was at least comforting her. Hoping it was enough.

When he looked up, Iris was staring at him, a soft smile on her face. She quickly schooled her features, but it was too late. Archer had seen the way she was looking at him. No, not at him, at him and his daughter, like maybe she had more than professional feelings for both of them.

And Archer found himself hoping that she did.

Chapter Twenty-Three

'Thank God, for modern medicine,' Iris said, clinking her wine glass against Archer's.

'Cheers to that.'

Iris breathed a sigh of relief as she took her usual seat at the kitchen island. The Tylenol had worked to bring Olive's temperature down and after an afternoon of *The Price is Right*, chicken soup, and coloring pumpkins—the closest food-related item to strawberries she could find in her new coloring book—she was slathered with Vicks, dosed with more meds, and peacefully sleeping in her bed. Iris could hardly believe they'd all survived the day.

She'd been a totally shitty nanny today, and if Archer hadn't come home when he did, she didn't really know what she would have done. As it turned out, she was right all along. Kids were terrifying and confusing, and she had no business taking care of one.

Which was half the reason she had to quit.

The other reasons were the equally terrifying and confusing feelings she'd had when she watched Archer brush the hair from Olive's forehead and tell her she was going to be okay. He was such a good dad, even if he didn't believe it yet. He came home and took care of that little girl even though he didn't know what he was doing, either. And it had done something to Iris's insides. Something scary. Something very different from all the horny feelings she'd been having about Archer since she arrived.

It made her feel tender and soft.

And she couldn't go feeling all tender and soft for a man with a child. A child who she'd already decided was far too scary to care for, so full circle, it was all a bad idea and she needed to get the hell out of here ASAP.

She took another sip of wine to fortify herself.

'Archer…'

'Yeah?' He looked up from his wine and he looked exhausted. He'd stepped up today but he was worried, too.

'I … uh…'

Maybe this was actually a terrible time to quit. It would be pretty shitty to abandon him now, wouldn't it? He'd have to scramble to find new care for Olive in the midst of her being sick.

Maybe she could tamp down those tender feelings for a few more weeks.

'I'm just sorry I had to call you to come home. Feels like I really dropped the ball.'

'Iris, I know you don't have a lot of experience with kids.'

'I … well…'

He held up a hand to stop her. 'And I hired you, anyway.

You've been exactly what Olive needs. She's happier. She *talks* to me,' he said with a little laugh. 'Did you see her holding my hand when she dozed off today?'

His face transformed as he talked about her. He wasn't exhausted anymore. He was practically glowing.

Damn it, there was that tender thing again.

'I did see it. You did a great job with her today.'

'Thanks.' His smile deepened. 'I was totally just winging it. But I couldn't have done it without you.'

Iris scoffed. 'You had your dad, the pediatrician, and WebMD. I think you would have been fine without me.' In fact, she'd done nothing today but panic and immediately call for back-up.

'Fine.' He shrugged. 'I wouldn't have *wanted* to do it without you.'

Oh, damn, damn, damn. Danger, Iris!

She smiled despite herself, and that tender spot grew.

'I'm tired of pancakes,' he said. 'I thought I'd make us some real food tonight.'

'Real food sounds good.' She sat back and watched as he cooked, marveling at his hands and the deftness of his movements. She let him hypnotize her as he chopped garlic and fresh parsley. The kitchen soon smelled amazing as the garlic hit the hot olive oil in the pan.

'What are you making?' she asked over the sizzling sound filling the kitchen.

'*Aglio e olio*,' he responded with a panty-melting Italian accent. *That* certainly didn't help anything.

'You going to translate that for me or just leave me guessing?'

'It's pasta with olive oil and garlic. It's really simple, actually.'

'Everything just sounds better in Italian.' Iris sighed wistfully. She'd never had the money to travel, but she had a list of places she'd love to visit someday. Italy ranked in the top five.

He smiled and his dimple deepened. 'Agreed.'

The pasta water boiled and he dumped in a handful of spaghetti and a large pinch of salt.

'I thought you exclusively cooked French food?'

'The last restaurant I worked in was French. But I've worked in a lot of places. I spent a year in Italy.'

'That must have been amazing.'

'It was. Some of the best seafood I've ever had.'

'You know,' Iris said, the teasing tone back in her voice because she just couldn't seem to help herself. 'The Pasta Palace in Northville is hiring. Since you have so much experience with Italian food, I'm sure they'd be thrilled to have you.'

Archer looked at her like she'd suggested they eat out of the trash and not that he work for a popular Italian restaurant chain. 'That place doesn't serve Italian food.'

Iris bit back her laughter, but she was struggling to keep a straight face. 'Are you sure? *They* seem to think that they do.'

His expression darkened. 'I don't know *what* that food is.'

Iris giggled. 'You have to admit, though, people go bananas for those breadsticks.'

'I don't have to admit anything.' He took a small mug and scooped pasta water into the pan with the garlic and the oil. Iris watched with interest. She was going to accuse him of being a food snob, but it all looked and smelled so good, that mocking him just seemed absurd now. He strained the spaghetti and tossed that in the pan, too, coating the pasta with the oil and garlic. Iris's stomach grumbled in anticipation.

He took two plain white bowls from the cabinet and twirled a perfect nest of pasta in each bowl, sprinkling some fresh parsley and parmesan cheese on each portion. Iris wanted to crawl inside and live in that pasta nest forever.

'That looks so good,' she nearly moaned. Damn this man and his pasta-making skills! Resisting his adorable dad-ness was one thing, but serving up a big ol' bowl of carbs and cheese was going to be another thing altogether.

'*Buon appetito.*'

'Jesus, man. Just give me the food and cut that out.'

Archer smirked and slid the bowl across the island.

As expected, the meal was incredible. Like insanely good. Like so good that an hour ago Iris was planning her 'I quit' speech and now she was considering declaring her undying love for this man and his food. It was concerning.

But she was full and exhausted from this stressful day and between the food and the wine and Archer's dimple, she had been lulled into a cozy contentment she hadn't felt in a very long time. Maybe not since those days in Josie's kitchen, watching her neighbor cook while she chatted to her about everything from her mom's latest boyfriend to the bike she wanted for her birthday.

Was this why people wanted a partner? This feeling at the end of a rough day that they'd survived something together? She had to admit it was nice. She'd always had her mom and her aunt and her cousin. She collected friends like she collected new careers. But maybe having a partner would be different.

Sitting here, laughing and drinking with Archer.

Decompressing after taking care of a sick kid all day, it was …
it was something she could maybe see herself wanting.

Someday.

Not today.

Because today he was still her boss. And today she didn't
want to hurt Olive. And she still wasn't convinced she'd ever
want this responsibility full-time.

Today was the most worried she'd been since the time they
were nine and Bex had flipped over the handlebars of her bike
and bashed her face on the sidewalk. Iris had never run home
faster, tears streaming down her face the whole way, screaming
for her mother to come help.

'Today was rough,' she said, pushing away her empty
plate.

'Yeah, but we figured it out.' They were in their usual
positions, Iris on her stool on one side of the island and
Archer standing on the other side, leaning against the
counter behind him. Per usual, his arms were across his
chest.

She wished he was closer. She shouldn't but she did. She
wished he would lean across the island like he had the last
time, the time when he'd sucked her finger into his mouth. She
wished he would do more things like that.

She shouldn't. But she did.

'I should get to bed.'

'Okay.' Archer was watching her, studying her with dark
eyes like he knew what she wished and that he did, too. But he
didn't budge. Just held himself still, only his eyes moving to
follow her down from her stool.

'Thanks for dinner.'

'Anytime.' His voice was low and deep, vibrating through

her. It was clear that he wanted her as much as she wanted him. But still, he didn't move.

He was protecting himself. He was protecting Olive.

A one-night stand with the nanny wouldn't help either of them. And in the end it wouldn't help Iris either.

Be strong, Iris.

'Goodnight, Archer.'

The muscle in his jaw ticked.

'Night, Iris.'

He held steady, but she felt the heat of his stare the whole way back to her room.

Olive was home sick the next day, of course. She obviously needed more time to rest, and Iris was not about to break the twenty-four-hour fever-free rule and piss off that school nurse. But she had convinced Archer that he could go to work today and she would man the sick kid. Now that she was armed with plenty of over-the-counter fever reducers and a working knowledge of Olive's names for various symptoms ('eyeballs hurting' meant she had a headache and the fever was on the rise, a 'scratchy neck' meant a sore throat), she was feeling slightly more confident than yesterday.

That, and Archer had assured her multiple times before he left this morning at the ungodly hour of 5am that he was just a phone call away and Iris could call at any time and he would come home regardless of what was happening at the diner.

She had to admit, that did make her feel better.

'How are we feeling so far this morning?'

Olive was curled up on the couch with her trusty narwhal

stuffy and a cup filled with OJ. Turned out the trick was ice and a straw to get her to actually drink it.

'Better,' she said, taking a sip of juice. 'Can I go to school?'

Iris plopped down on the couch next to her. 'Nope. Not today.'

'Why?'

'You're still sick.'

'I don't feel sick today.' Olive's face was too pale with dark circles under her eyes.

'You're definitely still sick. Sorry.'

Olive's mouth turned down in a pout. 'But it's library day and now I won't get new books.'

Iris glanced at the stack of unread books littering the coffee table. 'You have a ton of books.'

'But I want new ones.'

'Well, if I send you to school they will just send you back. That's the rules, kid. You don't want to get all your friends sick, right?'

Olive shrugged like she didn't really care if she got her friends sick, she just wanted new books.

'How about this,' Iris said, doing her best to avoid a meltdown from her or the child. 'Once you're better, I'll take you to the public library and you can take out as many books as you want.'

Olive's face lit up at that promise.

'Really?'

'Yep.'

'Can I take out one-hundred and fifty?' One-hundred and fifty was Olive's current favorite number.

'Can you carry one-hundred and fifty?'

Olive thought about that for a minute before declaring 'Probably.'

Iris smiled. 'I like your confidence. Now drink your juice.'

They settled in for the day, binge-watching Olive's favorite shows all morning until she dozed off with her head in Iris's lap. Her face was warm but not hot, which Iris found encouraging. She brushed a piece of dark hair from Olive's face. It was damp from sweat, but somehow Iris didn't find that as gross as she once would have. At the moment, she was just happy that Olive was feeling better and that she was napping, even though Iris now had to pee and was stuck until Olive woke up because she sure as hell wasn't going to wake her.

Before Olive had fallen asleep, they'd been watching her latest favorite cooking show. Iris watched three chefs come up with crazy concoctions based on surprise ingredients. She tried to focus on the show, but her brain insisted on drifting to Archer and how much she liked watching him cook. About the way his precise chopping and dicing contrasted with his messy hair and scruffy stubble. About how he looked when he was worried about Olive.

Okay, so Iris was still refusing to have daddy issues, but she'd be a big fat liar if she said it wasn't doing all kinds of things to her to watch Archer take care of his daughter. It was objectively hot. She was pretty sure it was some sort of evolutionary thing, right? As though her cavewoman brain was like, *Oh, a man who can take care of his offspring? Hot.*

Ugh. She nearly groaned out loud at her own stupidity, but the sleeping girl in her lap kept her quiet. Speaking of evolutionary urges, the small cuteness of this creature was obviously designed to lure her in.

She had never been one to coo over people's babies (she was pretty sure they all looked the same) or to volunteer to babysit her friend's children, but this one, Olive, whom she now knew as a complete person, well, the kid was kinda growing on her.

This whole thing was a mess.

She was here to do a job. She'd taken it in the first place because she felt bad that Archer was in this position and because she needed a reasonable place to live. She needed to remember that. Archer was doing much better in the dad department, so it wouldn't be so bad when she bailed, right?

Olive stirred in her lap, a little drool streaming onto Iris's leg. Okay, that was still gross.

She turned her head and blinked her big, please-don't-eat-me-because-I'm-adorable eyes open. The small smile Olive gave, like she was happy Iris was there, made Iris's heart feel weird.

'Hi, Iris.'

'Hey, kid. Have a nice nap?'

'I didn't nap.'

'Okay, sorry. My mistake. You just had your eyes closed and you were snoring like this…' Iris did her best super loud snoring impression and Olive giggled.

'I was not.'

'You definitely were.'

'Iris?'

'Yeah?'

'Are you going to be my mom soon?'

That heart feeling got even weirder. Some bizarre combination of panic and happiness shot through her body and made Iris dizzy.

'I'm your nanny, remember?'

Olive sat up and faced her on the couch. 'Yeah, but you're sort of like a mom.'

Iris frowned. How to explain this? 'I take care of you when your dad's at work, sweetie, but I'm not a mom.'

'But you could be.'

'I … well…'

'Because Addison at school said her dad got married again and now she has two moms and a dad and I don't even have one mom anymore and that's not really fair. So, if you married my new dad then I would have one mom and one dad and that would be fair.'

Oh, Christ.

'Well, families aren't really a numbers game.'

Olive frowned.

'What I mean is,' Iris went on. 'It's not really about how many of everything you have, it's more about having people who love you. And as long as you have some of those, then you have a family. And you have a dad and a grandma and all those new grandparents who love you so much and that's amazing.'

'And you? You're in my family, too, right?'

Those eyes! Iris swallowed the lump that had inexplicably formed in her throat.

'I am…'

What was she supposed to say? I'm on the staff? Your dad pays me to care about you? None of those things were right. She wasn't even sure they were true anymore. Not entirely. She did care about this little person.

'I am. I care about you, too, Olive.'

Olive's frown tentatively turned up at the corners.

205

'But I'm not your mom. And I'm not going to marry your dad.'

The frown was back.

'But you might.'

'No, Olive. Definitely not.' She had to shut this down right now. Sure, she had the hots for Archer, but she had no intention of marrying him or possibly anyone for that matter, and this whole conversation was dredging up way too many memories about the men her mother had dated and the hope that she, little Iris, had each time that maybe this one would stick around. *She* wasn't going to stick around, and she needed Olive to understand that. She wouldn't get this little girl's hopes up like hers had been so many times.

'But my teacher says, never say never!'

Iris pinched the bridge of her nose. Was that fever gone yet? Because this kid needed to go back to school ASAP.

'Look, Olive. I know you miss your mom, but I can't be your new mom. I'm sorry.' There. Just rip off the Band-Aid.

Shit. *Tears*.

Rip off the Band-Aid?! Kids hated that. Just last week she'd pulled off Olive's old Band-Aid too quickly and she had screamed and then cried about it until Iris bribed her with a lollipop.

'Come here.' She scooped Olive into her arms and made vaguely comforting noises into her hair until they were both a bit calmer. Marry her dad?! Become her new mom?! Yikes. Things had escalated at an alarming rate and Iris was a little afraid that if she stared into Olive's big eyes for much longer, she might just give in to it all.

And the longer she held Olive in her arms, the more she thought maybe that wouldn't be the worst thing in the world.

Which was crazy.

Iris did not want kids. She did not want to be a nanny. She shouldn't want to be here cuddling this sticky, sweaty child in her arms and yet, here she was, sticky and sweaty, and not wanting to be anywhere else.

She'd thought Archer was the problem, her undeniable attraction to him, her tender feelings when she caught him looking at Olive, like he was both terrified and delighted by her. But what if the kid was the problem? What if Iris fell in love with Olive?

How would she leave, then?

How would she explain to those big eyes that not only was she never going to be her mom, she also wasn't going to take care of her every day?

Iris had made some big mistakes. She'd clearly miscalculated this whole thing. And now she was stuck. Literally. Olive was wrapped around her like a slightly damp koala bear.

Iris smiled into her hair.

'Come on. I bought Popsicles. They'll help with your scratchy neck.' She stood up with Olive still clinging to her. 'What flavor do you want?'

'I want a blue one.'

'Blue isn't a flavor,' Iris attempted to explain as they walked out to the kitchen.

'Blue is the best flavor,' Olive told her as Iris set her down on a stool and grabbed a Popsicle from the freezer. She laughed, despite herself.

'Okay. Here's a blue flavored Popsicle. It tastes just like the elusive blue Popsicle plant that grows in the rainforest.'

Olive grinned. 'Thank you.' She took a big lick. 'I love you,

Iris,' she said, still innocently slurping on her Popsicle. Not realizing she was tearing Iris up inside with her words. 'And I love blue Popsicles,' she sang, happily swinging her feet below the stool.

'I'm glad you like them,' Iris said, swallowing the rest. This was just a job. A job like all the others she'd had and quit. And eventually, she'd quit this one, too.

But not yet.

Chapter Twenty-Four

No one was home when Archer got back from work the following Wednesday. Olive had been feeling much better and returned to school this week, and he wondered where she and Iris were. Sometimes Iris took her to the bookstore or the pool to practice her swimming, but she usually texted Archer about where they would be.

He dropped his stuff by the door and made his way into the kitchen when he heard Olive's now familiar giggle from the backyard. It still made his heart swoop in his chest to hear it.

When he walked out into the yard, Olive jumped up from her seat on the ground.

'Surprise!' she yelled, leaping into his arms.

'Wow! What is all this?' he asked.

'A picnic!' Olive squirmed out of his arms as quickly as she'd flung herself into them and led him to the blanket set up in the center of the lawn. After a month of rain, the sun had finally graced them with its presence and the grass was a deep green in the late afternoon sunshine. Everything smelled fresh and new. Whoever had rented the house before them had apparently planted perennials and the yard was lined with flowers, first daffodils and now tulips. They even had a cluster of irises along the fence.

The beautifully human Iris sat smiling up at him.

'Welcome home,' she said. And it felt true. It felt like home when he was here with the two of them. What a wild thought coming from the man who not even two months ago had to stand on the front step giving himself pep talks before he went in.

'Iris said it was the perfect day for a picnic because it's the first really warm day of spring and she found local strawberries at the market and we made strawberry shortcakes!'

'Wow,' Archer said with a laugh trying to absorb all the information Olive had just unloaded as she danced around the blanket.

'Yep. We cooked for you today, chef,' Iris said with a wink and thank God Olive was here because his desire to lean Iris back on this blanket and kiss her everywhere was very strong today. She smirked at him like she knew.

'Well, this all looks delicious.' He couldn't help it if his gaze wandered from the picnic feast to Iris's long legs and soft curves. An equally delicious blush worked its way up her neck. He rarely saw Iris in anything other than her PJs or her work uniform of yoga pants and a tank top.

But today, on this gorgeous sunny May day, Iris was wearing a navy blue dress with strawberries and white polka dots. Slender straps grazed her shoulders, and her hair was wrapped in a bun on top of her head, exposing the long line of her neck. The rose-gold strands of her hair glinted in the sunlight.

She looked positively edible.

But his daughter was here, and she was so excited to show him what she had made, and Archer was thankful for the distraction because he could no longer be trusted to make good and responsible decisions around Iris Fraser. He probably never could.

'Are you going to tell me how you made it?' he asked, taking one of the plates of strawberry shortcake. The plate was white and dainty and covered in little blue flowers. Archer wondered where they'd come from.

'Iris said not to tell you.'

'Oh really. Why is that?'

Iris rolled her eyes. 'Because you're going to get all chef-y on us and belittle our efforts.'

'I would never! And these look delicious.' There were plenty of ways to make strawberry shortcake, but they'd gone the traditional New England route: sweet biscuits layered with whipped cream and juicy strawberries. He cut his fork through and got the perfect bite, equal parts biscuit, fruit and cream.

He widened his eyes for full dramatic effect. 'Liv, these are amazing.' He'd taken to shortening her name and it felt good. It felt like they were becoming a real family.

His daughter beamed. 'They are?!'

'Oh, yeah. You did a good job.'

'Well, Iris helped with the oven part.'

'Just doing my duty as the sous chef,' Iris said with a grin.

'So, you're really not going to tell me your secret?' he asked.

Olive glanced at Iris and Iris shrugged. 'I guess you can tell him. There's enough secret recipes in his life already.'

Archer chuckled. 'Thanks for taking pity on me.'

Olive leaned in closer. 'We used a mix for the biscuits and whipped cream in a can.'

Archer leaned in and whispered back. 'Well, it tastes better than my strawberry shortcake.'

'Really?'

'Yep.' He planted a kiss on Olive's nose. 'Good job, chef.'

He didn't think it was possible for Olive to smile any bigger, but somehow she was doing it. And when he glanced at Iris, she was smiling at him, too. That soft smile she only did when she thought he wasn't looking. His favorite smile. The one that wasn't playful or mischievous. The one that he thought, *hoped*, showed her real feelings.

She looked away. 'Wow, Olive. Now I'm dying to try one.'

With that, they all dug into their cakes and washed them down with pink lemonade in delicate teacups. Archer complimented Olive's dress and the whole picnic-surprise idea, and she told him about her day, with Iris popping in to fill in pertinent details, and the sun warmed the earth beneath them and the flowers bloomed and the birds chirped and Archer once again felt his life flip upside down.

Because he *liked* this.

He liked coming home early. He liked talking to Olive. He liked having a picnic in the damn sunshine. He liked it a hell of a lot more than striving and pushing toward some unachievable career goal. This day, this life, felt like a different type of achievement. The type that only required his presence not his perfection.

And he *really* liked Iris sitting next to him. He liked that by the time the sun was getting lower and the air chillier that her body leaned against his. He wanted to pull her closer, to tuck her under his arm. He wanted to put Olive to bed together and talk about their day.

The man who had once only thought about his goals. About being the best. About perfection. About *himself.* Now just wanted a sunny afternoon picnic with his favorite girls.

How was that for a surprise?

'Okay, good. Now we're going to practice putting your face in the water,' Iris said, gesturing at the pool. Archer had left work early to rush over to the Y to catch some of Olive's swimming lesson with Iris. The girls hadn't noticed him yet, though. They were the only two in the pool and Iris's voice echoed in the big space.

Olive looked at Iris like she had lost her mind. 'I don't want to.'

'Trust me, it's important.'

'No, it's not. I can swim with my face up like this, see.' Olive doggie-paddled around the shallow end with her little face above the water and Archer had to stifle his laugh.

'That's nice, but what if you want to jump in?'

'Then you'll catch me.'

Olive's blind trust in Iris made his heart swell.

'What if you want to jump in by yourself?'

Olive shook her head. 'I don't want to.'

'I think you should at least try…' Iris trailed off as she glanced up and caught Archer lingering by the door.

'Hey.' He raised his hand in a sheepish wave. 'I hope it's

okay I came. I left a little early so I could see some of Olive's lesson.'

He left work early. That was a monumental statement from him and judging by the look on Iris's face she thought so, too. But everything had slid into place over the last few weeks. He was all in with Olive. This was right and he *knew* it now. He wanted to be a dad. He wanted this life.

'Of course it's okay,' Iris said, still studying him with a mildly surprised look on her face. Olive scrambled up the steps to greet him.

'Hey, Liv.'

She hugged him around his legs, completely soaking his pants with her wet body.

'You came to see me swim?' she asked, gazing up at him so adoringly that Archer was sure Iris was right about his face turning soft and gooey when he looked at his kid. He was basically a human puddle at this point.

'Yeah, let me see what you've learned,' he said, detaching her arms from his knees.

'Okay. But Iris has to catch me,' she said, coming to the edge of the pool and lining her toes up on the edge.

Iris came closer, her body rising out of the water in the waist-deep shallow end, and Archer was afraid he might have to excuse himself from the rest of the lesson. She was gorgeous. Of course she was. She always was. But she was in a bathing suit and his body was completely ignoring the fact that he should not be noticing that right now.

His gaze snagged on her bare arms, the curve of her breast in that utilitarian swimsuit that was sexy as hell, simply because she was the one wearing it. He lingered over the sight of her until she cleared her throat and his attention snapped back to Olive. Right. Not the time or the place for that. He tried to discreetly adjust his pants, but Iris caught him, a knowing smirk on her plush lips.

She shook her head at him and turned back to Olive. 'Okay, Olive. One … two … three…'

The little girl launched herself in the air and Iris caught her, not letting her head dip below the water. Archer's breath caught as she landed in the pool, but he trusted Iris, too. Completely. He knew she would keep Olive safe.

'Did you see that?' Olive called as she doggie-paddled back to the stairs.

'I did. That was amazing!'

'I'm gonna do it again.'

She jumped over and over, and each time Iris caught her and Archer cheered, and it felt like maybe Olive was going to be okay, maybe they'd mended something in her little heart.

'Hey, Liv. I think you're ready to put your face under,' he said, crouching down at the edge of the pool.

She crinkled her nose. 'I don't think so.'

'You can do it,' Iris told her. 'And I'm right here. I'll scoop you right up if you need me.'

'And I'll scoop you both up if you need me,' Archer said, catching the smile Iris tried to hide.

Olive looked between the two of them, and Archer could feel the shift, the moment Olive realized that maybe she trusted them too.

'Okay,' she said, slowly. 'But you have to stay right there.' She pointed to the edge of the pool.

'I won't move, even if you do a giant splash and get me all wet,' Archer assured her.

'Oh, that's a good idea,' Iris said. 'Let's see if you can splash your dad.'

Olive's face lit up with mischief at that idea.

Forgoing the countdown, she launched herself into the water before Archer could stand back up and completely soaked him.

She burst out of the water with a triumphant smile on her face. 'Did I get you?!'

Archer shook the water from his hair. 'You sure did.'

'Yay! I'm gonna do it again.'

'Wonderful,' Archer grumbled, but Iris caught his eye, a huge smile on her face to match Olive's and the whole thing was totally worth the wet clothes.

After their lesson was done, the girls changed into dry clothes and met Archer in the lobby.

'I'm really glad I came,' he said, nudging Iris's shoulder as they walked out to the car. 'You're a great teacher.'

'Well, you provided great motivation,' she said with a laugh.

'Will you come next time, Dad?' Olive asked, grabbing his hand as they walked out into the parking lot.

Dad.

She was holding his hand.

She wanted him to come to the next lesson.

How could he possibly say no?

Not to mention he'd be a fool to pass up the chance to see Iris in a bathing suit again.

Chapter Twenty-Five

'What's on the pancake menu tonight, chef?' Iris asked, wandering out into the kitchen after tucking Olive into bed, and reading her extra stories, and catching and releasing the spider that was living in the corner of her bedroom, and bringing her fresh water. It was a whole thing. Sometimes Olive insisted Iris do it and sometimes she demanded Archer do it and sometimes she liked them to do it together in a way that was uncomfortably domestic for Iris. They'd started the bedtime procedure over an hour ago and Iris was only mildly convinced that Olive was going to stay put.

Archer was in his usual position behind the kitchen island in his usual after-work outfit of a fitted T and gray sweatpants that made Iris absolutely feral, but instead of cooking he was reading over his notes from the town meeting two weeks ago.

'Just trying to figure out what to try next.' He frowned. 'Although half of these ideas are just new things people want to see on the menu.' He looked up at her as she slid onto her stool. 'Give it to me straight. Is this whole town just fucking with me? Like is there even an original recipe for these pancakes, or is this all some kind of joke to chase me out of town?'

Iris shrugged. 'It's hard to tell with this crowd. Probably a bit of both.'

His frown deepened.

'Don't get me wrong!' Iris continued. 'There's definitely a much-beloved pancake recipe out there somewhere, but there is also probably a good amount of fucking with you going on,' she added with a smile.

'Wonderful,' he grumbled.

'You're grouchy tonight.' She wondered if the increasing amount of sexual frustration building up in her was also the reason for his grouchiness. The way he looked at her, she thought maybe she was right. His eyes were dark and a slight flush had worked its way up his cheeks. His gaze kept wandering to where her oversized T-shirt had slipped off her shoulder.

She remembered what he'd said about that. About wanting to graze his teeth over the skin there. And God, did she want him to do that.

Realistically, if she had met Archer in some other circumstance, she was certain they would have slept together and moved on by now. They were fighting their natures by avoiding the inevitable this whole time, and honestly, she wasn't sure she could do it anymore.

Maybe she'd been blowing this whole thing way out of proportion in her mind. They didn't *have* to become some official couple and parade their relationship in front of the whole town and the freaking custody lawyer. What happened in this kitchen, stayed in this kitchen.

No one had to know.

Especially not Olive.

Fooling around with Archer did not have to be that serious.

She hopped off her stool and came to his side of the island, which, of course, was a terrible idea but Iris was no longer thinking with her brain. She was thinking with her lady parts. Her very keyed-up lady parts, who demanded to be closer to him.

'I'm going to be your sous chef,' she said with a smirk. 'Teach me what to do.'

He stared down at her like he was fully aware of what she was doing, and also fully aware that it was a bad idea. But he didn't tell her no.

'You want me to teach you to make pancakes?' he asked, his body close to hers, warm and solid. He always showered right after work, and he smelled like soap and the laundry detergent he used that made his shirts so soft. She was probably going to keep the one she slept in when they were drunk.

'Yes, chef,' she said, and his eyes sparked in delight.

'Okay, Iris. I'll teach you.'

Neither of them moved. They stood face to face just waiting to see who would break first. They were both sober tonight. Anything that happened now would be because they both chose it. Archer reached out and tucked a stray hair behind her ear, his knuckles brushing against her cheek and Iris's eyes fluttered closed.

Thank God.

'This hair makes me crazy,' he said.

'Because it's a health-code violation to have it down while I'm cooking?' she asked, opening her eyes and finding Archer staring at her hungrily.

He shook his head. 'No, Iris. That's not why.'

'Then why?' Her voice was just a breath.

He shook his head again like he wasn't going to answer, but instead he squeezed his eyes shut and said, 'Because I want to see it draped across my pillow; I want it wrapped around my fist. Christ, Iris. I want you so bad and I don't know what to do about it anymore.'

She wrapped her arms around his neck, pressing her body against his. He let out a soft groan.

'Give in,' she whispered.

His eyes were still closed. The muscle in his jaw ticked. Iris held her breath.

And then his hands were on her waist, his fingers digging into her flesh as he lifted her onto the counter of the island. Her surprised gasp was swallowed by his mouth on hers, greedy and hot. He kissed like he did everything else in this kitchen, with perfection and complete dedication.

He deepened the kiss, his tongue sliding against hers, his fingers in her hair. And all Iris could do was hold on. She wrapped her legs around his waist, pulling him closer as her hands roved across the muscles of his back.

This T-shirt has to go.

She grabbed his shirt from the bottom and pulled it up, breaking the kiss only long enough to get the shirt off and tossed to the side. She ran her hands across all the firm muscle and soft hair that combined perfectly to create Archer. God, he was hot. This was hot. Iris was melting. Or burning. Was it possible to come just from kissing? From kissing Archer Baer, maybe it was. Because Iris had never been kissed like this before, like she was Archer's last meal. Or his first after he'd been starving for years.

It was all-consuming, urgent and insistent. This wasn't just a kiss. It was an assault, a release of all the tension that had been building between them for weeks.

'Iris,' he groaned, pulling away and resting his forehead against hers.

'Don't say it.'

'This is a bad idea.'

It *was* a bad idea. She knew it was a bad idea except right now in this exact moment she was having a hard time remembering why it was a bad idea.

Because he was her boss? That only made it hotter.

Because of Olive? As long as she never found out, as long as Iris didn't make any promises she couldn't keep, everything would be fine. Iris could kiss Archer by night and care for Olive by day, no problem. It didn't have to get complicated. It could just be this, two people kissing like their lives depended on it.

Because of that tender part of her heart that kept flaring up every time she saw Olive and Archer together? That was easily ignored.

Especially right now, when Archer still had his fingers in her hair and his half-naked body pressed up against her. She could ignore the hell out of that tender spot.

She kissed him again, nibbling his bottom lip. 'I know, but let's keep going, anyway.'

His laugh tickled her face. 'What happens when this doesn't work out?'

LAURIE GILMORE

'When what doesn't work out? This fantastic make-out session? Because I think it's working out just fine.'

Archer pulled back a little further, studying her face. 'Just a make-out session?'

Iris smiled. 'Just a harmless make-out session between friends. No big deal.' No big deal at all. This was just a 'we need to make out or we will explode so let's just take care of it like adults' moment. It didn't have to be anything else.

'No big deal,' Archer echoed as she pulled him back in.

'Exactly.' She smiled against his mouth, and he slid his hands down to her ass, tugging her even closer so he was nestled between her thighs. She ignored the slight tilt of disappointment in his voice, the look on his face that said maybe he didn't want this to be just a make-out session between friends. She put those things in the same little box she'd put her tender feelings for him and tucked it right back behind her spleen, where she'd never have to think about it.

Archer must have tucked it away, too, because he was kissing her again, thoroughly and enthusiastically, his hands roving her body.

'Shit, Iris,' he murmured against her lips. 'You're so— This is just—' He kept starting sentences and then breaking them off with more kisses, never finishing his thought but making it pretty clear what he was thinking, nonetheless. 'Let me touch you?' His hand was on her inner thigh now, so close to the bottom of her tiny shorts that Iris felt like she would combust if he didn't touch her.

'Yes, chef,' she purred against the soft shell of his ear and smiled at his answering groan.

'You have got to stop doing that,' he said. 'Or I'm really going to embarrass myself.'

Iris's laughter was cut off abruptly by the feel of Archer's fingers slipping beneath her underwear. He didn't waste time. He found her clit and pressed with his thumb and Iris momentarily lost consciousness.

'Holy shit, Archer,' she breathed, and it was his turn to smirk.

'Like that?'

'Yes, like that and…' her voice hitched, 'and more and…' She wiggled her hips a little, side to side and Archer immediately caught on, moving his thumb from left to right with a little more pressure and, holy shit, was that good. This man was not screwing around.

Iris's moan was far too loud for how early it still was, and the fact that they were in the middle of the kitchen and that there was a child—hopefully, please Jesus—sleeping down the hall. Oh God, this really was a bad idea, but pleasure was seeping into all of her limbs, sparking and hot, and they couldn't stop now!

Archer covered her mouth with his, swallowing her moans and gasps and sighs, and that hand kept going, harder and faster until Iris couldn't breathe or think or care that this was a categorically terrible idea.

'Come for me, Iris,' he rasped, his forehead against hers and Iris whimpered, the pleasure building so fast and sharp and sudden, that if Archer hadn't kissed her again, she would have screamed loud enough to wake the neighbors.

'I knew it,' she said, pulling away, panting and shaking.

'Knew what?' Archer asked, his fingers still stroking her, slow and leisurely now and Iris trembled under his touch.

'I knew those hands were capable of all kinds of things.'

Archer's smile grew, pressing that thumb down again and

sending a second wave of pleasure coursing through Iris's body. She gasped and clamped a hand over her mouth, her legs shaking on the counter.

When he took his hand away and licked his fingers, his groan nearly as loud as hers, Iris practically melted clear off the counter.

'That was a bad idea,' he said, staring at where she was still loose-limbed on the counter.

She knew it was, but it still sucked to hear when she was in her post-amazing-orgasm state. 'It was?'

'Yeah,' his voice came out choked. 'Now that I've tasted you, I want more.'

Heat flooded Iris's body. 'Oh.'

Archer shook his head and took a step back and Iris immediately missed his heat between her thighs.

'That was too risky, though,' he said. 'Olive could have come out at any time.'

'It's like being a teenager but in reverse.'

Archer looked confused.

'Like being worried your parents are going to catch you making out on the couch, but now we're worried about your kid catching us.' And kissing Olive's dad in the kitchen probably wouldn't do much for her 'we're never getting married' argument.

'Right.' Archer huffed a pained laugh. 'And I don't think I can afford doubling her therapy sessions if she catches us.'

'Right,' Iris said, hopping down from the counter onto shaky legs. Archer steadied her with a hand on her elbow. 'Sorry, I shouldn't have—'

'Don't apologize.' His words were stern, final.

'But what about you?' Iris gestured to the front of his

sweatpants that were now even more obscene than usual due to the prominent erection pressing against them. Quite prominent.

Look away, Iris!

Archer flashed her a wicked grin. 'Just more fuel for the shower, I guess.'

Iris's eyes widened.

'Goodnight, Iris,' he said, planting one more searing kiss on her lips before turning and walking down the hall. When he went into the bathroom instead of his bedroom, Iris had to lean against the counter. Her legs were weak again.

Somehow that intense kitchen-counter orgasm wasn't nearly enough and now thinking about Archer in the shower, thinking about her...

It was too much.

Time for bed, Iris.

And good luck sleeping.

Chapter Twenty-Six

'You okay, chef?' Cyrus's question broke Archer out of his daydream. His very not-appropriate-for-work daydream.

He cleared his throat. 'Yes, fine.'

Cyrus smirked. 'Really? Because you just covered that plate of pancakes with salad dressing.'

Archer looked down at the mess in front of him. 'Shit.' He dumped the ruined breakfast in the trash. 'Can I get another batch?'

'Yes, chef.' Cyrus chuckled. 'What's got you so distracted?'

Not what, *who*. It had been two days since the kitchen-counter incident and Archer had not stopped thinking about Iris since. Her mouth and her heat and her sounds. Christ, her sounds, those gasps and moans were running on a loop in his head. An obscene soundtrack to his day. He'd barely spoken to her since, keeping Olive as a buffer between them during the day and quitting his night-time pancake-making in case she came out to join him. He didn't know what he would do if she did.

He wanted Iris in too many ways now.

'Nothing,' he muttered, certainly not about to explain any of that to his cook.

'Ah,' Cyrus said with a knowing nod as he poured more batter onto the griddle. 'It's a woman.'

'It's not … that's not it.'

The older man chuckled. 'Okay, sure. You just ruined three plates this morning because you're thinking about the weather.'

'Just make the damn pancakes, chef.'

Cyrus shook his head with another laugh. 'Yes, chef.'

'Hey, chef, the mayor's at table three. He wants to talk to you,' Jess said as she came skidding through the double doors into the kitchen.

'Slow down,' Archer barked as he strode past her. Jess gave him a mock salute. 'Cyrus, those pancakes!' he yelled on his way out of the kitchen, knowing he was taking his shitty, frustrated mood out on his staff, but unable to stop himself. And now the mayor wanted to talk to him. If the man had one more note about his latest attempt at the sacred pancakes, Archer might snap completely.

He *wanted* Iris. Bad. And in so many more ways than he should. And he didn't know what to do about it and it was bringing out his asshole tendencies.

He took a deep breath before stopping at the mayor's table. 'Good morning, mayor. Everything all right?'

Mayor Kelly smiled up at him.

'Hi, Archer,' Hazel said from the other side of the table. 'How's Olive feeling?'

'Hey, Hazel. Much better, thanks.'

'We love the new pancakes, Archie,' the mayor said, and Archer almost didn't hate the nickname when it followed a compliment.

'Wonderful.'

'And the specials board was a great idea.'

Archer glanced at where he'd listed 'Noah's Blueberry Pancakes' as today's special. He'd done it on a whim, remembering that it was Noah who'd requested blueberry pancakes at the meeting.

'Glad you like it, sir.'

The mayor waved away Archer's politeness. 'Call me Pete. Anyway, I'm sure the town will love this new idea.'

Dread started to seep into Archer's gut. New idea?

'People will love to see their name on the board and to try all the new pancakes.'

Was that his new idea? To make everyone's suggestions and then name the pancakes after them...

It wasn't the worst idea, actually. And maybe it would get everyone off his back about the damn original recipe.

'You know,' Pete went on. 'I had a dream that this diner was actually a pancake house.'

'You dreamt about the diner?'

Hazel huffed a laugh. 'He dreams about all kinds of things.'

Pete shrugged. 'I'm usually very accurate.'

Archer glanced between father and daughter and tried to figure out if they were serious. It was impossible to tell so he just nodded.

'I will keep that in mind.'

Pete smiled. 'Wonderful. And how are things working out with Iris?'

Heat rushed to Archer's face. Did the mayor somehow know what he did to his nanny on his kitchen counter?

'Is she working out as Olive's nanny?' The mayor prompted when Archer just stood there like an idiot.

'Oh … uh … yeah. Yes. She's a great nanny.'

'Glad to hear it. I'm really happy you're settling in here in Dream Harbor.'

Archer nodded dumbly. Settling in. Here. In Dream Harbor. That was what he was doing, of course. Settling in and wanting Iris to settle in with him.

'Right.' He cleared his throat again and Hazel gave him a little smile that said she knew everything he was thinking, which was highly alarming. 'I should get back to the kitchen.'

'Of course! Big breakfast crowd to feed.'

'See you later.'

'Bye, Archer!' Hazel called as he turned and made his way back through the crowded dining room and into the kitchen.

He needed to do something about Iris and fast. He didn't even recognize himself anymore. So distracted by a woman that he was screwing up orders, that he was fantasizing about things he'd never wanted in his life.

But what he didn't know was if he should push her away or pull her closer.

Iris was teaching an aquatic aerobics class, and she was pretty sure she was doing the movements correctly and calling the instructions loud enough and that she was totally tricking everyone into thinking she wasn't thinking about Archer's hands and lips and what he could do with those hands and lips and—

'Iris?'

Her name echoed through the pool room. Her playlist had ended.

She blinked to find a group of half a dozen seniors staring at her. Right, okay. So maybe she wasn't doing the best job of not being distracted.

'Sorry, ladies. Um, let's just cool down.'

'No way,' Marrisa piped up. 'What's got you so dreamy-eyed, Iris?'

Uh oh. The ladies sensed drama. And they loved drama. And over the years she'd set an unfortunate pattern of spilling the tea to her beloved students, but this wasn't some fling. This drama was about Archer.

And for a million concerning reasons that felt different.

'It's nothing, really.' Iris dunked her shoulders and lifted her feet out of the water, using her hands to stay afloat.

'Mmm-hmm, sure,' said Carol, swimming closer. 'And that's why you stopped telling us what to do about ten minutes ago and we've all just been flopping around like fish in here until the songs stopped.'

Iris's cheeks flushed.

'Okay, here's the thing,' she started, and the ladies gathered closer. 'Have you ever met someone that made you seriously reconsider everything you've ever thought you wanted?'

The women's eyes widened. Janet whistled. 'Wow, she's got it bad.'

'I don't. I don't have it bad.'

Estelle raised her eyebrows. 'Iris.'

'Okay, fine I have it a little bit bad. But here's the thing, he's making me like … want stuff I never thought I wanted and now I'm confused.'

'What kind of stuff? Like being tied up or something?' Marissa asked.

Iris splashed her. 'No! Not sex stuff, like actual life stuff. You know me, ladies. You know I'm not into keeping men around.'

'But you want to keep this one?' Janet asked.

'I don't know. It's complicated. There are other factors…' If she said the whole, he has a kid thing out loud they'd know immediately who she was talking about (and even though they probably already did, she didn't feel like admitting it yet). 'We probably just need to have sex and then I can stop feeling all weird about everything.'

'You haven't had sex yet?' The shock in Marissa's voice was enough to illustrate exactly how the majority of Iris's relationships went. Hot but quick.

'Well, let's just say he's very good with his hands.' Iris grinned and then sunk beneath the water, the sounds of the women laughing and hooting following her below the surface.

Maybe she was right. Maybe she needed to sleep with Archer and get all this pent-up sexual frustration out of her body and then she'd be able to think straight. Then she'd remember that she had no desire to have a serious relationship or a kid or a long-term anything.

This thing between them could be purely physical with no harm done to Olive.

Now she just had to convince Archer.

Chapter Twenty-Seven

O ne week after the kitchen-counter incident, they were sitting on the couch together watching a movie. Olive was not in between them. Olive wasn't even at home. She was having a sleepover at her grandmother's house. So they'd decided to take advantage of having the TV to themselves and watch a movie. And now here they were, in the cozy darkness of the living room, with no kid at home and an empty couch cushion between them and Archer had no idea what this movie was about.

He'd been staring at the screen for the past forty-five minutes but if asked, he could not tell you a damn thing about this movie. He *could* tell you that Iris was wearing a tank top and yoga pants and that her hair was piled on top of her head in a messy bun and that she smelled like vanilla and that she'd made happy sighing noises as she ate the dinner he'd made her and that every time she giggled at something in the movie his heart constricted. And that he was absolutely losing his mind being this close to her and not touching her.

This was ridiculous.

He was a grown man and this was his damn house, and if he wanted something, he should have it. Right? Just because he was a father now did not mean he had to be celibate. And Olive wasn't even here. This didn't have to affect her, at all. It didn't have to get messy.

'Iris?'

'Yeah?' She turned to face him with a mischievous smirk. It was almost as though she knew exactly what he'd been stewing over all night. All week, really.

'I want to kiss you.'

Her smile grew.

'So do it.'

He was across the couch and dragging Iris into his lap before the words were out of her mouth. She straddled him and ran her hands through his hair, tugging a little on the ends. He smiled up at her.

'I poured salad dressing on pancakes because of you.'

'What?' She giggled, and he kissed the sound from her lips.

'I can't stop thinking about you, Iris,' he murmured against her mouth, and he could feel her smile. 'It's becoming a problem.'

'For me, too,' she confessed. 'I basically stopped teaching in the middle of a class.' She nibbled his bottom lip and he groaned.

'So, what are we going to do about it?' he asked.

Iris lowered further into his lap, pressing her ass into his cock. 'I have a few ideas.'

'And when things get messy?'

'They won't,' she promised, grinding against him and his

breath caught. 'And if they do, I promise we'll protect Olive from it all.'

He breathed a sigh of relief at that. They'd protect Olive. Together. This thing between them didn't have to hurt his daughter.

'Okay, good.' His fingers dug into her hips and she rocked forward. 'But you have to stop doing that or things are going to get real messy, real fast.'

Iris laughed, her breath warm on his face. 'I want it messy and fast. I don't want to wait any more for this.'

'Jesus, Iris,' he breathed.

'This time,' she said, already shucking her yoga pants and Archer barely had time to register her bare legs, her bare ass. 'Next time we can go slow.'

Next time. His thoughts snagged on that little promise.

'Please, Archer.' Iris's desperate voice snapped him back to reality. She was half naked in his lap, her cheeks flushed pink, asking him to do the one thing he'd not stopped thinking about since she moved in.

'Yes.' Yes to her please, yes to everything. And then her hands were on him, tugging his sweats down, wrapping around him with such single-minded determination that Archer nearly laughed, but it died in his throat. Iris stroked him once, twice, three times before raising up on her knees and notching him at her entrance.

She held his gaze. Hers was hungry.

'I'm on the pill,' she said, and he nodded. 'Okay, Archer?' He knew what she was asking.

'Yeah, it's okay. I've been tested.'

'Me too.'

He kissed her hard and desperate as she slid down, both of

them gasping when she was fully seated. Christ. It was too good. He wasn't going to last. But Iris was already moving, already moaning like maybe she wasn't going to last either.

She rocked her hips hard and fast, and Archer wished she wasn't still wearing her top and he wished he'd gotten a chance to taste her and he wished he had seen her body, but she rocked and rocked and the words *next time, next time*, rolled through his brain.

He held tight to her hips, kissing her as she rode him.

'I'm close,' she gasped. 'So close.'

Archer gritted his teeth. So was he.

Iris rolled her hips again, her fingernails digging into his shoulders, a low moan coming from her lips. He hadn't had time to pay attention, to take it all in, Iris in his lap, Iris sighing and gasping and moaning. It was too quick, too short, too lightning fast, but he couldn't stop it. He couldn't stop Iris moving against him or his own pleasure from barreling into him.

'Come with me, Archer,' she said and he did, thrusting up into her as she clenched around him. Luckily the house was empty because neither of them were quiet. The moment was loud and breathless and frantic, weeks of tension finally coming to a head. But it wasn't enough.

'Holy shit,' Iris said, slowing her movements and resting her forehead against Archer's.

'Yeah.' He huffed a laugh. 'That was…'

Amazing, hot. Insufficient to purge this need for Iris from his system.

'Yeah.' Iris smiled. 'That was.'

The pleasure had barely subsided before Archer felt a surge of panic that now that Iris had gotten off, there wouldn't be a next time. Now that the tension had worn off, she wouldn't need a next time.

And he shouldn't care. A one-night stand was nothing new to him. One-night stands were perfect for the old Archer. They'd almost always worked in the past for getting an attractive co-worker off his mind so he could focus on the one thing that really mattered to him, his work.

But he didn't want that anymore. Not with Iris. His work wasn't the most important thing in his life anymore. In fact, it ranked a distant third at the moment. The tension was gone, but he still wanted her. He wanted her in his life. Period. Whether they were having sex or not, he wanted Iris Fraser around.

Shit. *He* was the one who was going to make this complicated. *His* feelings were the ones that were going to get hurt.

Somehow, he had not seen that coming.

She leaned forward and planted a kiss on his cheek. 'I'm gonna go clean up.'

'Yeah, of course.' Archer was slowly coming back to his senses, to what they'd done and to how much it had affected him.

'But I wouldn't mind company later,' Iris said. 'You know where to find me.'

'Yeah, okay.' He wasn't even sure Iris heard him; she was halfway down the hall by the time he answered. What the hell just happened?

After he cleaned himself up with a towel from the kitchen, he sat back on the couch and tried to piece together the last half hour. He should feel relieved, right? Satisfied to have finally had the thing he'd wanted for weeks.

But it wasn't enough. It wasn't just about getting off.

At least it wasn't for him. Not anymore. But Iris had run off immediately after they were finished so maybe it had been just sex for her?

She'd told him she never planned on having kids. And if they were together in any sort of real way, the whole arrangement came with an automatic child in the mix. So where did that leave them?

Archer dropped his head back on the cushions. He'd thought he could compartmentalize his feelings for Iris. He'd thought that he could handle having her living in his house. He'd thought he could just control this whole thing, like he was so used to doing, but none of this was going how he thought it would.

And now he was left with a choice.

This could be it. They'd gotten the forbidden-sex thing out of their systems and he could let the whole thing go. Move on. He should probably even look for a new nanny. And kids were resilient, right? Olive would be okay. She had him. And he was proud of that. Proud that he was here for her. They'd get through Iris's departure together.

Or…

He could take Iris up on her offer to keep her company later.

It took him exactly three seconds to decide on choice number two. He didn't know what Iris wanted in the long run, but if there was an inkling of a chance that she wanted him, then he had to take it.

Iris stood under the warm spray of the shower and tried not to freak out. Okay, so she'd finally slept with her boss. And it was amazing. And then she'd quite literally run away, while also extending an invitation for more fun later.

Good lord, what was wrong with her? She was all over the map. Was Archer as confused as she was right now? Maybe she shouldn't have bailed so quickly afterward, but it was all so fast and hard and good, and then she didn't know what to do with herself!

He probably thought she was just using him to get off because she kinda was, but she also kinda wanted more and she *liked* him. Genuinely, actually liked him and it had been creeping up on her all this time and then it just slammed into her and she panicked.

It had been a very long time since Iris had liked a man and wanted to be around him when their clothes were on. She didn't really know what to do with that.

Okay, breathe, Iris. First you need to get out of the shower because you've been in here for a really long time and Archer is going to start to think it's weird.

She turned off the water and stepped out of the tub only to realize that she hadn't thought to bring in a change of clothes, or even the ones she'd stripped out of in the living room. She had her tank top and sports bra and absolutely no bottoms. Perfect.

She didn't bother wrangling herself back into her tank top and instead just wrapped a towel around her and prayed that she could get to her bedroom without being caught.

She opened the door and walked straight into Archer's chest.

'Oof.'

'Sorry.' He grabbed her arms to steady her. 'I was getting worried. Thought maybe you hit your head in there or something.'

Iris laughed. 'Nope. Just … thinking.'

'Yeah, me too.' Archer's gaze was steady on hers, dark and serious in the dimly lit hallway. Iris was hyper aware of her lack of clothing. Her skin prickled beneath the towel, every nerve ending standing to attention.

'And what were you thinking about?' she asked.

Archer's gaze flicked down to the bare skin above her towel and back to her face.

'I was thinking that that wasn't nearly enough.'

'Really?' Her voice was embarrassingly breathy, but Archer still hadn't let go of her arms and he was so close Iris felt dizzy.

'Was that your way of trying to end things between us, Iris? Bang out a quick one and we can move on with our lives because if it was—'

'No,' she responded before she could think. 'No, that's not what I want.'

Archer's lips curved into a relieved smile. He moved closer until her back was against the wall.

'What *do* you want?'

'I'm not sure.'

He frowned and moved to back away, but Iris wrapped her arms around his neck and pulled him close again.

'Iris, if you want to stop, we'll stop. I never meant to pressure you into any of this.'

She reached up and brushed a chaste kiss on his lips. 'I do want *this*. I want this physical thing between us. A lot. Trust me.'

Archer let out a small chuckle, but he was waiting for her to go on.

'But … I don't know about anything else … and I don't want to hurt you or Olive. I can't make you any promises, so if *you* want to stop, we'll stop.' She held his gaze and in that moment she wished she could make him a promise, but she still just didn't know about any of it. About if this was a life she even wanted for herself.

'Thank you for being honest with me,' he said, his mouth brushing against hers as he spoke. 'Just physical is just fine with me.' His mouth had moved down to her neck and he licked the drips of water from her skin.

'Are you sure?' Iris gasped.

'Very sure.' He ran his fingers along the top of the towel. He raised an eyebrow in question and Iris nodded, happy to be heading far away from this conversation and into safer territory.

Archer gave a gentle tug and the towel slid down her body and puddled at her feet. He groaned, his hands grazing along the curve of her waist and over her hips. His eyes were dark, drinking her all in.

'Last time was far too quick.' He scooped her up in his arms and she gave a little squeak of surprise. 'This time, I plan on savoring you.'

Iris clung to his shoulders, not sure she would survive whatever he had in mind, but very excited to find out.

Chapter Twenty-Eight

Archer laid her on his bed, her towel long forgotten.

'I've been picturing you like this for weeks.'

Iris smiled. 'I hope I'm living up to the fantasy.'

'Far exceeding, actually.' Archer shucked his T-shirt and crawled up her body, planting a searing kiss on her lips. 'You've been so fucking tempting, Iris. Like some kind of siren.'

Iris crinkled her nose. 'Don't sirens lead sailors to their deaths?'

Archer's mouth was on her neck now, sucking and nipping the delicate skin. 'Something like that.'

'Well, I don't go in the ocean, so you might need to come up with a different mythical creature.'

Archer's head popped up. 'You don't go in the ocean?'

'Nope.'

'You grew up in a beach town.'

'Right, so I know all the creepy crawlies that live in that water. No, thank you.'

Archer kissed the frown from her lips. 'Okay, so you're not a siren.'

Iris wriggled beneath him and wrapped her legs around his hips. Archer moaned. 'Not a siren,' Iris agreed. 'Just a really hot human.'

He laughed and Iris soaked in the sound. She loved it when he laughed. Loved that he was having fun with her, that he wasn't stressed about work or his daughter in this moment. *See*, things could be simple between them. She could make him smile and he could make her come and everything would be great. And normal. Par for the course for Iris.

But then she remembered how stressed and worried she'd been when Olive was sick and how Archer had been there for the both of them. How he had taken charge, how he'd shouldered everyone's emotions until the crisis passed.

Maybe Archer was different.

Maybe she could want different things with him.

'You are really hot,' he agreed, kissing along her jawline to her ear. 'And kind and funny and playful and dedicated.'

'Dedicated?' She'd never heard that one before.

'Yeah, to your students and to Olive. To your friends. To this town.' He kissed down her neck as he listed all the things Iris had dedicated her life to and for a brief moment, she felt like maybe she hadn't spent her adult life drifting around, like maybe she had done some things that mattered to people.

Emotion rose tight and uncomfortable in her throat. Oh no… She swallowed hard but the tears were already streaming down her face. Shit. She never cried. Not unless she was watching those damn commercials they played during the Olympics or encountered an elderly veteran in literally any scenario.

And now she was crying during sex?!

Her body language must have shifted, despite her best efforts, because Archer's head rose again. His eyes widened when he saw her tear-stained face.

'It's nothing,' she sniffled, trying to frantically wipe her face. 'It's just been a long, weird day.'

Archer's eyes were soft and his mouth sweet when he said, 'For me, too.' He kissed the tip of her nose and got off the bed, leaving her naked and crying and vulnerable, and Iris was about to get up and retreat to her room, because who wants to sleep with a crying person? No one *she* wanted to sleep with, frankly.

But Archer grabbed a fresh T-shirt from his drawer and handed it to her.

'You can sleep in this,' he said, as though he had no intention of sending her back to her own room, as though it was a given that she would sleep here with him even if they didn't have sex.

And the shirt was so soft and smelled so good and Archer's smile was also so soft and *he* smelled so good, that Iris just gave in. She gave in to the temptation to sleep there, to let this be more than sex, at least for the moment, to let that tender spot in her heart for Archer grow just a little bit more.

Because it had been a long, weird day. A long, weird few months. And having sex with Archer hadn't solved any of it. Big surprise there.

'Thanks.' She took the T-shirt and pulled it over her head. Archer folded down the sheets and climbed in on his side of the bed. Iris got in after him and he immediately wrapped his arms around her, tucking her little spoon into his big one, her back to his front.

LAURIE GILMORE

'Do you want to talk about it?' he asked, his breath tickling the hair at the nape of her neck.

She let her fingers trace over the corded muscles of his forearms where he held her gently around the waist.

'It's nothing really, I just ... it was nice to hear that about myself, I guess. I usually think of myself as pretty flighty. *Dedicated* was ... new.'

He pressed his lips to the back of her neck, softly. It was barely a touch but still, she felt it down to her toes. 'I think you're amazing, Iris. Despite my best efforts not to.'

Iris laughed. 'Oh yeah?'

'Of course.' Archer's hand was splayed on her belly, his thumb tracing idly on the underside of her breast. Iris forced herself to focus on his words. 'Sleeping with the nanny is a big faux pas, but having a full blown crush on the nanny, I think that's an even bigger one.'

'You have a crush on me?' The question sounded far too innocent for the situation, that thumb tracing higher, nearly grazing her nipple now, Archer's erection pressed against her still naked ass.

'A big one.'

'I might have a crush on you, too,' she admitted.

She could feel Archer's smile on the back of her neck. 'Oh, yeah?'

'Of course I do,' she said with a huff. 'You've been feeding me food I've only dreamed about. You take care of your daughter in a way that does very confusing things to my insides. And the way your forearms look when you chop things ... well, I want to lick them.'

Archer let out a surprised laugh at that and tugged her closer. 'You think I'm doing a good job with Olive?' he asked

246

and she could hear the hesitation in his voice, the fear that maybe he wasn't doing a good job at all.

'You *being* here is amazing. You making an effort, you *trying*, you just … loving her … it's all perfect, Archer. Trust me.'

She was glad she wasn't facing him because a few more tears slipped down her cheeks, but he must have sensed it anyway. His arms tightened around her.

'This can be whatever you want, Iris,' he said. 'But just know, I'm here for you, too. If you want me to be.'

Iris sighed. 'You had me with those forearms, you didn't have to be all sweet too.'

His mouth was on her neck again. 'Can't rely solely on these good looks.'

'I'm still not making any promises,' she said, her voice going breathy as Archer sucked on the delicate skin where her neck met her shoulder.

'I'm not asking for any.' He slid his hand higher until he cupped her breast through her shirt. 'This okay?'

'Mmm-hmm,' Iris murmured, letting her body take over. Archer's movements were slow and languid now, his hands roving across her skin, savoring her like he said he would. He let one hand slide up her shirt, brushing his knuckles over the curve of her breast and grazing the nipple. Iris sucked in a breath, and he chuckled in her ear, doing it again.

His other arm was still wrapped around her, his hand pressed to her belly, holding her tight against him. Iris felt hot and restless all over, his touch too unhurried, too light.

'Archer,' she breathed. '*Do* something.'

He chuckled again, his laugh coasting over her skin. 'I am

doing something, Iris. I'm finally touching this sweet body of yours, and I'm not going to rush this time.'

She groaned in frustration, wriggling against him, feeling the hard, heavy weight of him on her backside.

He bit back a groan. 'Iris,' he ground out, his hand snaking between her legs. She lifted her top leg over his, resting it on top of his thigh. His fingers found her wet and waiting, but instead of pressing right to her clit like he had that first night, this time he used soft strokes she could barely feel, light flicks that made her want to climb out of her skin.

'Archer,' she nearly growled. 'Please.'

'Do you always want it so hard and fast?' he asked, still teasing her, still tracing his fingers over where she wanted him, but never with enough pressure.

'Usually, yes.'

'No one's ever taken their time with you?'

'I never wanted them to,' she confessed.

'Do you want me to?' he whispered, using his other hand to cup her breast, rolling the nipple between his fingers. Pleasure shot through her body, hot and sharp. What *did* she want? Pinned to Archer's body, his hands torturing her, slowly, softly; did she want him to take his time? Did she want to be savored? Wasn't that dangerous? Sex had always served one purpose in her life and one purpose only: to get off and move on.

But this didn't feel like that, at all. This felt like sinking further into whatever this thing was between her and Archer. Did she want that?

'Yes,' she said. And just because she liked to mess with him, even when she was vulnerable and needy in his arms, she added a 'Yes, *chef.*'

Archer groaned and rocked his hips against her in a way

that suggested maybe he was reconsidering his idea about taking his time, if only just for a second.

'Christ, Iris. How am I going to go to work if I get hard every time I hear 'Yes, chef' now?'

Iris's laughter was cut off by her moan when Archer finally pressed his fingers harder, moving them in tight circles.

'Like that,' she crooned as Archer's hand worked between her legs. Iris let her head drop back against his chest and gave in to the feeling of Archer's touch on her body, to the pleasure he was slowly and tortuously bringing. He brought her close and then backed off, his touch going from hard to light and back again until Iris was a whimpering, writhing mess in his arms. She turned her head, straining to find his mouth and then it was there, on hers, kissing and licking and biting more pleasure from her body. She felt heavy and slow, hot and languid and frantic for more all at once. She let herself sink into it. Time slowed down. All she knew was Archer's hard body at her back and his soft, warm mouth on hers, and his hands, those hands she'd admired so many nights, working and working. She forgot about coming. She forgot about why this was a bad idea. She forgot everything except her body pressed against his.

By the time Archer had shucked his sweatpants and pressed into her from behind she was so keyed up she nearly came just from the feel of him filling her.

'Iris,' he groaned into her hair and all she could do was whimper. His thrusts were shallow from this angle, but he was hitting something perfect and intense inside her and his fingers still pressed against her clit and Iris couldn't hold on any longer.

Pleasure broke around her, a low keening moan tearing

from her lips. She shuddered and trembled through it, Archer's arms still banded around her. Fireworks, stars, earth-shattering, none of the usual descriptions could quite grasp how Iris was feeling as Archer continued his assault on her body. She was nothing but nerve endings and every single one was firing.

'No more,' she gasped, grabbing his forearm. She couldn't take any more. It was too much. She'd never in her life of quick hook-ups and frantic, festival fucking felt like this during sex. It was like she'd spent her entire sexual life playing in the minor leagues and she just got called up to the majors. And she wasn't sure she was ready for that.

He stopped, his hand sliding from between her legs.

'Okay, sweetheart. No more,' he whispered in her ear. 'You did so good.' Heat coursed through her already overwrought body. And there were those damn tears again. What was wrong with her today?

He was still inside her and it suddenly felt very important that he feel half as good as she did right now. She pushed back against him, taking him deeper and he groaned.

'Iris, you said you were done. I can take care of it…'

'No.' She clenched around him, eliciting another cracked moan from his lips. 'I said *I* was done. It's your turn. I want you to come, Archer. Please.' She sounded desperate and half crazy, and maybe she was. Maybe she'd finally lost it, but her body was still humming with everything he'd done to her, and she wanted him to feel it, too. She wanted him to feel good.

'It's not going to take much,' he said, thrusting into her again. Pleasure immediately started to build again with each shallow thrust, and as his breathing increased so did hers. She could feel his heartbeat racing against her back and when he came, gasping and moaning into her hair, she came again too, fast and hard and perfect.

They lay there, melded together, limbs tangled, and Iris could feel every bit of blood flowing through her body, every fast thump of her heart. Eventually, Archer pulled out and Iris rolled to her back, she was sweaty and sticky and she couldn't stop smiling. Archer kissed the shoulder that was peeking out of his T-shirt. She'd never taken it off.

'You okay?' he asked.

'Mmm-hmm,' she murmured. 'You?'

He was looking down at her now, propped on an elbow, and there was something warm and tender and dangerous in his expression. And all the reasons this was a bad idea came flooding back in. She was going to hurt him and that little girl.

'I'm good,' he said with a soft smile, the one that poked that tender place in her own heart and Iris knew she was in so much trouble. 'Want another shower?' And Iris was so thankful in that moment that he was offering a practical thing to focus on instead of the crazy feelings swirling around inside her.

'Yes, definitely.'

She got up and let Archer pull the T-shirt over her head, let him get in the shower with her, let him shampoo her hair, scrubbing those magic fingers over her scalp. She let him help her out and wrap her in a fuzzy towel and escort her back to bed. She let him tuck her in and wrap his body around hers again.

But she didn't let herself think about any of it.

About what it meant.

About why she liked it so much.

About what she was going to do next.

It was morning and a bright spring sunshine was streaming through the windows and Iris was still in his bed. And this time she was here on purpose.

She was snoring lightly, her hair spread across his pillows. Archer's heart constricted at the sight of her. He liked this girl. A lot. And last night had been incredible.

But she'd been honest with him. She wasn't sure she wanted anything beyond the physical. So he was just going to have to be content with that for the moment.

Iris was still naked from last night, soft and warm next to him. It wouldn't be that hard to keep things purely physical. It should be ideal, actually. Archer ignored the voice in his head claiming that it wasn't ideal at all. That voice needed to calm down. Iris wasn't a Michelin star, she wasn't a head-chef position, she wasn't an immaculate kitchen. He couldn't just set his mind to this goal and achieve it. All he could do was be here and hope she chose him.

But, in the meantime...

He kissed her and she stirred in her sleep.

'Iris,' he whispered. 'Wake up.'

She frowned, a little crease forming between her eyebrows, but didn't open her eyes. 'Why? Don't you have the day off?'

'I do. But I need your consent before I go down on you.'

Her frown flipped into a slow grin.

'Okay, I'm awake. I consent.' Her eyes were still closed, but he'd take it.

He worked his way down her body, kissing and licking points of interest along the way, in ways he still hadn't gotten a chance to do last night. She was gorgeous in the morning, all supple, pliable limbs. He swirled his tongue around her nipple, sucking it into his mouth and Iris's breathy gasp had him immediately hard. He worked his way down her stomach, letting his hands trace the curves of her hips.

He nudged her legs apart and Iris complied, her hand coming into his hair. He hummed in approval.

Archer had traveled the world, he'd worked in some of the best kitchens, with the best chefs, and so he'd had the opportunity to taste the best of the best, but nothing in his life tasted as good as Iris.

Her hips bucked as he licked and sucked, her fingers digging into his scalp and God, was it good. So damn good he couldn't stop thrusting into the mattress. Iris's taste, her sighs and moans, her hands on his head, he was going to come like this. He was going to come with his mouth on Iris, with his tongue sliding against her clit and her legs trembling on his shoulders. She was surrounding him and he breathed her in, thinking he could die like this, thinking he wouldn't mind if he did and when he could feel her getting closer, when her fingers tightened in his hair, her hips moving against his tongue, he thrust harder into the bed, pleasure quickly shooting down his spine.

'Archer!' She shouted his name when she came and that was enough to do him in completely. He came on his sheets, too happy and full of Iris to be at all embarrassed by that. By the time he dragged himself back up the bed, Iris's eyes were open and she was smiling at him.

'Well, you sure know how to wake a girl up.'

'Better than an alarm clock?'

She laughed. 'Do you want me to return the favor?'

'Uh … nope. I … uh…'

LAURIE GILMORE

Iris's eyes widened. 'You came from doing that to me?'

He felt his cheeks redden but he held her gaze. 'Yeah.'

'You liked it that much?'

'Of course.' He decided to leave out the part about Iris being his new favorite meal, but the way she was smiling now, he thought maybe she wouldn't mind. He grinned, diving down to kiss her neck and Iris squealed.

'Archer!' she said with a giggle, and he loved the way his name sounded that way, too. He sat up, running a hand through his hair, savoring the way she looked in his bed, naked and flushed with orgasms and laughter and he could picture life being like this every morning.

He *wanted* life to be like this every morning.

He'd been worried at first about taking days off, but Gladys had insisted that he have one day off a week to spend with his family. Work, life balance she'd called it and now he finally understood. He finally wanted that. He didn't need to be in a kitchen every day of his life. He didn't need to be striving and striving all the time.

He could be home cooking for the people he loved.

Loved. The word thundered through him.

'How about some pancakes?' he asked, refusing to meet that word head-on. He couldn't love her yet. That would scare her off, for sure. Even if it was true.

She rolled her eyes. 'Archer, if I have to eat another pancake, I may turn into one.'

He laughed. 'Understood. How about an omelet?'

'An omelet sounds perfect,' she said with a smile.

When they were showered and the sheets were changed and she was at her usual seat at the island and Archer was

254

cooking, he still had that feeling like he wanted to do this every day.

'So, what time do we need to pick up Olive?' Iris asked, as he scrambled the eggs.

'Around noon.'

Olive, right. What were they going to do about her and all this?

'I don't think we should tell her. I mean about us … about any of this,' Iris said, getting to the heart of the matter, and of course that made complete sense. Why would they tell a five-year-old that they'd fooled around but it was probably just physical? That would be weird. But a part of him wished there was something to tell her.

'Definitely. We don't want her thinking…'

Thinking that you're going to stick around.

That we're dating. That you're going to be more than just her nanny…

Iris huffed a laugh. 'We don't want her thinking I'm going to be her new mom just because me and you are…'

Her new mom.

'Right, yeah, that would be too much because we're just…'

The playful expression she'd worn in bed this morning was gone.

'Archer.'

'Don't say it, Iris.'

'You know we shouldn't do this.'

'Do what?! We haven't done anything yet!'

'I tried to be honest with you. I told you…'

He was around the island before she could finish, planting himself between her splayed knees. 'You told me and I heard you. Just physical. I know. And we won't tell Olive. It's fine, Iris.' She was right of course. Olive couldn't know about this, and neither could anyone else. Would Kaori and the custody court allow him to keep his daughter if he was caught fooling around with the nanny? Would they question the environment he was keeping her in? He honestly didn't know but he couldn't risk it. Not now. Not when he knew he wanted to keep Olive forever.

She frowned. 'I don't want to hurt you.'

He forced a laugh. 'You're not going to hurt me. I know exactly what this is, okay? Olive is the one we need to protect. You were right. We won't tell her, and life will go on as usual.'

'With what, the occasional booty call?'

The smirk on his face was fake but maybe Iris wouldn't notice. 'It's a great commute for a booty call. Right across the hallway. Can't beat it.'

Iris was still studying him so he forced the smile wider. 'It's the perfect plan.'

She gave a little sigh, and he took the opportunity to kiss her, soft and sweet until her body relaxed into his.

'Okay, as long as you're fine with it.'

'Totally fine,' he lied, returning to his place on the other side of the island. 'Now, mushrooms or peppers in your omelet?'

'Both.'

'You got it.'

Mushrooms, peppers, his whole damn heart. She could have all of it.

Chapter Twenty-Nine

I t had been nearly a week since they'd had the SEX. It was always in big, bold letters in Iris's mind whenever she thought about it. The SEX had been incredible, five stars, would recommend, but they hadn't done it since. And she wasn't sure why. And she wasn't sure if she wanted to or not. Or if Archer wanted to. Or if he had lied about the whole being-fine-with-having-a-purely-physical-relationship thing. Or if she wanted things to be purely physical.

Or if she was completely losing her mind!

So, she'd been avoiding him as much as humanly possible while living in his house. Which was pretty damn hard. On Monday, she ran headfirst into his naked chest as he emerged from the bathroom, right as she was hurrying down the hallway to her room. He'd grabbed her arms to steady her and she'd just stood there, frozen like a deer caught in the headlights.

'Good morning, Iris,' he'd rumbled, his voice all raspy from sleep and Iris had stuttered some excuse about having to check on Olive, an obvious lie since Olive was still sound asleep, before running away.

On Tuesday, she'd managed to avoid him until he got home from work and then she was subjected to him in all his chef-coated, post-work, messy-haired glory. He'd been polite, asked her how their day had gone and that was it. He hadn't pushed anything. Hadn't asked for anything. She'd almost wished he had, wished he would just decide for her.

Wednesday was a real nightmare. She'd accidently peeked into Olive's room and found Archer curled up beside his daughter in bed, reading her favorite bedtime story with all the silly voices and everything. That had nearly broken her, the two of them side by side, their heads tipped together. It was too much. She was so happy for him, for them, for how far they'd come. Archer and Olive were a family now. And why did that hurt? Why did she want to picture herself there with them? Her brain felt completely scrambled, this new version of what her life could be playing on a loop in her head.

She'd managed to run out of the house on Thursday as soon as Archer had returned home and hidden out at Kira's house until past Olive's bedtime. Although it didn't escape her notice that she was disappointed to find the kitchen empty when she got home. She wanted to see him there, mixing up a new batch of pancakes. She wanted to sit and tease him. She wanted to discuss Olive's latest therapy session and all the progress she'd made.

She wanted to be a part of his life. A real part. Not a hired-help part or a booty-call part. It was all very concerning.

And now here they were, Friday, and they were at the diner for lunch since Olive had a half day of school and she wanted to see her dad. And Iris was more than a little afraid of what would happen when Archer stepped out of the kitchen. Would she run? Would she propose marriage? Would she stand on this table and proclaim her new and entirely unexpected love for him?

'Iris! Earth to Iris.' Bex waved a hand in front of her face, snapping her out of her slow descent into madness.

'Sorry, what?'

'Olive was talking to you.'

Olive squirmed next to her in the booth.

'Sorry, kid. I guess I fell asleep with my eyes open.'

Olive scrunched her nose like she didn't believe that excuse for a minute. Iris was just glad the little lie detector couldn't tell she was having wildly inappropriate thoughts about her dad.

'What were you saying?'

Olive sighed the long-suffering sigh of a five-year-old surrounded by incompetent grown-ups.

'I said, when are we going to start our garden?'

'Soon.' Iris reached over and opened the little pack of crayons that the kid's menu came with.

Olive grabbed them and started coloring, but Iris saw that her frown had deepened. She had learned that 'soon' and 'maybe' were Olive's least favorite words. She did not appreciate stalling.

'We were waiting for the threat of frost to pass! But we'll plant it soon. I promise, okay?'

Olive nodded as she colored. 'And when are you going to teach me to dive?'

'You need to finish learning to swim first.' Olive's swimming lessons had quickly become Iris's favorite part of the week. After just a few lessons, Olive had gone from thrashing around rather ineffectually in the water, to being able to do a front and back float and a pretty solid doggie paddle. Iris had been surprised by the swell of pride she felt when Olive's little tummy rose above the water, her head back, limbs like a starfish, and she'd done it. She'd floated! Even now, Iris felt a bubble of excitement inside her when she thought about it.

But Olive wasn't satisfied with a promise to garden and dive. She wanted more.

'Can we watch Narnia tonight?' she asked.

'Maybe.'

'Iriiiiis…' she dragged out the last half of Iris's name on a long whine.

Bex cringed and Iris just shook her head. 'What's with all the demands today?' She brushed the hair from Olive's face.

Olive laid her head on the table, her cheek sticking to the children's menu she'd scribbled all over. 'I want to do all the things.'

'I know. We have plenty of time, babe,' she said. But was that true? It was already May. If she stuck to her original plan, she'd be handing in her notice by June. Had Olive somehow sensed that she'd been planning to cut out early? Did she know that Iris was bound to disappoint her?

'But what if we don't.'

'We do.' A month and a half was a long time. Even if she did leave at the end of June, they would still have plenty of time to do everything Olive wanted. Unless she kept adding to the list. Or unless Iris decided to stop being a coward and acted on her newfound feelings.

Olive scowled.

Bex mouthed 'Yikes' from across the table. Yikes was right.

This kid had a lot of plans and Iris had made a lot of promises, and the thing was, she actually wanted to keep them. She wanted to plant a garden with Olive and teach her to dive and watch Narnia and do all the millions of other things they'd talked about. And that only complicated her feelings even more.

But at that moment, Archer entered the dining room from the kitchen, carrying a tray heaped with food. As soon as his eyes found hers, his face split into a smile. Iris couldn't help but return it, her insides immediately turning to goo.

'Oh. My. God,' Bex hissed. Iris kicked her under the table. Now was not the time to catch her cousin up on just how close she and her employer had become, but apparently, Iris wasn't imagining the way Archer was looking at her. They were obvious as hell.

'Look, there's your dad.' Iris nudged Olive with her elbow and Olive raised her head.

'Yay!' Olive waved to Archer, as though he wouldn't find them at their usual table. 'Dad! Over here!'

At the sound of Olive's eager 'Dad' shouted out across the diner, Archer's smile grew even wider and Iris's heart ached at how sweet he looked staring at his daughter.

'Hello, ladies,' Archer said, laying the plates on the table, he caught Iris's gaze and held it a beat too long to be normal. Iris's face heated.

'Let's see, we have one Olive Special.' He put the plate with the strawberry pancakes and whipped cream in front of their namesake. Iris started cutting the pancakes into little pieces for Olive.

'One Noah special.' Blueberry pancakes landed in front of Iris. 'And the "as close as I can get to the original" pancakes for

261

Bex.' He laid the last plate down with a flourish. Naming pancakes after the people who suggested them was a huge hit. Of course, this town absolutely loved the idea of having menu items named after them. They'd even almost forgotten about the original pancakes. Almost. Iris knew for a fact that Archer was still working on them, not that she'd been brave enough to venture out to the kitchen the last few nights to join him.

Archer ruffled Olive's hair. 'Hey, kid. How was school?'

Olive shrugged. 'S'okay,' she said with her mouth stuffed full of pancake.

'Just okay?' That worried crease appeared between his brows. The one that said he would literally march down to that school and do whatever he needed to do to ensure his daughter was having a good day.

Olive swallowed her pancakes and gulped down half her chocolate milk. 'Can Iris come to the Mother's Day breakfast?' she asked as soon as her mouth was clear, and Iris wanted to immediately stuff more pancakes back in. Of course Olive had waited to drop that bomb until Archer was here. Her gaze snagged on his over Olive's head. This kid wanted so much from her. She wanted everything. She wanted Iris to be a part of her family, and Iris still didn't know if she could promise her that. If she had it in her. Panic fluttered in her belly.

'I'm uh … going to go wash my hands before I eat,' Bex said, slipping out of the booth and bee-lining it for the bathroom. Iris desperately wanted to join her, but Olive was looking at her with those large, dark eyes.

She opened her mouth, hoping the words would just come to her once she started speaking but she was saved from having to figure it out by Archer's answer.

He cleared his throat, pulling his gaze from Iris and turning his attention to Olive. 'Mother's Day breakfasts are not in Iris's job description, Liv. But I can come. Or Grandma Paula, if you'd rather.'

Olive frowned and the feeling that Iris was letting her down weighed heavier than she wanted to admit.

'It'll be fun, okay?' Archer went on, running his finger through Olive's whipped cream and putting a dollop on her nose.

She giggled and tried to reach her tongue out far enough to lick it off.

Bex came back from the bathroom, her eyes flicking back and forth between Iris and Archer. 'Should I go wash them again?' she asked.

'My dad's going to come to the Mother's Day brunch,' Olive told her.

'That's great,' Bex said, breathing a little sigh of relief. Iris wished she felt the same way, but the panic had shifted into something else. Something like regret. Or longing.

She tried to catch Archer's eye again, but he stayed focused on Olive.

'Enjoy your lunch and be good for Iris, okay?'

'Okay.' Olive slid a finger through her whipped cream and reached her hand up to Archer's nose. He bent over so she could dab the cream on his nose. He smiled, that dimple popping in his cheek.

'Thanks, Liv.'

Olive grinned.

'See you later,' he said and Iris willed him to look at her, but when he did, she instantly regretted it. Written on his face was everything he wanted.

He wanted Iris. And his daughter. He wanted a family.

'See you at home, Iris,' he said and all she could manage was a feeble wave.

As soon as he was gone, Bex leaned across the table. 'We need to talk,' she hissed. 'What the he—heck is going on?'

'Were you going to say hell?' Olive asked.

'Uh … no. Of course not.'

'My dad says I'm allowed to say hell as long as I don't say it at church or school. Or in front of my grandma,' Olive said, still swirling her finger through the cream.

'That seems reasonable,' Bex said, digging into her own pancakes. 'These still don't taste like the original.'

'I know,' Iris said. 'But he's trying.'

'Has he tried Bisquick?'

'He gets very offended if you suggest using a mix.'

Bex raised an eyebrow. 'Kinda high maintenance. Are you sure you want to get into all this?'

'All what?' Olive asked, her little ears perked and listening.

Iris shot Bex a look that said 'shut the hell up in front of the kid!' Or at least she hoped it did.

'Nothing. I was thinking of opening a competing diner and making my own pancakes, but I don't think I will.'

Olive stared at her.

Iris attempted a smile.

Olive frowned like she was disappointed in her.

'Hey, isn't that Hazel and Noah over there?' Iris pointed out Hazel and waved at her. 'Why don't you go say hi.'

'Okay.' Olive slid out of the booth slowly like she knew they were just trying to get rid of her, but as soon as she was with Hazel and Noah, she was giggling and dancing around next to their table.

'Seriously, Iris. What the hell is going on?'

Iris kept her gaze on Olive to make sure the kid didn't make a run for it. She hadn't tried to escape the house in a while, but Iris didn't trust her not to see a bunny outside or something and try to follow it.

'We may have slept together.'

'You what?!'

'Bex,' Iris hissed. 'Keep your voice down!'

'Sorry. You what?!' she whisper-shouted.

'We slept together, and it was amazing. Like, earth-shattering, and now I don't know what to do.'

'Do what you always do.'

'What's that supposed to mean?'

Her cousin sat across from her with her arms over her chest. They looked nothing alike. Apparently, Bex looked like her dad, tall and strong with wild blond curls, and a booming voice. Iris looked like hers, and neither took after their mothers.

'You are the queen of one-night stands, Iris. When was the last time you actually dated a guy?'

Iris sighed. 'Eleventh grade.'

'Exactly.'

'But he has a kid, Bex. This is serious.'

'A kid you already love and take care of all day long.'

Iris looked at where Olive was now reciting some kind of poem or song or something for Hazel and Noah. When she'd first started working for Archer, Iris remembered how closed off Olive had been, how lonely and sad. She'd come a long way.

And maybe Iris had, too.

She'd been terrified of kids before, convinced she never wanted any of her own. And now, maybe, she could picture a life with Olive in it.

'Look, Iris, it's like any other relationship. Maybe it will work out and maybe it won't, but judging by the way you two were looking at each other, I think it's worth a shot.'

'But what if it doesn't work out?'

'Then it doesn't.'

'But what about Olive? Bex, you know how things were when we were kids. You know the men that waltzed in and out of my mom's life, and mine. Every time, I got my hopes up, and every time, they left. I don't want to do that to Olive.'

'Iris Lyn Fraser, you are being crazy.'

'Thank you. I feel crazy. That's very validating.'

Bex smiled. 'You are nothing like those dudes. Look, I love your mom, but she made bad choices in men. A lot of bad choices.'

'But those men weren't bad. They were kind and funny. I *liked* them. And then she'd just … get tired of them.'

'Okay, I'm confused. Are you afraid you're like your mother, or the men she brought home?'

'Both?'

'Iris.'

'Help me! I don't know what to do.'

'I think you do. I think you know exactly what to do but you're too afraid to admit it.'

Iris scowled. This was why she didn't talk to Bex. Her cousin knew her too damn well. And Iris did not feel like being called out right now. She felt achy inside.

Luckily for her, Olive was skipping back to their table.

'I'm back!'

'Oh good.' Iris sent a smug smile at Bex and her cousin

returned the gesture by sticking out her tongue. 'How are Hazel and Noah?'

'Good. I showed them my new dance.'

'I'm sure they loved it.'

'They did. They're going on a trip to an island and they're going to bring me back a souvenir.'

'Wow, lucky you.'

Olive grinned at her, right before she swiped the remaining whipped cream from her plate and dabbed it on Iris's nose.

'Got you! Now you match me and Dad!' she squealed with delight.

And for some crazy reason the whole thing made Iris want to cry.

Chapter Thirty

'Hey, Dad.'

'Hey, Arch. How's it going?'

Archer sighed.

'It's going okay.' He leaned back against his headboard. Olive had just finished her weekly chat with his dad and Iris had taken her to bed. When Iris had scooped her up, Olive giggling and shrieking in her arms, Archer was a goner.

They all just made sense together. Didn't Iris see it?

He'd been losing his mind over the past week. He'd been trying to give Iris space. He didn't want to push her into anything she didn't want, but now he had no idea what was going on in her head. She'd barely spoken to him about anything other than the basics for Olive's day and it was making him crazy.

'It's clearly not okay, so why don't you just tell me what's going on.'

'Things with Iris have … escalated.'

His father arched a gray eyebrow. 'Escalated? In what way?'

In what way? In a way that they'd slept together and it had altered Archer's entire brain chemistry, and now he had been left in a torturous limbo and he was tiptoeing around his own house.

'I think I accidentally fell in love with her.'

The shock on his father's face through his laptop screen would have been comical if Archer wasn't feeling destroyed inside.

'You fell in love with her?'

'Yes.'

Yes. He was in love with Iris.

He'd never been in love with anyone in his entire life, but here he was, in love with the woman he'd hired to take care of his daughter, the woman who was apparently allergic to long-term relationships and the idea of motherhood, and he didn't know what to do about it.

His father sat back in his desk chair, swiveling slightly from side to side. Archer had thrown him for a loop. His dad did not fidget. He had an opinion about everything. He never held back. And now he was looking at Archer like he had no idea what to say or how to handle the situation.

It was not comforting, to say the least.

His stepmother's face appeared on the screen. 'Sorry to butt in,' she said, 'but I couldn't help overhearing your problem, Archie.' Probably because she had been sitting in the same room as his father, working on her latest cross-stitch pattern. Archer had received more pillows with Bible verses stitched on them than he knew what to do with. They were currently all shoved in a hall closet.

'How does Iris feel about all this?' Cathi asked, her face now completely eclipsing his father's.

'She … uh…'

Cathi frowned. 'Well, there you go.'

'What does that mean?' Archer snapped.

'You need to *talk* to her, Archie. Like, really talk to her. Find out what she wants.'

That was the problem. He had talked to Iris, and she told him what she wanted. She wanted this to be purely physical. She'd been upfront about that from the start. He was the one who wanted more. He was the one hoping she'd change her mind.

He was an idiot.

'Thanks, Cathi. You're right.'

His stepmother smiled. 'Good. Glad I could help.' And with her job done, she disappeared from the screen.'

His father came back into view, a confused crease still between his brows.

'What is it, Dad? Why are you looking at me like that?'

His dad shook his head. 'Sorry. It's just … you've never talked about anyone like this before. It's good, Arch. I'm happy for you.'

Archer scoffed. 'Well, don't get too excited about it. I don't think we want the same things.'

'People change their minds about what they want all the time.'

'Maybe.'

'I'm proud of you, anyway.'

'Proud of me for falling for a woman who doesn't want me? Gee, thanks, Dad.'

His dad chuckled. 'I'm serious. Work was all you cared

about for years, Arch. And while I'm proud of you for pursuing that dream, it's nice to see you finding other things to pursue. Even if it doesn't work out with this girl, it's good that you're trying.'

It didn't feel good. It all felt pretty shitty, actually, but Archer didn't have time to explain that before Olive tore back into his room, freshly bathed and sporting her new jammies.

'I need to show Grandpa my sloths!' she said, climbing back up onto his bed and crawling into his lap. Archer readjusted the laptop to accommodate her.

'Hey, there's my little Livie again.'

'Look! Sloths!' Olive pulled out her pajama top to display her sloths.

'Oh, wow, look at those! Very stylish.'

'Move over, Jim, I want to see her jammies too.' Cathi was back, nudging his dad to the side and Archer had to laugh. His parents were so happy about having a granddaughter. His mother had sent multiple postcards from Chile and Olive had them all over her bulletin board. So between his three parents and Cate's mom, Olive had no shortage of doting grandparents and Archer was so thankful for that.

He could never have done this alone.

He glanced up and found Iris hovering in the doorway, her expression dreamy as she watched Olive talk to her new grandparents.

He *hadn't* done any of this alone.

Iris caught him watching her and she gave him a shy smile. 'Sorry. I tried to tell her it was your turn to talk to your dad, but she was very determined about showing off her jammies,' she said quietly.

Archer slid Olive and his laptop off his lap and let her finish her conversation. He joined Iris in the doorway.

'It's okay. She's excited.'

'Yeah.' Iris's gaze kept flicking back between Olive and his face. 'Sorry I've been so weird this week.'

He shrugged. 'It's a weird situation.'

'I don't want you to think I regret anything, because I don't.'

Archer's heartbeat ramped up, but he kept his face neutral. 'Me neither.'

'Maybe we can go out somewhere later, just you and me. I can call Kimmy to babysit.'

Archer grinned. 'Sure. Meet me in the kitchen at nine.'

Iris smiled back. 'I'll be there.'

'Hey, Mom.'

'Hey to you, my little flower. It's been a while.'

'I know, sorry.' She loved her mom but neither of them were very good about setting aside time to catch up.

Iris hung her head over the side of her bed, letting her hair brush the carpet, her phone held to her ear. It was eight o'clock. She had an hour before her 'date' with Archer and she felt weird and nervous.

'Anything wrong?' her mom asked.

'Not particularly.'

'Hmm … okay. So, what's new? How's the new job?'

'It's fine.'

Her mom laughed and the sound was familiar and

273

comforting. Her mom had a good laugh. 'So, you called to tell me you're okay and your job is fine.'

Iris sighed, somehow her mother still had her powers of mom perception, even long-distance.

'Mom, did you want to be a mom?'

'Of course, I did!'

'Too fast of an answer, Mom. I want the truth. When you found out you were pregnant with me, were you happy? Or scared? Did you always dream about being a mom or was it an accident?'

'Iris, honey, where is all this coming from? Are you pregnant?'

Iris started coughing and nearly choked on her spit. She rolled over, bringing her head back up onto the mattress.

'God, no,' she said when she'd caught her breath. 'I just... I've just been thinking about it a lot lately.'

'Oh.'

'I'm not like going to judge you or anything. I'm just wondering how you felt at the time. I know you love me, and I always felt loved as a kid.'

She could feel her mother's sigh through the phone. 'Well, that's a relief. I loved being your mom.'

'I know.'

'But if I'm being honest...'

Her mother paused for so long that Iris held the phone away from her ear to see if they'd been disconnected, but then her mother started speaking again.

'I wasn't married, obviously, and I had no intention of marrying your father. He wasn't ... the father type. So, yeah, I was scared, of course I was.'

'I get that.'

'Your aunt took me to the clinic, you know. She said she would help me with whatever I decided, and I did the same for her two months later... But in the end, I decided I wanted you. Even though I was still terrified.'

'You were terrified?'

'Of course! Every mother is. And if they say they aren't, they're lying. Motherhood is terrifying and complicated and not for everyone. But I never regretted my decision, even for a second, even when you refused to sleep between the hours of 2am and 4am for the first four months of your life.'

Iris let out a little laugh. 'Sorry about that.'

'Forgiven. Now, did I answer your question? Did that help?'

'It did. Thanks.'

'Good.' She could hear her mother's smile through the phone.

'One more question.'

'Wow, Iris! Are you writing a book about me?'

'Not yet,' Iris said, dryly. Lord knew, she had enough material to fill several volumes. 'But have you ever been in love?'

Her mother didn't hesitate this time and Iris wasn't surprised by her answer. 'Plenty of times.'

'But you've never stayed with any of those men.'

Her mother blew out a long sigh. 'Just because I loved them didn't mean I could stand living with them.'

Iris's heart sank. Was she like that, too? Would she tire of this relationship with Archer and hurt him and Olive in the process? She hated the idea of getting Olive's hopes up about being a family and then squashing them. It had happened to her one too many times as a kid.

'Some of us just aren't built for monogamy, babe,' her mother said. 'I am sorry if that affected you as a kid, but moms are people, too, you know? I did my best.'

'I know, Mom. You did great.' And she had done great. Iris's childhood had been filled with laughter and dancing around the kitchen and dinners with her aunt and cousin and it was beautiful and fun, and her mother had done her best.

Maybe Iris could do her best even if it wasn't perfect. Maybe it would be enough for the people she loved.

Her mother laughed. 'Well, good because we can't go back and redo it now.'

'No, and I wouldn't want to.'

'I love you, Iris.'

'Love you too, Mom.'

They said their goodbyes and Iris promised to call more often, as she always did, and her mom promised, too, and then she hung her head back over the side of the bed. She didn't know if she felt better or worse about her ability to commit to a real-life relationship.

But she did know one thing, one thing she'd somehow managed to forget. She may not have had a father, but she'd always had a family who loved her. Her mom and aunt and Bex, their own little female-only commune. Iris knew how to be part of a family.

So if she decided she wanted more with Archer, if she decided she wanted to join his family, she could do it. Even if she was still a little bit terrified.

Chapter Thirty-One

'So, is this a date?' Iris asked from her stool when Archer met her in the kitchen.

She looked beautiful, as usual, but gentler tonight, less like she was trying to drive him to distraction and more like she just lived there. Like she was comfortable there in his kitchen in her jeans and a sweatshirt, her hair still damp from her shower. She looked cozy and sweet and like she belonged there. He shook his head, refusing to dwell on how much he wanted that. Permanently. As his girlfriend, not his kid's nanny.

But one step at a time.

'Do you want it to be a date, Iris?' he asked, leaning over the island, just a little, just enough to get a bit closer to her, to smell her shampoo and watch the flush wash over her cheeks.

She looked up then, caught his gaze and her mouth tipped into a smile. 'Maybe.'

'Maybe?'

'Yeah.' Her smile grew more mischievous. '*Maybe* I want this to be a date. *Maybe* I want to date you.'

Archer felt like he wanted to shout how fucking happy that made him, but instead he went with a very cool, 'I'll take it.'

Iris laughed. 'You'll take a maybe?'

'For now.'

'Well'—Iris hopped down from her stool— 'I know just the place for our *maybe* date.' She grabbed his hand and Archer let her lead him out of the house.

They ended up at the ice cream store he'd passed a bunch of times but had never gone in. They should bring Olive here, he thought and then almost laughed at how she was never far from his thoughts these days.

Iris stood in line, examining the giant list of flavors hung up behind the counter.

'What do you recommend?' he asked, leaning down to whisper in her ear and to watch the shiver run through her when he did. God, he just wanted to be close to her.

'I like to mix and match. My favorite combo is a scoop of Strawberry Cheesecake with a scoop of Death by Chocolate. In a waffle cone.'

'Wow.'

Iris turned to smirk at him. 'You're not the only fancy-pants foodie around here.'

He laughed. 'I guess not. You've been keeping it a secret.'

She shrugged. 'I didn't want to intimidate you.'

'Oh, was that it?'

'Yep. Can't go bruising that ego of yours.' She laughed, her eyes dancing as she teased him.

They stepped up to the counter and he ordered two Strawberry Cheesecake and Death by Chocolate combos in waffle cones from the young guy at the register, who was busy staring at Iris. At first Archer wasn't sure the guy had even heard him, he was so distracted, but Archer couldn't really blame him. It was impossible not to stare.

Iris smiled at him, and Archer thought the poor kid might expire on the spot.

'Hey Carter,' she said. 'How's your grandpa's new hip?'

The question about his grandfather seemed to snap Carter out of it.

'It's okay. But my grandma said she might put a pillow over his face while he's sleeping and put them both out of their misery.'

Iris threw her head back and laughed, her hair like a fiery stream down her back. 'Wow, that woman is dark,' she said when she'd caught her breath.

'Yeah,' Carter said with one more shy smile at Iris before he went and scooped their ice creams.

'Do you know every senior citizen in this town?' Archer asked while they waited.

'Pretty much.'

'You know that's remarkable, right?'

'Is it? I've lived here my whole life. It would be weird if I didn't.'

He didn't really have a response for that, except he knew it wasn't just because she'd lived here her whole life. It was because Iris cared about people. She paid attention to them. And that's why people couldn't help but want to be near her.

It was why he wanted to be near her.

That, and he knew what she tasted like and he desperately wanted more.

But for now he would settle for strawberry and chocolate.

'Want to walk while we eat?' Iris asked as they grabbed their cones.

'Sure.'

They headed out into the warm night air. The town smelled like magnolia blossom and salt air. He followed Iris's meandering lead, enjoying being with her.

'It's not just Olive that I'm worried about,' she said, after a while. 'I mean, that's not the only reason I'm hesitant. About us.'

'Okay. Do you want to tell me the other reasons?'

Iris took another bite of her ice-cream cone. 'I don't usually do things like this.'

'Wander the streets at night while eating way too much ice cream?'

She laughed a little, her soft gaze flicking to his. 'No, I do that plenty. Date people, is what I don't do. Well, date one person for like a long period of time.'

'Yeah, I kinda got that.'

'You did?'

'Iris, you tried to make our first time sleeping together a hit-and-run.'

She laughed harder at that. 'A hit-and-run?!'

'That's what it felt like,' he said with a laugh.

She cringed. 'Sorry about that.'

'I'm not saying I didn't enjoy it.'

She smirked and shook her head at him.

'Look, Iris, I'm on unfamiliar ground here, too. With everything. With Olive, with the diner, with you.' He swallowed hard, refusing to let this conversation get too far ahead of him. 'I didn't really do relationships in the past either.

I didn't have time for them. So maybe we just take this slow. See how it goes.'

'See how it goes?'

'Yeah, we see how it goes. We figure it out together.'

'And what about the whole custody thing?'

'I'm allowed to date, Iris. I just need to provide a good home life for Olive. If and when we decide we're going to do this for real, we'll deal with the lawyers and the town's busybodies then. But us dating isn't going to harm Olive.'

She didn't look convinced, and maybe he'd been unsure of that fact at first, too. He didn't think it was a good idea to have a fling with the nanny. But this wasn't a fling. He knew Iris's heart now. He knew she wouldn't hurt Olive.

She glanced at him from the corner of her eye as they walked and he held his breath as he waited for her to respond. Had he said too much, pushed her too far already?

'And what about the fact that you're still my boss?' she asked.

'Are you going to report me to HR, Iris?' he teased, nudging her gently, but the look on her face was serious. 'Do you want to stop being Olive's nanny?' She had a right to say no, of course she did, but still he hoped she'd stay.

Iris made a humming sound in the back of her throat as she thought. 'Well, if the goal is to disrupt Olive's life as little as possible, then I should probably stay on as her nanny.'

'Are you sure? I really don't want you to be uncomfortable with this whole thing.'

'I know you don't. So let's just take it slow and see how it goes. Like you said.'

Her hesitant smile had him breathing a sigh of relief.

'Okay, good.'

'But we still don't tell Olive,' she said, her brows drawing together in concern, and he saw it then, her love for Olive. It just reinforced his faith in her. She didn't want to disappoint his little girl. And he didn't want to either. He wanted to be able to tell Olive and the lawyers when this whole thing was on more solid ground. But he understood that Iris needed more time.

'Agreed.'

'And she's like a little detective so we need to be discreet.'

Archer laughed. 'Definitely.'

They'd come to the end of a dead-end street and the harbor stretched out ahead of them. Iris walked out onto one of the big rocks that separated a small beach from the residential street they'd just come from. She sat and he followed suit.

The waves lapped quietly at the shore, the moon hanging low over the water.

'This is one of my favorite spots,' she said, tipping her head onto his shoulder.

'It's a good spot.' Any place where Iris rested her head on him was a good spot.

'Did you know that Olive wants a bunny now? She's moved on from puppies,' she said.

'She's mentioned that to me several hundred times, yes.'

Iris laughed, and he felt the sound down to his toes. 'So are you going to get her one?'

'A bunny? Hell, no.'

'We'll see. I predict she talks you into it.'

Archer shook his head. 'The last thing we need in this house is a pet.'

'If she flutters those long lashes enough, you'll get her one. You'd do anything for her, Arch.' *Arch*. The teasing was gone from her voice, replaced with a sweet tenderness that made Archer feel like his heart was too big for his ribcage. That little shortening of his name, something people did all the time, sounded like the sweetest endearment from her lips. Oh Christ, he had it bad.

He cleared his throat. 'I'd do a lot. But I draw the line at bunnies.'

Iris lifted her head and turned toward him on their sun-warmed rock. She looked beautiful in the moonlight, like a character out of Olive's book of fairy tales.

He leaned forward and brushed his lips over hers. 'I'm really glad I moved here,' he said because it was true, so much truer than he ever thought it could be. How was it only a few months ago that he was scrambling to figure out a way to leave?

He felt Iris smile against his lips. 'Me too.' She kissed him, tangling her hands in his hair and he pulled her closer, wanting all of her but willing to settle for her sighs and whimpers and the feel of her soft curves beneath his fingers in the moonlight.

Later as they walked into the house, Iris whispered, 'This was a nice date,' with her fingers still twined in his. And her confession that it was a date felt like a win to Archer.

'Yeah, it was. I'll walk you to your room.'

Iris giggled. 'You'll walk me to my room?'

Archer smirked. 'I have to make sure you get home safely.'

They snuck quietly down the hall, past Olive's bedroom, peeking in to make sure she was fast asleep under a pile of stuffed animals. They stopped outside Iris's room and she looked up at him and he wanted to take her to his room and kiss her everywhere, but he also wanted to show her he wanted more than that.

He dipped his head and she rose to meet him, her lips warm and soft on his. The kiss was slow and sweet and tasted like strawberries and chocolate. Iris sighed and pressed her body against his, every curve teasing him. And Christ, did Archer want to lean into it, but he pulled away, resting his forehead against hers.

'Goodnight, Iris.'

Her eyes were big and dark, her cheeks flushed.

'What do you mean, "goodnight"?'

He smiled. 'I mean, will you go on a date with me again tomorrow night?'

She stared at him for a minute and he thought maybe he'd overplayed his hand, but then she gave him a small nod.

'Great, nine o'clock, the kitchen. I'll see you then.' He planted another chaste kiss on her lips before leaving her stunned in the hallway.

Chapter Thirty-Two

A rcher was wooing her.

Or something like that.

They'd met for their 'dates' every night for a week. Their dates, where Archer had cooked for her—all sorts of amazing dishes—and sometimes Kimmy had come to babysit and Iris had shown Archer more of her favorite places in Dream Harbor. They'd talked about everything under the sun, about growing up, about how they felt about their parents, about Olive, about the way they thought their lives would go, about how maybe that's changing, and they kissed, God, how they kissed, slow and sweet and delicious. Those kisses made Iris weak, they made her unable to think and her knees feel like jelly.

And it was really freaking nice.

She was having a hard time remembering why she was worried about this whole situation in the first place. What could possibly be a bad idea about letting an insanely talented chef cook for you and then letting him kiss you until you forget your own name? It sounded like an amazing idea, actually.

At the moment, she was pressed up against the wall outside her bedroom, with Archer's mouth on her neck and she only knew her name was Iris because Archer kept murmuring it against her skin.

'We've been dating for a week now,' she said, her voice breathy and far away.

'I know,' Archer said, his teeth grazing her throat.

'I think we should sleep together. Again, I mean.'

Archer pulled back just enough so she could see his face in the dim light of the hallway. 'Oh yeah?'

'Yeah, don't you? I mean it's been a whole *week*.'

He chuckled at the way she emphasized 'week' like it had been an eternity but with the way he was kissing her, it felt like it had been a century since they'd had sex. She wasn't sure how much more she could take.

'If we have sex again, are you going to freak out and tell me it's all just physical between us?' he asked, brushing the tip of his nose along her cheek until his mouth was on hers again, coaxing little sighs from her lips.

'I don't think I can claim that anymore,' she said and felt his lips tip into a smile. How could she possibly claim it was just physical, when she very clearly liked this man. She still wasn't really sure how it had happened. Somewhere in between the pancakes and the pasta and the kissing and the talking, she'd maybe fallen in love with him.

The thought sent a dizzy thrill through her body.

This had never happened to her before.

'Good,' he said. 'Because I can't pretend I'm okay with that anymore.'

His gaze met hers and she saw it, she saw that maybe he had fallen in love with her, too, and she couldn't help the grin that broke out across her face.

'So…' she said, running her fingers through his hair. 'You want to sleep over?'

Archer's grin followed hers, the dimple popping in his cheek.

'You know I do.'

The dizzy feeling grew.

'But…' He glanced down the hall toward Olive's bedroom.

'We'll be so quiet,' Iris promised, running her hands across his chest. She'd forgotten that Olive had been safely tucked away at Grandma's house the last time they did this. 'And we have the bells in case she sleepwalks. And you know nothing can wake her once she's passed out. And—'

Archer cut her off with a searing kiss, pressing her back into the wall and she groaned in relief. If she had to spend another night alone, she might not survive it. Her vibrator certainly wouldn't.

'You've convinced me,' he murmured, leaning his forehead against hers.

'Good.' She smiled and he kissed her.

They broke apart barely long enough to get through her bedroom door and close it behind them before they were kissing again. She couldn't get enough of it. Of him. Of this. Archer had broken every rule she'd had about men. Every idea that all she needed a man for was sex.

His lips were familiar now, the feel of his tongue against hers, his hands grabbing and holding her body, the way he moved, the way he groaned as she raked her hands through his hair. It was all familiar. And she'd never had that before.

Relationships had been fleeting, hot and heavy for a few weekends, at most. Never this. Never this feeling of longing and desire wrapped up with comfort and friendship.

Never with this feeling of home and family.

It was cozy and nice and still made Iris want to tear Archer's pants off.

And if that wasn't love, then she didn't know anything.

But she didn't tell Archer any of that, because at the moment she was trying to get him out of said pants and he was trying to get her to slow down.

'Iris,' he grumbled. 'Wait.' He grabbed her hands and she huffed in disappointment.

'We can go slow,' she said. 'I promise. Just take your clothes off.'

Archer stared at her with heat in his eyes and a little smirk on his lips.

'Please, *chef*,' Iris purred, and he immediately dropped her hands and yanked the shirt over his head. His pants soon followed and Iris was left with a nearly naked Archer standing in her bedroom.

He tried to pull her in close again, but she swatted his hand away.

'No, no, no,' she scolded. 'We're going slow, remember?' She gave him a wicked smile as she slowly began her perusal of his body. And it was a good body. Strong and broad, not like he worked out a lot but like he could carry you out of a burning building if needed.

She dragged a fingernail across his chest and he shivered.

'What are you doing, Iris?'

'Savoring you.'

Archer groaned, but by the way his cock strained against

the front of his boxer briefs, Iris didn't think he hated it all that much. She made her way around his body, letting her finger trail along, in and out of the dips of his muscles, over his shoulder and around to his back. She trailed a line down his spine and he shivered again. She let her finger catch in the top of his briefs and pulled them down just enough to appreciate the curve of his ass. And to get a glimpse of a tattoo.

'I knew it!'

'Knew what?' he said, looking over his shoulder.

Iris tugged his shorts down further. 'A tattoo.'

Archer smirked. 'You didn't notice it before?'

'I didn't exactly get a good look at your ass before. But now that I'm here…' She dragged his boxers the rest of the way down his legs and Archer kicked them aside.

'What is it?'

'An olive branch.'

'You have an olive branch tattooed on your ass?'

'It's not on my ass. It's above it.'

'Barely.' Iris traced the stem and leaves over the top curve of Archer's cheek. 'So why an olive branch?'

Archer shrugged and Iris watched his shoulders bunch and flex. 'I was headed to Italy. I guess I thought I was being clever.'

'So, you got this before you left?'

'Yeah.'

'You had it when you slept with Cate?'

'Yes.'

'And then she named your baby Olive?'

'Maybe? I don't really know; it could just be an odd coincidence. Is it weird?'

'That the woman you were hooking up with named the

baby you didn't know you had after a tattoo you have on your ass? Nope. Not weird at all.'

Archer laughed.

Iris leaned her forehead against the warm muscles of his back, her fingers still making paths on his body. 'It's nice, in a way. Like she wanted you to be part of naming Olive.'

She felt the sigh that rumbled through him.

'Do you think she would have told me about Olive?' he asked, his voice quiet and sad.

Iris wrapped her arms around his front, pressing her cheek against his back, holding him close. 'I don't know.'

He let out another long breath. 'Maybe she didn't tell me because she thought I would be a bad father…'

Iris held him tighter. 'She wouldn't have listed you on the birth certificate if she thought that.'

'I guess not.'

Iris tried to summon memories of Cate, this woman she barely knew but had seen countless times around town. She was kind, from what Iris knew, sweet to neighbors and quick to offer a smile. Iris had never heard a bad word spoken about her.

'She was probably trying to do what she thought was best for all of you,' Iris said, thinking about how Archer must have been back then. Driven and determined. Focused on his goals. Cate would have wanted him to achieve them.

'I wish she'd told me. I wish…' Another shuddering sigh. 'I wish I hadn't missed so much.'

Iris ran her hands over the broad planes of his chest. 'I know.' They were quiet for a while, Iris finding his heart and leaving her hand over its reassuring beat. 'Just because Cate *thought* she was making the right choice, it doesn't mean she *was* making the right choice. You're a good dad, Archer. And a good chef.'

He lifted her hand and pressed a kiss to her palm, whispering his thanks.

'Thank God you didn't have a spatula tattoo,' she said, shifting back to teasing, wanting to ease Archer away from his sadness. 'That'd be a much weirder name.'

He let out a surprised laugh as he turned and pulled her close again. 'Or a whisk,' he said, eliciting more giggles from her.

'Although Knives would have been an awesome name,' Iris added.

'I'll keep that in mind for the next one,' he murmured as he kissed down her neck.

The next one. The next child he planned on having with … who, exactly? Her? Iris Lyn Fraser? Did Archer just ask her to carry his baby and give it a totally amazing and badass name like Knives?

Did she want that now? Did letting Olive sneak into her life open her up to the idea of having offspring of her own one day?

Was it possible for a uterus to do a somersault, because that might have been what Iris's was doing, although whether it was in excitement or terror was still unclear. But now was not the time to untangle that mess of emotions.

Instead, she let Archer's body and mouth and hands distract her as he peeled off her clothes, leaving them both bare in the middle of her room.

'I haven't been in here since you moved in,' he said, backing her up to the bed, erasing all thoughts of kids and babies and motherhood. 'It looks nice.'

She hadn't done much. Added the comforter in varying shades of purple that Bex got her last year for Christmas to the bed, a few framed prints from local artists on the walls, and the bedside lamp she found at one of the Dream Harbor garage sales to her dresser. All the usual bedroom stuff, but all of that was in the periphery right now because Archer was leaning over her, pressing her into the mattress with his weight. His mouth on hers, his biceps bracketing her face.

'I'm in love with you, Iris,' he said, in between kisses, like it was normal, like they said it to each other every day, like it didn't suck the air from her lungs to hear it said out loud. 'I know it's fast, and I know it's maybe not what you wanted. But I do. I love you. I love every damn thing about you.'

He kissed her and kissed her and burned the words into her skin with every kiss and bite and lick.

'At first it was just physical. You were so damn hot. I should have never hired you, Iris. I knew it was going to be a problem from day freaking one when you showed up in that flimsy tank top.'

He moved down her body, kissing and talking.

'But then it was just you. It was you when you were happy and playful, and you when you were worried, and you when you were scared and when you needed me and when you didn't, and when you play with Olive and when you kiss me and it's just all of it, Iris.'

She still hadn't said a word and the way he looked up at her she thought maybe she was already breaking his heart.

'You don't have to say it back,' he said, his head resting on her stomach. 'You don't have to feel it. I just … this has never happened to me before and I wanted to say it.'

She ran her fingers through the soft waves of his hair, still not able to speak but wanting him to know she was there. He shifted again and took her nipple in his mouth, sucking until Iris whimpered, her grip tightening in his hair.

And finally, all her feelings for this man collided, the fun and the fear and the comfort and the lust and the friendship. And it was scary, but it was perfect.

'I love you, too,' she whispered.

His gaze shifted to hers even as he kept her nipple between his lips. He licked her once more before letting go.

'You do?'

'I'm pretty sure.'

He sighed against her damp skin and she shivered.

'I'll take it.'

He moved his way back up her body and she spread her legs for him. He pressed into her slowly until she was filled with him. They both breathed out a sigh. He moved slowly, deliberately, taking his time with her and she liked it, liked this feeling of being pressed down, of being surrounded by him, of being held.

By the time his thrusts became sloppy and fast, she was so close it hurt.

'What do you need, sweetheart?' he whispered against her temple.

'Can we roll over?'

He moved them without breaking contact, settling on his back with Iris on top. 'Better?'

She gasped as she rocked forward, the angle just right now. 'Much.'

She leaned forward and he took her nipple in his mouth again as she moved, her clit rubbing perfectly against his pubic bone, his cock still filling and stretching her. It didn't take long.

The orgasm rolled through her, slow and heavy and tortuous, spreading and building and crashing. Archer held tight to her ass, his mouth never leaving her breast, amplifying her pleasure until she was shaking and crying with it. He clapped a hand over her mouth, a not-so-subtle reminder that they were supposed to be quiet. She whimpered against his fingers.

When she finally came down, Archer smiled up at her. 'Again.'

Iris shook her head. 'I can't.'

'You can. Give me another one, sweetheart.'

Okay, maybe she really did love this man.

Three orgasms later, Archer finally let go and came inside her, his stare never leaving her face. When they were done, she collapsed on top of him, and they didn't untangle themselves until morning when Archer snuck back to his own room.

Because whatever the hell they were doing here, it was still way too soon to tell Olive.

Chapter Thirty-Three

'Iris!'

'What?' Iris opened one eye to find Olive's face frighteningly close to hers.

'It's strawberry day!'

Iris groaned. Strawberry day. Dream Harbor's latest festival. How could she have forgotten? The town had been abuzz with strawberry-themed preparations for weeks. Every business on Main Street was draped with strawberry bunting and displayed Strawberry Festival signs in their windows. Resisting an eye-roll, Iris sighed, this town really did go over the top for any seasonal festival.

'Iris!' Small hands shook Iris's shoulder. 'Iris, you said you would come with me and Dad, remember? You said. Iris! Remember?'

Iris reached out from her covers and put a hand over Olive's face. 'Where's the snooze button?'

Olive giggled.

'Liv?' Archer peeked his head around the door. Iris

burrowed further under her blankets. 'I told you to leave Iris alone. This is her day off. Sorry, Iris.'

Iris pulled down her covers to find both father and daughter staring at her, Archer with concern and Olive with unrestrained impatience.

'But she said she would come to the strawberry festival with us!'

Unfortunately, that was true. But that was also weeks ago. The promise was made before she'd caught whatever weird bug that Olive must have brought home from school. The little carrier had been fine all week, but Iris had been exhausted and queasy.

She rubbed her face and sat up slowly, letting the wave of nausea pass.

'She's right. I did say I would come.'

'Yay!' Olive clapped her hands and did a happy dance around Iris's room. Archer scooped her up in his arms and she squealed.

'Okay, well let's at least let Iris get ready in peace.'

'But the strawberries!'

'They'll be there all day, I promise.' Archer deposited Olive in the hallway and then peeked back into Iris's room. 'You okay? I can take Olive alone, if you'd rather stay here.'

She'd much rather stay here, but she'd promised, and with her new tender feelings toward this damn man and his damn kid, she didn't want to let them down.

'I'm fine. Just a little off this week. No big deal.' She forced a smile. 'I'll get dressed and be ready soon.'

'I'll make you some breakfast.'

Iris couldn't help her real smile. This man's need to feed her was one of her favorite things about him. 'Okay.'

'Eggs and bacon?'

Except at the moment, food was tricky. Iris's stomach turned. 'How about tea and toast?'

Archer frowned. 'That's all you want?'

'That's all I want, really. Thank you.'

He was still watching her from the doorway in that intense way of his.

'I promise, I'm fine.'

'Okay.' He finally cracked a smile. 'I'm glad you're coming with us.'

'Me too.' And she meant it, even though she still felt a little bit like she was going to barf. This would be their first outing all together since she and Archer had started sleeping together, since the L word had been spoken between them. It had been going well for the past two weeks. The sex had been incredible, but more importantly, every time he whispered he loved her, his body pressed against hers, his breath warm and fast against her ear, it felt real and true and right. And when she whispered it back, she *meant* it.

But when they were with Olive, they had to keep their distance. No kisses, no touching, and it was harder than Iris had thought it would be. Especially with a kid who was always watching and listening. It had started to feel like they were lying to her, and Iris didn't like that feeling. She didn't want to lie to this kid who trusted her. Not to mention, it was just really hard to keep her hands off of Archer. She wanted to hug him when he got home from work. She wanted to hold his hand and brush the hair from his face. She wanted to feel like they were a real couple and not like she was the hired help fucking her boss. It turned out that fantasy was less hot the longer it went on. And even though they'd agreed they would date *and* she would stay on as Olive's nanny, that whole plan was starting to feel worse every day.

So this outing to the first annual springtime Strawberry Fields Forever Festival felt like a big deal. Almost a test to see if they could be a family. A real family, out in public.

If today went well, maybe they would tell Olive.

The idea made Iris's stomach swoop again and luckily Archer was gone when she leaned over the bed and threw up into her trash can.

———

Like most lifelong Dreamers, Iris loved a festival. It was in the DNA of the town. These people just loved a reason to gather. So even though this was only the first year of the Strawberry Fields Forever Festival, the place was packed.

Logan Anders was hosting the event at his farm, and his fields were filled with craft vendors, snack stands, and more strawberry-flavored treats then Iris knew existed. Olive was vibrating with excitement beside her, and Iris had to admit that now that she was out in the fresh air with a nice layer of plain toast in her belly, she was feeling much better.

The air was warm and the sun was shining. It was the perfect June day. Everything felt new and fresh and hopeful. Iris had her eyes closed and face tipped toward the sun like a thirsty flower when Olive's shriek cut through her peaceful springtime thoughts.

'Baby animals!' the little girl squealed. 'Iris! Baby animals!'

Iris looked down at where Olive was tugging on her hand and her heart surged with affection. Her little rain-boot clad feet were squished down in the mud and she was already wearing the new strawberry hair clips that Archer had bought her at Bernadette's craft stand, and she looked so damn cute. She stared up at Iris with anticipation in her large brown eyes.

'Can we go see them?'

'Of course.'

'Let's go.' Olive started tugging Iris along to the pen with the animals. 'Dad! Come on!' she called to Archer, who'd been buying them a giant strawberry lemonade from Jeanie's stand to share.

'I'll catch up with you, but don't try and sneak any baby bunnies in your pockets.'

Olive laughed but Iris made a note to check her overall pockets before they moved on to the next attraction. Iris did not trust Olive not to try and smuggle out a bunny. She'd caught her a few days ago with carrots and a shoe box in the backyard attempting to rig up some sort of trap.

They made their way across the field, avoiding mud puddles and ruts in the grass to get to the animal pens. Dozens of kids swarmed around the fences to get a better look at the baby goats and piglets. Iris spotted a few familiar faces in the crowd.

'Look, Olive, Ivy and Cece are here.' She pointed to where the girls were giggling over a pair of baby goats nibbling on the wire fence.

Olive ran to meet them shouting about her new strawberry hair clips and her love of baby goats the whole way. By the time Iris caught up to her, all three girls were jumping up and down together, with a slightly frazzled Hazel and Noah looking on.

'It's possible we've given them too many strawberry-themed sweets already,' Hazel said.

'Nah,' Noah said with a grin. 'They're just having fun.'

Iris gave him a bemused smile, still too out of breath from her near jog across the field to contribute much else.

'Uncle Noah'—Cece tugged on Noah's arm—'can we have more quarters for the goat food?'

'You girls wiped me out,' he said, reaching into his pockets and coming out empty-handed.

'Olive, ask your mom if she has any,' Ivy whispered to Olive. Iris watched in horror as Olive's face transformed from joy to sadness in the blink of an eye.

'She's not my mom,' Olive said, and Iris's heart splintered.

'Oh…' Ivy squinted up at Iris in confusion. 'Your aunt?'

'No. She's just my nanny.'

Just my nanny.

'Okay,' Ivy continued with zero regard for how this little conversation was tearing Iris apart and really bumming out Olive. 'Then ask your nanny if she has any quarters.'

Shit. She definitely didn't have quarters. Who carried around pockets full of quarters?! Did moms do that?

'Sorry, kid. I didn't bring any.'

The disappointment written across Olive's face cut Iris to the core. This was exactly what she was afraid of. This little girl wanted so *much* from her and she was bound to disappoint her.

'I've got some more!' Hazel said, shaking her small purse until quarters rained down and the girls shrieked with joy. Thank God.

Iris blew out a sigh of relief. 'Thanks, Hazel.'

'No problem. We made the mistake of taking them to the zoo without quarters once and it was a complete nightmare.'

Noah slung his arm over Hazel's shoulder. 'I do appreciate you letting the girls stay over with us.'

Hazel smiled up at him. 'Of course. They're little nightmares but I love them.'

Noah grinned, planting a kiss on the tip of Hazel's nose. They'd make good parents one day, Iris thought, fun and loving. Iris could picture how their house would be filled with books and dance parties and a dad that would do anything for his kids and a mom who would adore them.

Could Iris build something like that with Archer and Olive?

'Did you know they have bunnies here?' Cece said to Olive as the baby goats licked the last of the food from their sticky palms.

'I know!' She turned to Iris, the earlier infraction of not having quarters already forgotten. 'Iris, can we go see the bunnies?'

'Let's go!' Cece said, pulling Olive along with Ivy right on their heels, not waiting for a response from any of the adults.

Noah laughed. 'Well, I guess we better follow.'

'I don't think we have a choice,' Iris said, tracking Olive through the crowd of kids. The girls made it to the bunny hutch and Kira was stationed out front.

'Hey, ladies.'

'Hi Kira, can I hold a bunny? I'll be so careful,' Olive said.

Kira laughed. 'Wow, coming in hot this morning, huh, Miss Olive?'

'Very hot. To hold a bunny. Please.'

Kira laughed again. 'You got it kid. But you have to sit down and be very quiet so we don't scare them, okay?'

Olive sat on the nearby bale of hay and nodded her head solemnly. Cece and Ivy followed suit. Iris smiled.

'At least they have to be quiet for a few minutes,' Hazel whispered, and Iris laughed.

'Okay, this one is called Cookie.' Kira lowered a caramel-colored bunny wrapped in a baby blanket into Olive's arms. Olive practically glowed with excitement, but she stayed completely still and silent, just staring at the animal in her arms.

Kira lowered a white and black bunny named Alexander into Cece's arms and a tiny gray one named Stormy into Ivy's.

'Well, that's the cutest freaking thing I've seen all day,' Iris said, and Kira grinned.

'I know, right?'

'So, you have bunnies now?'

Kira shrugged. 'It started with just a couple.'

'That's how it goes with bunnies,' Noah said with a laugh, and Hazel rolled her eyes.

'Aren't they cute, though!' Kira said with a dreamy smile.

'How do Bennett and the dogs feel about them?' Iris asked.

'Very protective of them. The dogs keep watch all day, and I've caught Ben checking on them in the middle of the night several times.'

Iris laughed and Olive shushed her. 'You're going to scare him,' she whispered.

'Sorry,' Iris whispered back.

'If you're very careful you can stroke his little head like this.' Kira demonstrated and then Olive followed suit, petting the bunny's head with such gentle love and care that Iris felt the inexplicable urge to cry.

'You okay?' Kira asked, looking at her with concern.

Apparently, it wasn't just an urge. Iris wiped her eyes. 'It's been a weird day.'

Kira was still looking at her with a furrow between her brows when Archer found them.

'God, that's cute,' he said when he saw Olive and the bunny.

'Dangerously cute,' Iris agreed.

'We're not getting a bunny.'

'Right. We're not getting a bunny.'

They caught each other's eye and started laughing. Kira was staring. Luckily, Hazel and Noah were too busy snapping pictures of the girls to notice.

'What is—' Kira started.

'Can I hold a bunny too?' A young boy with freckles and a strawberry stained mouth tugged on Kira's apron, distracting her from whatever it was she was going to ask, and Iris was definitely not going to answer. What would she say anyway, 'Oh, right, I forgot to tell you Kira, I fell in love with this man and his daughter and we're here trying to pretend we're a family and I'm not sure if it's working or not but I can't look at Olive without wanting to cry and I can't look at Archer without wanting to fling myself at him, so … yeah … that's what is going on.'

Kira flashed her one more raised eyebrow, like she'd heard Iris's thoughts, before turning to the rabbit hutch to pull out the next one needing a snuggle.

Iris took the opportunity to distract herself from her feelings and take in the scope of the festival. It certainly wasn't as big as say the fall festival or even summer, but it was a good showing for the first year. There were several booths selling strawberry shortcake. Iris noticed Annie's bakery had multiple varieties of strawberry-flavored cookies and cupcakes for sale. The Pumpkin Spice Café had a booth, too, serving up strawberry lemonades and strawberry smoothies. There were the baby animals, an arts and craft tent, and a bounce house for the kids. And more craft vendors than Iris could count. Not bad at all for year one. She even spotted Logan giving tractor rides, an activity usually reserved for the fall. Jeanie must have talked him into that.

'So how do we get her away from the bunnies?' Archer asked after they'd been standing around sipping lemonade and watching Olive snuggle Cookie for far too long. Cece and Ivy had gotten bored and convinced Noah and Hazel to take them to the bounce house, but Olive hadn't wanted to give up her bunny yet.

'I saw something about a puppet show starting around noon. Maybe we can lure her away with that.'

They both looked skeptically at Olive. Her face was filled with deep and abiding adoration for this bunny. They were so screwed.

Archer leaned into her, his shoulder warm and solid against hers.

'You sure you're okay?' he asked.

Iris let herself press against him, just a little. 'Yep.'

His hand brushed against hers, his pinky hooking around hers. A secret touch just between them.

Or it was secret until Olive's head shot up, her gaze zeroing in on where their hands were linked. Her smile grew. Iris dropped Archer's pinky in a panic. Maybe she wasn't ready for this. Maybe it wasn't time. Just thinking of Olive's disappointment over the lack of quarters was enough to make Iris want to reconsider this whole experiment. How disappointed would she be if she thought Iris was going to be her new mom and then it didn't work out?

'Kira!' Olive called. 'I'm done with my bunny!' She passed Cookie back to Kira and scampered over to Iris and Archer, looking at their hands, frowning in disappointment to see they were separate again.

'What's next?' Archer asked her, and Iris knew he was trying to avoid the inevitable.

'Dad, were you holding Iris's hand?'

'Uh…' Archer raked a hand through his hair. 'I was just making sure she didn't get lost.'

Olive's nose crinkled. 'You were?'

'Yep. It's crowded today. We have to stick together.' He grabbed Olive under her arms and lifted her up onto his shoulders. She squealed in delight on her way up.

'Her boots!' Iris said, watching in dismay as Olive's muddy boots got dirt all over Archer's shirt. But when she looked up, Olive and Archer were grinning at her with matching dimples and the boots didn't matter, the shirt didn't matter, her own doubts didn't matter. Maybe it was time. Maybe she was ready for this.

'Dad, hold Iris's hand again so she doesn't get lost,' Olive instructed.

He looked at her, the question clear on his face, so Iris nodded and grabbed his hand and they marched off to the puppet show. Together. As a family.

Chapter Thirty-Four

I ris stood at the back of the audience for the puppet show with the rest of the parents. The kids were all seated on hay bales lined up in front of the makeshift stage. Olive had managed to snag a front-row seat with one of her friends from school, but Iris could still spot her little pigtailed head from back here.

Iris was using the time to lean against a tree in the shade and collect her thoughts while Archer went to get them yet another strawberry-shortcake sample.

This wasn't so bad, she mused, her eyes scanning the other parents watching over their kids as the kids watched a somewhat creepy rendition of *Little Red Riding Hood* acted out by marionettes that would for sure haunt her dreams. But she could do this. She could date Archer for real. She could be a bigger part of Olive's life. Sure, she'd forgotten the quarters, but they'd been right on time for the puppet show.

Isabel caught her eye from the other side of the crowd and

mimed how horrified she was by the show. Iris laughed and nodded in agreement.

Look at her, just being a regular mom-type person out here in the world. She liked Olive. She more than liked her dad. And it was totally fine. She was totally managing it. She was—

Wait a minute.

The show had ended with the gruesome axing of the wolf and now all the kids were up and moving and the parents were in her line of sight and she could no longer see Olive, and where the hell was that kid?

Her thoughts became more frantic as she moved through the crowd toward where Olive had been sitting just a moment before. She had been right here! But now the hay bale was empty and her friend was nowhere to be seen and the audience had thinned and Iris still couldn't find her. Where was she?

'Oh shit, oh shit, oh shit,' Iris cursed as she circled the stage. Olive wasn't here.

She had LOST Olive!

'No, no, no, no…' This was not possible. Everything had been going fine. It had been going great. She was handling this. She'd become good at it. Hadn't she? Hadn't she bonded with Olive? Hadn't she learned what she liked to eat and what made her laugh? Hadn't she figured her out?

This could not be happening.

'Iris?'

Archer stood next to her, hands filled with strawberry-flavored treats, his brows drawn together, staring at her. Staring at her and wondering where the hell his kid was.

His kid that she had lost.

Oh God.

She was going to puke.

'Iris, what's going on? Where's Olive?' Archer's stern voice broke through her panic.

'She … I … she was right here and now…'

'And now?' Archer's voice rose, his panic matching her own.

'And now … I don't know.'

'You don't know?'

'I—'

'Jesus Christ,' Archer swore, leaving all the snacks behind and striding off across the field, his head swinging back and forth as he searched.

'Olive!' he yelled. 'Olive, where are you?'

Iris hurried along behind, panic and horror and great big sweeping bouts of nausea rolling through her. She'd lost Olive. She'd fucked everything up. And to think, she'd actually believed she could handle this. She'd thought she could have a kid?! She'd thought she could play at what? Being an actual mother to an actual human child?

She had been unqualified from the start and now she'd ruined everything. What if Olive was in danger? What if she'd been kidnapped? What if she'd gotten hurt or fallen down or broken a bone or wandered into the road?

What if…

What if…

What if…

Iris stopped at the nearest trash can to empty the contents of her stomach as one awful scenario after another raced through her head. She had never known terror as acute as this. She had never known worry as debilitating.

This wasn't a game. This wasn't a fling.

This was Archer and his real-life daughter, and she'd let them both down so terribly, so completely…

Her whole body was shaking when Kira appeared beside her and wrapped an arm around her to steady her.

'It's okay,' she soothed. 'Everyone is looking for her, Iris. They'll find her in no time.' Kira pressed a kiss to Iris's temple and Iris clung to her friend.

'What if they don't… What if…'

'Hush,' Kira commanded, taking charge. 'They will find her. She's only been gone a minute, Iris, and the whole damn town is here. They will find her, and she'll be fine. Everything will be fine.' She said it with such certainty that Iris was forced to believe her, but she held tight to Kira's hand as they walked the festival calling Olive's name.

When Logan's tractor pulled into view with Olive on the seat beside him, grinning from ear to ear, Iris didn't know if she wanted to hug her or strangle her.

She ran to the tractor, leaving Kira behind. Archer beat her to it though, already lifting Olive from her seat, already scolding and crying and hugging her all at once.

'Never do that again,' he said, pulling back from his hug to look her in the eye. 'Never again, do you hear me?'

Olive nodded, her smile long gone. She took Archer's face between her small hands. 'Sorry, Dad. I just wanted to pick some *fresh* strawberries in the field.'

Archer glanced up at Logan.

'I found her wandering around the back of the farmhouse, happy as a clam, picking strawberries from my grandfather's personal garden.' Logan had a bemused smile on his face but Archer was clearly not ready to join him in that.

'Thanks, man. I really appreciate it. I'm sorry she got away from us.'

Not *us*. Away from *her*. It had been her fault, and Iris couldn't do anything but hover in the background as relief and regret swirled through her. All she could do was watch as Archer scooped up his daughter and smothered her in kisses and told her over and over again to never wander off like that again and that she'd scared him and that he loved her. And the longing to be a part of that hug was so sharp and so strong it nearly brought her to her knees.

But it was a different realization that forced her to sit. A realization that struck her so hard it felt like her entire world had flipped upside down. Iris didn't have a stomach bug. Of course she didn't. Olive wasn't even sick. And a stomach bug didn't make you want to throw up only in the morning. And it didn't make your boobs hurt. And it didn't make you weirdly emotional. And a stomach bug didn't make you skip your period.

Iris was an idiot.

And she was pregnant.

Iris was pregnant and she'd just proven to herself, to the entire town, and most importantly, to Archer that she was completely ill-equipped to be a mother.

———————

After an incredibly tense car ride home, followed by a tense dinner, and several stern talking-to's Olive was tucked safely in her bed, although Archer knew he would probably sleep outside her room tonight. And possibly for the rest of her life.

God, he'd never been so afraid in his life as he had been

today. The idea that Olive had just disappeared still sent waves of icy terror through his body. For someone that had only been in his life for a few months, she'd made a permanent mark, and now he couldn't possibly imagine his life without her.

And that went for someone else in this house, too. Someone who hadn't spoken more than two words since they'd returned home, since she'd apologized profusely, tears streaming down her beautiful face. Iris had retreated to her room when they got home, and he hadn't seen her since.

He knocked softly on her door.

'Come in.'

'Iris, I—' he stopped mid-sentence, taking in the scene in Iris's room. 'What are you doing?'

'Packing.' She didn't look up from where she was pulling clothes from her dresser drawers and tossing them onto the bed.

'Packing? Why are you packing?'

She didn't stop. More clothes made it to the pile on the bed. What the hell was going on? A panic similar to the one he'd felt when Olive was lost shot through his chest. Impending doom.

'Iris, look at me. Why are you packing?'

She stopped, her gaze rising to his. Tears glimmered in her eyes. The panic swelled.

'I'm tendering my resignation.'

Fuck, no.

'What are you talking about? No, you're not.'

She huffed, tossing a sweater onto the pile. 'I am. I quit.'

Terror, sharp and hot sliced through his gut. 'No,' he said, again like he was a fucking child. But she couldn't quit. 'Olive needs you.'

I need you.

Iris let out a noise somewhere between a laugh and a cry. 'I *lost* her, Archer. Do you know what could have happened to her today? Do you know how many ways that could have gone so much worse? And it was my fault! I wasn't watching her close enough. I wasn't paying attention.'

She was fully crying now, great big sobs and sniffles and he couldn't stand it. He stepped closer, reaching out to touch her but she backed away, kept the distance between them and he hated that, too.

'Iris, listen, it wasn't your fault. She does this, remember? She wanders off. She's done it to me plenty of times. Right out of my own house. It's not your fault.'

'It is my fault. And it's going to reflect poorly on you, Archer. How will this look in court? I jeopardized your whole case for custody. I messed up everything.'

She shook her head, her fiery hair wild around her shoulders. Her skin was pale and there were dark circles under her eyes. What was going on with her? What had he missed?

How had he fucked this up so thoroughly?

He stepped closer again and this time she let him touch her, let him brush the hair from her wet face, let him tip her chin up so she had to look at him.

'I'm sorry, Iris. I'm sorry if I made you feel like it was your fault today. I was just scared. I'm sorry I hadn't noticed that you were sick. Maybe you just need some time off.'

'I'm not sick,' she whispered.

'Okay, okay, sweetheart, then whatever it is, we'll figure it out. The court will see how well we've taken care of Olive. She's thriving because of you. You don't need to leave. This was just a bad day.'

Her lips tipped into a sad smile. 'No, Archer. This wasn't just a bad day. I never should have had this job in the first place and we both know it. I have no qualifications to be a nanny.'

'Fuck qualifications. Olive loves you. *I* love you. I don't want you to be her nanny anymore anyway, Iris. I want to be with you. I want you to live here for real. I want my bedroom to be *our* bedroom. I want you in Olive's life. In my life. Okay? You're fired, Iris.'

She was crying again, and he wiped the tears from her cheeks, pressing his forehead against hers.

'Please, sweetheart. Don't cry.'

'I can't—'

'Just sleep on it, okay?' He cut her off. He couldn't bear to hear what she couldn't do. 'Don't make a decision today. Too much has happened.'

She nodded, her head moving slightly against his. 'Okay,' she whispered, and that one little word sent such relief through his body he nearly sagged to the floor.

'Okay,' he echoed, kissing her head and stepping back. 'We'll talk more tomorrow. Just get some sleep.'

He wanted to stay. He wanted to wrap himself around her and take her to bed, to keep her there, but she clearly didn't want him to. Her arms were wrapped around her middle, her eyes dark and sad. He would give her space to think. By morning she would see, she would see that this was just a bad day, that it wasn't her fault, that everything worked out fine in the end.

She would see that she belonged here.

'Goodnight, Iris.'

'Goodnight, Archer.'

He made the mistake of sleeping in his own room instead of keeping watch in the hallway, but it wasn't Olive missing in the morning. It was Iris.

She'd left three things on the kitchen counter that Archer found the next morning at 5am. A note for him, a note for Olive, and a box of Bisquick pancake mix.

'But where is she?' Olive asked for the twelfth time.

Archer wanted to scream.

'At her cousin's house,' he answered calmly, for the twelfth time.

Olive scrunched her nose. 'Do I have any cousins?'

'No.'

'But why is Iris at her cousin's house? Is she coming back?'

'Because she needs a break, and I don't know.'

'A break from what?'

Us.

'A break from being a nanny.'

Olive's frown deepened. She looked back down at the note Iris had left. It was more of a doodle than a note. A stick-figure Iris and a stick-figure Olive were holding hands in the picture with a rainbow over them. Iris had written:

Dear Olive, I really loved being your nanny, but my cousin needs my help for a little while. Take good care of your dad. All my love, Iris.

Honestly, it was better than the note she'd left him, which just said: *I'm so sorry for everything.* At the bottom, she'd included the name and number of a replacement nanny and a suggestion to try Bisquick. And that was fucking it. No *'all my love'*, no explanation, no promise to come back. Was she quitting as his nanny or breaking up with him? Both, apparently.

He glared at the box of pancake mix.

'Are you going to take a break from being my dad?' Olive asked, and his heart, the heart that was barely holding on after yesterday and this morning, officially tore in two.

'No, Livie, I'm never going to take a break from being your dad.' That thought would have sent him into a state of despair just a few months ago but now it just felt true. Olive was his forever. And he wouldn't have it any other way.

She smiled at him. 'Okay, good.'

'And your mom, even though she's not here anymore, she's always your mom. Forever.'

'Okay, that's good, too.'

'Yeah, it is. Maybe we can finish that garden you and Iris started and put something special for your mom there. Something to attract hummingbirds, maybe.'

'Yes! And maybe we can get a bunny!'

'Don't push it, kid.'

Olive pouted. 'Can I at least have a Pop-Tart for breakfast?'

Archer sighed, thinking about all the ways Iris had imprinted on their lives. She'd been here from the start with Olive. And now it was just the two of them.

'Sure.'

'Yay!' She clapped her hands, her mood immediately improved by the promise of an overly processed breakfast treat. 'And don't worry, Dad. I think Iris is going to come back.'

He swallowed hard, not wanting Olive to get hurt anymore than she already had in her short life. 'I don't know, Liv. She might not.'

'But she might.'

'But she really might not.'

'Never say never, Dad.'

He looked at her then, her round face and dark eyes so much like Cate's, but her mouth, her smile, and that dimple were all him. He thought about all the years they had ahead of them, of all the things he still needed to figure out, to learn how to do. There would be birthdays and holidays and skinned knees and broken bones and heartaches and toothaches and trouble at school and trouble with friends and it was a lot. But looking at his daughter's face, so full of hope, he couldn't be the one to take that from her.

'Okay, Olive. I won't say never.'

She grinned and bit into her Pop-Tart. It all felt heavy and real, but Archer thought maybe he could carry it. Even if he had to carry it alone.

Chapter Thirty-Five

'What's going on?' Iris grumbled, emerging from her pile of blankets. She had cranked Bex's window air conditioner as high as it would go so that she could properly wallow. It was too hard to wallow when it was hot. And she had a lot of wallowing to do.

Not to mention she still felt sick and more exhausted than she ever had in her entire life.

'I called in reinforcements.' Bex plopped down next to her on the couch. Kira took the floor at her side and Isabel lowered herself gingerly into the ancient armchair Bex had inherited from their grandmother.

'For what?'

'Oh, you know, to help figure out what the hell you're going to do about the whole, falling in love with Archer, missing Olive, unplanned pregnancy situation,' Bex said, patting her roughly on the leg.

'I don't want to talk about it.'

Kira and Bex exchanged concerned glances.

'Iris…'

'I *can't* talk about it.' She already felt the tears creeping up her throat. She couldn't talk about this without completely losing it. And she didn't want to do that. She wanted to move on, like she always did. She wanted to be able to walk away from this job like she had from every other job she'd ever had.

But of course, this wasn't just a job. It was Archer and Olive and her debilitating fear that she'd ruined all three of their lives and didn't know how to fix it.

And she was pregnant. A pretty huge and concrete reminder that she did in fact need to sort this all out. Soon.

'Okay, here's what we're going to do. Let's just take one problem at a time,' Kira said. 'Any preference where we start?'

Iris shook her head, letting her hair fall around her. It was dirty and tangled. She was a hot mess. It had been two weeks since she'd quit and moved out of Archer's house and she hadn't done much more than cry on Bex's couch and eat sugary cereal. It was the only thing she could keep down.

'So … the pregnancy…' Kira started, watching Iris to see if she would completely fall apart at the mention of it. Iris nodded, swallowing the surge of emotion that happened every time she thought about carrying Archer's baby.

'I don't even know how it happened,' she said, as if figuring that part out would solve anything. 'I'm on the pill.'

Bex snorted.

'What the hell does that mean?' Iris snapped.

'You've never exactly been reliable when you take that thing, Iris. It's only effective if you take it regularly and even then…'

'Oh, like you're so damn perfect, Bex!'

'I'm just saying!'

Isabel whistled, bringing the attention of both women to her. 'This isn't getting us anywhere. It doesn't matter if it was a damn immaculate conception. Do you want to continue with the pregnancy, Iris? Because you have options.'

All three women were looking at her now. She had options, thank God. She didn't have to keep this pregnancy if she didn't want to.

But what if she did?

That was the part that actually scared her. What if she *did* want to keep it? Then what?

'What would you do?' Iris asked quietly, knowing that only she could make this choice but still wanting to know what her friends would do in this situation.

'Well, you know I'm a dog mom for life,' Kira said. 'But I have no plans to have human children, probably ever.'

'I used to say that, too,' Iris said.

'And you're allowed to change your mind,' Kira said. 'Or not.'

'I think I would keep it,' Bex said, surprising everyone. In all her relationships with men and women, Bex had never mentioned wanting to have kids.

'Really?' Iris asked, sitting up straighter on the couch.

'Yeah, even if Archer's not in the picture anymore, you could do it, Iris. Our moms did it.' Bex shrugged. 'I think you'd be a good mom. And I think I would be, too. And I would help you.'

Tears slid down Iris's cheeks again and she pushed them away. 'Thanks, Bex.'

'Jane was a surprise,' Isabel chimed in. 'We were definitely not ready for kids yet and I considered not going through with it.'

'You did?' Iris turned to Isabel, surprised again by her friends' choices.

'Definitely. We were broke. I still had a year of college left to go. It was objectively not a good time to have a baby, but…'

'But?' Iris was on the edge of her seat.

Isabel smiled. 'But, I don't know. I *did* want to be a mom. And I loved Marc and we decided to keep the baby.'

Iris sighed.

'And it was really fucking hard.'

'Oh.'

'Iris, it's always going to be hard, and scary and you are going to mess up. All the time.'

'Wow, Iz, very comforting,' Bex said with a laugh.

'It's true! You will make a lot of mistakes and you will always be questioning if you're doing it right. That's just part of the job.'

'Mistakes like losing the damn kid?' Iris asked, the panic of that day still thrumming through her veins when she thought about it.

'Yes, exactly like that. I never told you about the time Jane wandered off in Target and they had to call her name over the PA system and I felt like the worst mom in the entire world?'

'No, you never mentioned it.'

'Well, there you go. Every parent has plenty of stories of the mistakes they've made but all you can do is your best to love them, Iris. That's it. So whether we're talking about Olive or this pregnancy, if you decide to keep it, it's the same thing.'

'Yeah, Iris,' Kira agreed. 'You've been all, oh, Archer's so great for showing up and just trying to be there for his daughter, and that *is* great, but it's great when you do that, too! Why does he get a gold star just for showing up and you don't? You were there for that little girl when she needed you, and just because you made one mistake doesn't undo all of that.' Kira was fired up now and Iris couldn't help but smile through her tears.

'Thanks, guys.'

She still didn't know what she was going to do but she felt so loved surrounded by her best friends that she knew whatever she decided, she'd be okay, and they'd have her back, no matter what.

'And what about Archer?' Kira asked, moving down the list of issues.

'I don't know,' Iris admitted, and it was true. She didn't know what to do about Archer. She missed him so much it physically hurt, and sometimes she daydreamed about going back, about telling him about this baby, about scooping Olive up in her arms. And sometimes she wanted that so badly it took her breath away. But what if Archer didn't want that? What if one surprise kid was enough for him? What if he couldn't forgive her for leaving, for breaking Olive's heart? That was the one thing she couldn't seem to forgive herself for, letting Olive down. She'd just left without even saying goodbye to a kid who had already lost her mother. Who did that?

If she was Archer, she wouldn't forgive her for it.

'Well, do you want to be with him?' Bex asked.

'It's not that simple.'

'Why not?'

'Maybe he doesn't want to be with me,' Iris said. 'Maybe he doesn't want me messing with Olive's emotions any more.'

'I'm sure Olive is fine,' Isabel said. 'I saw her the other day, getting a lemonade at The Pumpkin Spice Café, and telling everyone who would listen that her dad bought her a bunny.'

A laugh burst from Iris so unexpectedly she clapped a hand over her mouth. 'He bought her a bunny?'

Isabel laughed, too. 'Apparently, yeah.'

The pain of missing them was sharp; a blade to her heart. She should have been there. She should have helped pick the bunny out. They probably named it something absurd. She should have been there to name it.

Iris shook her head, trying to force the longing from her lungs. 'I miss them,' she admitted.

Kira ran a hand down her arm, giving her hand a squeeze. 'Then maybe you should give him a call.'

'I can't.'

'Iris.'

'I just … I need to figure out this pregnancy thing first. I need to figure out what I'm going to say.' She should, right? She should know how much she was asking of Archer before she asked anything at all.

'Okay, that's fair,' Kira said, giving her hand another squeeze. 'But don't wait too long. Don't torture yourself for one mistake.'

'Okay, I won't.'

'Now, let's get you up and showered!' Bex said, patting her on the back.

'Okay, okay, I get it.' Iris swatted her cousin away and emerged from her blankets. 'I'm up.'

'I'm leaving ginger tea in your kitchen!' Isabel called as she hustled inside. 'It'll help with nausea!'

'And call me if you need anything at all,' Kira said, giving her a hug and kiss on the cheek. 'It's up to you, babe. Whatever you want to do.'

'Thanks,' Iris whispered through her refreshed tears.

'Love you.'

'Love you, too.' Iris hugged Kira and Isabel again on their way out the door and locked herself in the bathroom as Bex began her trumpet practice for the day. Maybe the shower would drown out the noise.

Decisions needed to be made sooner rather than later for more reasons than one.

Chapter Thirty-Six

A few days later, Iris somehow found herself at the monthly meeting of the Dream Harbor Book Club. Well, actually, she knew how she got there. Isabel had come over and physically lifted her from the couch and insisted that she get out of the house and now here she was listening to Linda and Kaori debate the appeal of 'the single-dad trope'.

The single-dad trope.

Somebody kill her now.

'Sorry!' Isabel mouthed from across the circle. She apparently hadn't had time to read this month's book and had no idea it featured a sexy single dad.

'I don't know, I still don't see the appeal,' Linda said, leaning back in her seat. They were in mismatched chairs in their usual corner of The Cinnamon Bun Bookstore. It wasn't a Sunday so there were no actual cinnamon buns to be found but Iris would swear the whole place smelled like cinnamon sugar and she could really go for a gooey treat right now.

'Kids aren't sexy. I really don't need them in my romance novels,' Linda went on.

'Agreed,' Nancy said with a nod, and if Iris was a retired kindergarten teacher she probably wouldn't want kids popping up in her romance novels either.

'Yeah, but there's something about the juxtaposition of a strong, masculine man cradling a baby in his arms that just does something for me,' Kaori argued.

Isabel and Jacob practically purred in agreement and then burst out laughing.

And now Iris had the very unhelpful image of Archer holding a baby flashing through her mind. Seeing him hug Olive was bad enough, but what would he look like rocking a baby? *Their* baby.

Okay, maybe she understood the appeal.

'What do you think, Iris?' Jeanie asked, turning toward her, and the whole group followed suit. She hadn't told anyone else about the pregnancy, but if anyone could figure it out it was this crew. Iris felt their stares boring through her.

'I ... uh ... I didn't read the book.'

Jeanie smiled. 'That's okay. I was just wondering in general if you like kids in romance novels.'

'I personally don't think a baby epilogue is required for a happy ending,' Isabel chimed in in a valiant attempt to save her.

'That's different than the single-dad trope, though, don't you think?' Jeanie asked, pulling her gaze back to Isabel and Iris breathed a little sigh of relief.

'True,' Isabel agreed. 'The baby epilogue implies a couple can only be happy if they bring a baby into the mix, whereas the single-dad trope is more about a hero who is nurturing.'

'Unless we throw breeding kink into the mix,' Jacob said with a grin.

'Oh God, breeding kink has way too much semen talk for me!' Kaori nearly shouted and Hazel's head shot up from where she was working behind the counter.

'Guys, please, keep it down,' she whispered, wide eyed. 'There are kids here!'

'And how do you think they got here, Hazel?' Jacob asked, raising his eyebrows suggestively. 'Semen,' he stage-whispered, and the book club cackled in delight. And Iris knew she was safe. This meeting had officially gone off the rails. But as she sat back in her worn out armchair, pulling another saltine cracker from her bag, she noticed Nancy and Linda watching her with knowing smiles.

She felt the panic rising in her chest. She hadn't made up her mind yet. She hadn't told Archer anything. She couldn't have the whole town knowing her secret.

But Nancy just held a finger to her lips and tipped her head in a silent nod. A promise to keep her secret safe.

Iris mouthed a silent 'Thank you,' and the older woman just smiled in return. She was safe for another day, but who was she kidding, walking around with a sleeve of saltines was a dead giveaway! This town would sniff out her pregnancy in no time and then what? Archer couldn't hear about this from anyone but her, that much was true.

She just…

A familiar head bobbing by the book display in the front window stopped Iris's thoughts in their tracks. Olive. And Archer was right beside her. And they were coming into the bookstore. *Now.*

Iris skittered from her seat and hid behind the closest bookshelf before they entered the shop.

'Olive!' The book club halted their bodily fluids discussion to greet Olive as she skipped into the shop. Iris pulled a book from the shelf she was hiding behind so she could peek through. Olive held a gift bag in one hand and a giant cookie in the other. Her hair was up in lopsided pigtails, but her hair ties perfectly matched the shorts-and-tank-top set she was wearing. She looked adorable.

And it felt like a kick to Iris's softest places.

Archer had done her hair. He'd picked out that outfit. He'd bought Olive that cookie. And Iris had missed all of it. She thought she would suffocate from the longing and that was before she made the mistake of looking up.

Archer.

She couldn't breathe. She was going to die here in the self-help section. How ironic.

He still looked so damn good. His hair was messy, but his face was cleanly shaved. A tight white T-shirt hugged his biceps, and on his arm hung a canvas bag filled with wildflowers. They must have just come from the farmers' market. It must be Archer's day off. It must be summer vacation. So many little pieces of their life that she was missing. Missing, because she was hiding, because she was a coward. Afraid of loving this man and his little girl. Even though they clearly loved her. Even though her mother had never shied away from love, even if it didn't last.

'We brought you a gift!' Olive said, reaching up to the counter to pass the gift bag to Hazel.

'A gift?'

'A wedding gift! My dad said you and Noah got married

on your trip and he said that when people get married you get them a gift. So we did!'

Hazel came around the counter to give Olive a hug and Iris's arms ached with the memory of holding the little girl.

'Thank you so much. That's very sweet.'

'We were going to bring it over later, but Olive really wanted to give it to you now,' Archer said, his voice low and familiar. It was the first time Iris had heard it in weeks and it burrowed into her heart and she never wanted it to leave. She wanted to hear it every day. She'd been so foolish.

'And Dad said I can get a new book!' Olive said, racing off between the aisles.

'One book!' he called after her.

Hazel laughed. 'Good luck with that.'

He gave her a rueful smile and then turned and noticed the entire book club was still staring at him. Iris held her breath, praying they wouldn't say anything about her being there.

'Uh … hello, everyone.'

'Hi Archer,' the group said in unison.

He blinked. 'Right. Okay, well…' he pointed in the direction Olive had disappeared like he planned on following her, but Kaori stopped him with a question.

'How's that new nanny working out?'

Oh God, did this store have an emergency exit so she could crawl out right now?

Iris watched Archer swallow, watched his Adam's apple bob above his shirt collar, remembering the way his T-shirts smelled, how soft they were against her skin.

'The new nanny is good, thanks.'

Good.

Fine.

It was good that the new nanny was good.

But was he Iris good?

'It's too bad it didn't work out with Iris,' Kaori continued, and Iris made a mental note to murder her later.

Archer winced. 'Yeah, it is too bad.' He opened his mouth as if he was going to say more and Iris wished he would say more, if only so she could hear his voice for another minute. He turned to walk down the children's book aisle but then stopped and turned back around. The book club waited.

'Have you seen her lately?' he asked. 'Iris, I mean. Is she...' he shook his head like he was being ridiculous. 'Is she okay?'

To their credit, not a single book-club member glanced toward the shelf she was hiding behind. But still Iris was scared of what they were about to say.

'You should probably ask her yourself,' Isabel said.

Traitor!

'Yeah, give her a call,' Nancy said. 'Or text, or whatever you people do now.'

'You people?' Jacob laughed. 'Just text her, Arch! I'm sure she would like to hear from you.'

Archer stood considering the book club's advice, a torn look on his face. 'Yeah, maybe,' he said before wandering off after Olive.

Maybe.

Why would he text her? She was the one who left. She was the one who messed with his kid's feelings. With all of their feelings, actually.

She was the one who had to fix it.

Because there was one thought that wouldn't leave the whole time Archer and Olive were in the store, as they picked out books and chatted with everyone, and Iris watched from her cowardly position behind the books, there was one word that echoed loud and clear through her heart.

Mine.

They were *hers*.

Archer.

Olive.

And this little baby that apparently was currently the size of a gummy bear, were all hers. And she wanted them. All of them.

Now she just had to hope that Archer did, too.

Chapter Thirty-Seven

A rcher was in the kitchen when there was a knock at the door.

'I'll get it!' Olive yelled, hopping up from her position on the couch where she'd been watching her favorite after-school show. It was some kind of kids' baking show and if contestant number three burned their caramel sauce one more time, Archer was going to have a stroke.

'We'll get it together,' he said, wiping his hands on the dish towel as he followed Olive to the door. The neighborhood welcoming committee had slowed their visits considerably, which he took as a sign of their budding confidence in him, but he wouldn't be surprised if it was one of the ladies with a freshly-baked something on his doorstep.

It was a typical Tuesday night. He'd gotten home from the diner and relieved the new nanny, Will, who did *not* live here, and then he'd started on dinner for him and Olive. The diner wasn't the only place where he'd been working on new recipes. While he had a whole repertoire of pancakes named after townsfolk now, at home he'd come up with lots of compromises. Food that Olive would eat and that also tasted good. Tonight, he was making her favorite: homemade chicken nuggets.

And like any other weeknight, they'd eat dinner together and she'd tell him every minute detail of her day and he'd try his very best to listen. Then a bath filled with rubber ducks and bubbles, far too many bedtime stories and, if he was lucky, a few quiet hours to himself.

Those hours were the hardest. The hours when memories of Iris would creep back in after keeping them at bay all day long. It had been weeks since she'd left, and Archer had given up on any hope that she was coming back. She'd made her choice. She didn't want this life and he couldn't force her to want it.

Just because he'd changed his mind about how he wanted his life to go, didn't mean she ever would.

'Maybe it's trick-or-treaters!' Olive said, hopping from foot to foot in front of him.

'Liv, it's July.'

She gave a little shrug like the month was inconsequential and Archer laughed. It was impossible to stay melancholy for too long with this kid around.

He opened the door, rattling the jingle bells he still kept there, even though Olive hadn't sleepwalked in weeks, expecting it to be a neighbor or a politician with a clipboard, or frankly even trick-or-treaters would have made more sense to his unsuspecting brain than the person who stood on his doorstep.

'Iris!' Olive shrieked and flung herself at Iris.

'Hey, kid,' Iris said, scooping her up and letting Olive wrap her legs around her waist. She held her tight, her face pressed against Olive's little cheek. 'I missed you.' The confession was barely a whisper, but Archer heard it and he stood frozen in the doorway because he didn't know what to do. He didn't know what this meant.

'I missed you, too! But I knew you were going to come back. I told Dad. I said you were going to come back and here you are!' Olive was petting Iris's hair now and squirming in her arms. 'Guess what?!'

'What?' Iris asked, her eyes shining with tears, and still Archer didn't know what was happening. Was she *back*? Or was this some kind of visit? Did she feel guilty for leaving Olive?

Did she care about leaving him?

'I got a bunny!'

'A bunny! Wow!'

'Yep. I named him Sir Reginald Hoppington.'

A choked up laugh left Iris's mouth. 'Wow, that's quite a name. You've improved.'

'Thank you. I call him Reggie.'

'That's a good name.'

Iris still hadn't looked up, hadn't taken her eyes off Olive, and Archer still stood in the door, waiting, aching for her.

'Do you want to come see him?' Olive asked, and finally Iris lifted her gaze. Their eyes met over the top of Olive's head. Archer's heart leapt back to life in his chest.

'I ... uh ... I need to talk to your dad first.'

'Oh.' Olive deflated in her arms.

'But I'd love to meet him later. Maybe have a cup of tea or something.'

Olive laughed. 'Bunnies don't drink tea.'

Iris frowned. 'That can't be right.'

'They don't!' Olive said, delighted to correct a grown-up. 'They only drink water.'

'Hmm. Well, if you say so. Maybe you should go check on him?'

'Good idea!' Olive squirmed down from Iris's arms and ran back into the house, leaving Archer without a buffer, without anything between him and the woman who'd left him.

'Hi,' she said, her voice still a raspy whisper.

'Hi.'

'Can I come in?'

He wanted to say no. He wanted to say she could only come in if she promised she was staying, if she promised not to hurt him again, if she promised…

'Yeah, of course.' He moved out of the doorway and let Iris follow him to the kitchen. He supposed it was only right that they have whatever this conversation was in their usual spot, a counter separating them. 'What's up?'

She raised an eyebrow. 'What's up?'

He blew out a long sigh, resting his hands on the counter in front of him. 'What do you want me to say, Iris? Why are you here? Why haven't you responded to my texts? Where the hell have you been? Why did you leave?'

She winced a little and it broke his heart all over again.

'I'm pregnant.'

Archer's thoughts stopped, his words stopped, the actual rotation of the earth stopped.

'You're—'

'I'm pregnant, and I'm sorry and I kind of freaked out, but I thought about it and I want to keep it—and it's yours by the way, of course it's yours—and I wanted to tell you, but I know you already have Olive, and I know I hurt you both and I'm so sorry but I was scared and I—'

He was in front of her, holding her face in his hands before she could finish, before she could say any more. He dropped his forehead to hers.

'You're having my baby?'

A tear slid down her cheek.

'Yes.'

'Iris...' Her name was cracked and raw, torn from his throat.

'You don't have to be involved if you don't want to, I just ... I wanted you to know.'

'Jesus, Iris. Of course I want to be involved.'

'You do?'

'Yes.' More than anything. He wanted this, Iris, a family, his *baby*. More than anything.

'Do you still love me?' she asked.

He huffed a disbelieving sigh. How could he have stopped loving her? 'God, yes.'

He could feel her smile more than he could see it, the way her cheeks lifted beneath his palms. 'Do you still love me?' he asked.

Her hands were on his arms now, squeezing, holding him in place. 'Yes. I love you and I'm so sorry for leaving.'

'It's okay.'

'It's not. But I promise not to do it again.'

'Good.'

He pulled back, letting his hands slide from her face down the sides of her body, over the small swell of her belly.

'You're having my baby,' he said again to make sure it was real.

'Well, it's *our* baby,' she corrected with a grin, putting her hand over the top of his.

'*Our* baby.'

'So, you're not freaked out?' she asked, her gaze searching his face.

'Of course I am. I barely have a grasp on a five-year-old. A newborn is going to be a shitshow.' His life was about to turn upside down again but this time he wouldn't fight it. This time he wanted it, however crazy it was. He wanted it with Iris.

Iris laughed, tears still filling her eyes.

'But I'm happy,' he said. 'And I'm so fucking happy you're back.'

'Dad, don't say that word.' Olive sauntered back into the room, holding Reggie. The caramel-colored bunny dangled from her little arms looking entirely unamused.

'Sorry.'

Olive looked from his face to Iris's and back again and then her gaze held on where their hands were resting on Iris's stomach.

'Does Iris have a belly ache?'

'Uh … nope…' There probably wasn't any hiding this from Olive but he didn't know how Iris wanted to handle it. His gaze met hers and her mischievous grin grew.

'Hey, Olive,' Iris said, turning toward his daughter. 'How about I move back in and me and your dad kiss more often, and in a few months we all have a new baby?'

Olive's little nose scrunched as she considered it and Archer bit down on a smile even as his heart thundered in his chest, even as everything he wanted seemed to hang in the balance waiting for the approval of a kindergartener.

'I want you to move back in,' Olive said. 'And kissing is

yucky, but I guess if you want to…' She shrugged a little at the mystery of grown-ups. 'And can I name the baby?'

'No,' Archer and Iris answered in unison.

Olive scowled.

'But you can help change all the diapers you want,' Iris told her, and Olive squealed in disgust.

'Ew! No way.'

Iris grinned. 'Okay, fine. Dad can change the diapers and you can be in charge of snuggling and…'

'And teaching the baby new songs!'

Iris laughed. 'Sure. New songs.'

'And dances!'

'Yep, definitely dances. The baby will need all the musical training it can get.'

Archer was holding back a laugh, but Olive was beaming.

'Yay! Okay, we can have a baby.'

'So glad you approve, since it's already in my belly.'

Olive frowned again. 'How did it get in there?'

'Uh…' Iris looked at Archer in panic and the laughter pushed further up his throat.

'How will it get out?! It's trapped in there!'

Olive looked truly concerned now about the baby's well-being.

'Oh God,' Iris groaned.

'Liv, why don't you go put Reggie to bed and we can talk about all this later, okay?'

Olive narrowed her eyes at him, knowing full well he was trying to stall for time, but Reggie was getting heavy and slipping further and further down her arms.

'Okay,' she relented. 'But I still want to know how we're getting that baby out!' she said as she left the room.

When he turned back to Iris, her eyes were wide and a smile played around her lips. 'Oops,' she said. 'I didn't really think that through.'

Archer chuckled. 'We'll figure out what to tell her.'

'We should probably be honest, right?'

'We should probably google it,' he said and Iris burst out laughing.

'We are so bad at this,' she said between giggles.

'We'll get better,' he said. 'Together.'

'Yeah,' she said, and her voice was gentle and sweet. He stepped between her legs again and she wrapped her arms around his neck. 'I'm really glad you took me back,' she said.

'There was never any question about that, sweetheart. You belong here, with us.' He leaned forward and pressed his lips to hers. And it had only been a few weeks since he'd kissed her, but God, how he'd missed it.

She kissed him back, her hands in his hair. 'I missed you both so much,' she said, her lips leaving his to murmur the confession.

He smiled. 'We missed you, too.' He kissed her again and again, his lips and his tongue and his teeth retracing all their old steps. He would have done more, he wanted to do more, but it would only be a few minutes before Olive would be back with her questions.

He pulled back and grinned at the sight of Iris's flushed cheeks and swollen lips. 'Later,' he said. 'I want you in my bed.'

Iris grinned. 'Well, technically, it's *our* bed now.'

Archer laughed and his heart could barely stand it all. Our bed. Our baby. Our family. Christ, it was too much. It was everything.

'You're lucky you missed the barfing part of this whole thing,' Iris added.

'Oh, God. I'm such an asshole. How are you feeling? Should I be doing things like rubbing your feet or feeding you weird pregnancy food?'

Iris was looking at him like she couldn't love him more, and he would do anything to keep that look on her face.

'I don't think I need anything like that right now,' she said. 'My feet feel fine and the only weird thing I've been eating is copious amounts of frosted flakes.'

'If you're craving sweets, I can bake.'

She grinned. 'I know you can.'

'And we should get you one of those pregnancy pillow things.'

Still smiling she ran her fingers through his hair again. 'Okay, sure.'

'Anything, Iris. Just name it.'

Her fingers felt so good he let his head tip back and his eyes close. She leaned forward and kissed a trail from his jaw down to his neck, and he groaned.

'Okay, Archer. But we're a team. I'm here for you and Olive, too.' She licked over his pulse point, and he shivered.

'Later, sweetheart,' he murmured, and Iris's breathy laughter blew over his wet skin.

'Later,' she agreed, and he lifted his head to meet her gaze again. 'But I'm serious. You don't have to convince me to stay. I'm here for real. I promise.'

He pressed his forehead to hers again, needing the closeness. 'Okay, I know. But you are carrying our baby, and it is my job to make that as comfortable for you as possible. So you have to let me.' He planted one more kiss on her smiling lips right as Olive stormed back into the room.

'Kissing already?' she asked, climbing onto the stool next to Iris.

'Yep. Super gross, right?' Iris said, pulling Olive closer and planting a kiss on her forehead. Olive grinned.

'Super gross.'

'Okay, ladies. I have chicken nuggets to prepare,' Archer said, retreating to his side of the counter.

'Nugget night? I picked the right time to come back,' Iris said, and Olive nodded in agreement. They sat side by side, watching him move around the kitchen and Olive filled Iris in on everything she'd missed in the weeks she'd been gone. Iris commented and laughed or sighed or groaned at all the right places. She clapped when Olive sang her latest song and demanded retribution when Olive told the story about her favorite rainbow crayon being stolen at school.

And in between dredging chicken in his secret bread crumb mixture and pan frying them and chopping veggies for Olive to dip in copious amounts of ranch dressing (another compromise), Archer paused to look at the woman he loved loving his daughter, and he could hardly believe he was the same person who landed here a few months ago. That guy had wanted to return to his old life as quickly as possible. He wanted to go back to the grueling hours and that cramped apartment and those toxic relationships. Archer didn't feel an ounce of regret for the job he'd lost or the apartment he'd given away.

As he watched Iris's fair head tilt toward Olive's brunette one, he couldn't help but feel sorry for his old self. That guy that wanted nothing more but to work himself to the bone, to spend countless hours striving for perfection in kitchens around the world, kitchens that were slowly draining him of the joy and fun of cooking.

When all he really needed to do was to perfect his chicken-nugget recipe and feed it to the people he loved most in the world.

'Is it ready?' Olive asked.

'It's ready.' Archer carried their plates to the dining room and the girls followed him. *His* girls.

Olive immediately dug in, but Iris caught his eye across the table. She was glowing.

'I think you're the best chef in the world, Dad,' Olive said between bites.

Iris grinned. 'I agree. Nuggets and pancakes. What more do we need?'

Archer smiled back. This food with these people. He didn't need anything else.

Chapter Thirty-Eight

I ris stood in front of the diner looking up at the new sign. It was still covered with a white tarp, waiting for the big unveiling. The building itself had been painted a bright red and strawberry bunting hung from the roof. Everything looked adorable, but other than the new exterior, Archer had been very quiet about the other secret changes. And against all odds, somehow even Olive was keeping the secret. Iris had moved back into Archer's house, or *their* house as she was practicing thinking about it, a week ago, and she'd swear this kid had done nothing but talk to her since she got there.

Not that she minded. She loved being caught up on all that she'd missed. She was still anxious about the next steps headed her way, but between Olive's attention during the day and Archer's attention at night, Iris felt more loved than she had in a long time. It made her feel less terrified, especially when Archer told her he was scared, too, but promised they'd figure it all out together.

But despite all the love and attention the two of them had

been showering her with, they had still managed to keep the big diner overhaul secrets to themselves. So now Iris was standing on the front sidewalk with the other Dream Harbor residents milling around and waiting for the unveiling, just as in the dark as they were.

'Hey!' Kira said, draping an arm over Iris's shoulders. 'This is a lot of fanfare for a diner.'

Iris laughed. 'I know.'

'This town…' Kira shook her head, but her smile gave away how much she loved this quirky place.

'Oh, you love it. And it's this type of enthusiasm that will only help when you get that barn fixed up and ready for events.'

'I know!' Kira was nearly vibrating with excitement. 'I forgot to tell you! I booked my first event.'

'You did? Who?'

Kira leaned closer and whispered in her ear. 'A certain farmer and a certain café owner are getting married at Christmas time, and we're hosting!'

'Really?' Iris turned to face her friend and Kira grinned.

'Yep.'

'That's amazing.'

'I know! Sure to be the social event of the season.' A frown crossed Kira's face. 'Now I just have a million things to do to get ready before then.'

Iris patted her friend's shoulder. 'It was very bold of Jeanie to book a venue with no roof.'

'Shh!' Kira glanced around wildly at the crowd surrounding them. 'It's a secret, and you know how these people talk.'

'I sure do.' The news that Iris had moved back in with

Archer and that she'd been eating suspicious amounts of saltine crackers had already spread across town. She ran a hand over her lower belly, even though there was barely a bump there. Let them talk. She'd let everyone know when she was ready.

'How are you feeling?' Kira whispered.

'Much better lately.'

'Good.'

'There you are!' Bennett made his way through the crowd to Kira's side. 'Big turnout for a diner reopening,' he said, planting a kiss on Kira's upturned face.

'These people love their pancakes,' Iris said with a laugh. She spotted Archer through the crowd. Easy to do, since Olive was perched up on his shoulders. Gladys stood beside him in front of the new diner.

'Hello, everyone!' Gladys called above the din of the crowd. 'Hello!'

A sharp whistle cut through the noise.

Gladys cleared her throat. 'Thank you, Mindy.' She nodded to the deputy mayor. 'And thank you all for coming to the reopening of our beloved diner. As you know, we've had a new chef with us over the past few months, and thanks to his hard work and to so much helpful community feedback, we've revamped the place and we hope you love it.' She gestured to Olive to pull the rope that released the tarp over the new sign.

THE STRAWBERRY PATCH PANCAKE HOUSE

Pancake house? Iris nearly burst out laughing. Archer caught her eye with a grin on his face. This man, this world-renowned chef was now the proud cook at a pancake house.

'I picked the name!' Olive said from her perch, and the crowd cheered.

'Excellent name, Olive!' Tammy called from her spot next to Kaori and the rest of the book club.

'Thank you,' Olive said, with a huge smile on her little face.

'We hope you like the new menu,' Archer added. 'It's filled with many of your pancake suggestions, as well as some of the menu items we added this spring that you all liked the best. And I suggest trying the "Original Pancake". I think you all will find it very familiar.'

'Can we come in and eat now?' Jacob asked with Darius on his arm.

'Absolutely. Come on in.'

Iris followed the crowd until she met Archer and Olive at the door.

'Pancake house, huh?' she asked with a grin.

Archer shrugged. 'It just made sense.' He leaned down and brushed a kiss to her cheek and Olive patted the top of her head, making Iris laugh again.

'My dad's here somewhere,' Archer said, glancing around the crowd.

'There he is!' yelled Olive from her perch.

Archer's dad, Jim, and stepmom, Cathi, fought their way through the crowd to get to them.

'Grandpa!' Olive called, shimmying down from Archer's shoulders. 'You're here in real life,' she said, delighted to see him beyond a computer screen.

'I sure am.' He squatted down and pulled Olive into a big hug.

'Hey Cathi,' Archer said, hugging his stepmom before introducing her to Iris.

'Iris!' Cathi pulled her into a tight hug. 'We're so glad to finally meet you and we're just so over the moon about the news,' she whispered loud enough that Iris was sure half the diner heard her.

'Thanks. It's so nice to finally meet you guys.'

Cathi pulled away with tears shimmering in her eyes, while Jim stood up, giving Iris the same dimpled smile Archer had.

'We are so happy for you two.'

'Thanks, Dad,' Archer said.

'And you're a proud pancake chef now, too!' His father beamed and Iris knew this was exactly why Archer was such a good dad. He had a good example. A dad that loved him whether he was a Michelin-starred chef or he was flipping pancakes at a diner.

Iris immediately loved him.

'Yep, proud pancake chef. Should we go in?' Archer gestured for everyone to enter ahead of him.

The diner, or pancake house, was stuffed to the brim. The waitstaff hustled between tables as customers called out orders bearing their own names in delight. Archer led Jim, Cathi, Iris and Olive to a booth with a reserved sign sitting in the center of it.

'I'll assume this is your best table,' his dad joked, patting Archer on the back.

'Of course. Only the best for my family,' Archer said, and Iris let the word seep into her bones. His family. She was a part of it now and he was a part of hers.

He planted a kiss on her cheek as she waited for Olive to scramble into the booth.

'Let me just check on the kitchen and I'll be right back,' he said, leaving Iris with Olive and his parents. She'd spoken to them before (she'd thought Cathi might try to crawl through the screen to hug her when they'd announced their

LAURIE GILMORE

pregnancy) but this was the first time they were all together in person.

'So, Iris,' Cathi said now, 'how are you feeling?'

'Really good, at the moment.'

'Archer mentioned it was tough in the beginning.'

Iris winced. It had been tough for several reasons, some of which were very much her own fault.

Archer's dad reached across the table and patted her hand. 'You two are going to be just fine. You have each other.' He gave her hand a squeeze and Iris felt tears spring to her eyes. Apparently, she just cried all the damn time now.

He gave her one more smile and then turned to his granddaughter. 'Now, Livie, what's good here?' he asked, opening the menu and Iris was thankful for the moment to pull herself back together again.

Cathi gave her a kind smile and opened her menu as well. 'The Noah,' she read. 'A stack of blueberry pancakes with whipped cream.'

'The Jeanie: pumpkin-spice pancakes with real maple syrup. That one sounds good,' Jim said.

'Oh, listen to this one!' Cathi said, continuing to read down the list. 'The Andy: lemon poppy-seed pancakes served with creme fraiche.'

Archer was back at their table and slid into the booth beside Iris.

'These all sound delicious,' she said as his parents continued to ooh and ah over the selections. Olive scribbled on the children's menu on her other side.

Archer smirked, that dimple popping in his cheek. 'Of course they do. I've been trying to tell everyone, I'm a very good chef.'

Iris rolled her eyes, but the laugh was already escaping her lips.

'Don't you need to help feed all those people?' Iris asked, glancing around the packed dining room.

'Uh … yes, eventually. But the kitchen is a well-oiled machine. They'll be okay without me for a few minutes.'

'What do you recommend, Arch?' Jim asked, putting down the menu.

'How about I bring you some of my favorites?'

'The chef's favorites? Sounds perfect!' Cathi said. 'We are just so proud of you, Arch.'

And Iris had to bite down on a smile. These people adored this man, and she really couldn't blame them. She did, too.

'Thanks, Cathi. I'll be right back.'

While they waited, Cathi and Jim picked Iris's brain on all the best things to do in Dream Harbor during their visit. For Jim, Iris suggested a fishing tour with Noah, since the man loved to fish; a massage at the spa for Cathi, and a trip into town to shop and eat at all of Iris's favorite places. Olive chimed in that they had to get cookies from Annie and that she wanted to take them to the bookstore.

'Of course, Livie. Anything you want,' Jim told her with a laugh, and Iris decided not to warn him that that was a very dangerous statement.

Archer appeared back at their table with a tray of food.

'The Jeanie, for Dad,' he said.

'How did you know I was eyeing that one?'

'I know you by now, Dad,' Archer said with a chuckle.

'The Mayor Pete—double-chocolate dream pancakes for Cathi.'

'Oh my gosh, these look divine!'

'Well, the mayor saw them in a dream, so who am I to argue?' Archer said with a laugh.

'And a Lost in the Strawberry Patch special,' he said, putting the plate down in front of Olive. The pancakes were piled high with strawberries and whipped cream. She clapped her hands in delight.

'And The Original for Iris,' he said, laying another plate in front of Iris.

'The Original, huh?'

'Yep.'

'Hmm … we'll see.'

Archer sat beside her and watched as she cut her pancakes and added syrup. She took her time, letting the syrup drip from the tiny metal pitcher he'd brought it out in.

He groaned with impatience. 'Just try them!'

Iris smirked, bringing some pancake to her mouth. 'I don't know why you're in a hurry for me to tell you these aren't like the originals…' She chewed, her eyes widening. Suddenly, she was ten years old again, sitting in this diner with her mom and her cousin on Sunday mornings, and then after prom, when she and her friends had stopped here for a late-night meal— and the day after Josie's funeral when she'd just wanted familiar comfort.

It was the perfect, diner pancake.

'How did you—'

Archer's grin grew. 'Bisquick mix, with a splash of vanilla, cooked in far too much butter.'

'You used the mix?'

'I used the mix.'

Iris laughed. 'Oh my God, Archer! You could have just listened to me from the start!'

He leaned back, watching her, love and pride and happiness mixing on his face. 'I know. I was an arrogant asshole who thought he knew better.'

Iris shoveled more pancakes into her mouth. 'You sure were,' she said between bites.

'Good thing you helped me taste-test for all those weeks.'

'Good thing.' Her gaze snagged on his, remembering all the other things they'd done during those taste tests.

'Dad, can I go sit with Ivy and Cece at their table?' Olive cut in.

Archer's attention switched to Olive. 'Directly to their table, do not leave this diner or you will not live long enough to attend first grade.'

'K! Got it!'

'How about we walk her over?' Cathi suggested. 'We'd love to meet some of her friends.'

'Okay, if you don't mind.'

'Of course we don't mind,' Jim said. 'We're here to spend time with our granddaughter. And you, but you're busy, anyway, so we'll see you later. The pancakes were delicious.'

'Thanks, Dad.'

Olive scampered off with her new grandparents in tow and Archer's gaze returned to Iris.

'You're a good dad.'

'I'm trying.'

'And a good chef.'

'I know.' The smirk was back and Iris leaned forward to kiss it off his lips. He kissed her back slowly and tortuously until she was dizzy with it.

'I wish you didn't have to help cook,' she said when he finally pulled away, his fingers still tangled in her hair.

'I know.'

'But I'll see you at home.'

His smile grew at that.

'Yeah, I'll see you at home.'

'I love you, Archer.'

'More than pancakes?' he asked, glancing at her empty plate.

'Don't push your luck,' she said, patting his shoulder in consolation. His laughter trailed behind him as he strode back to his kitchen.

Epilogue

SEVEN MONTHS LATER

Archer Baer had just become a father. Again. And still not in any way he'd expected.

He'd expected to have time to drop Olive off at her grandmother's house and to arrive in plenty of time at the hospital to get Iris settled in her room. He'd expected to have their birthing playlist on and to make sure Iris had her cozy socks and plenty of ice chips. He'd expected to follow all the coaching pointers he'd learned from their birthing classes.

Archer had a plan this time.

He was *here* this time.

He was in control this time.

But the joke was on him once again. His son had other plans.

Iris went into labor two weeks early, right in the middle of her seniors aerobics class—much to the delight and excitement of her students. It was Janet and Carol who had driven her to the hospital while Archer raced across town from the pancake house to get there. Olive, who was at school, had to be picked up by Hazel, their emergency contact, and brought back to stay at her house since Archer's parents were not expected in town for another two weeks.

Due to the ice rain that had started falling and the flooding on Main Street, Archer had barely made it to the hospital in time. By the time he slid into the labor and delivery room, hustled Carol and Janet out, and grabbed onto Iris's hand, the baby was crowning.

And then it had been all her.

All his beautiful, strong Iris, bringing the baby into the world in a screaming fury that scared the absolute shit out of him.

She looked up at him now, her sweaty hair pushed off her forehead. The baby, their son, slept on her chest.

'Well, that was wild,' her voice was hoarse and tired.

'I'm sorry I nearly missed it.'

'It happened so fast,' she said. 'Everyone says the first baby never comes that fast.'

He leaned over, kissing her forehead. 'You did so good, sweetheart. You were amazing.'

Iris hummed softly in thanks. 'You should hold him,' she said.

'I ... he's so small.'

'I know. But the nurses wrapped him like a little burrito. Makes him easier to hold.'

Archer reached down and took the snug package that was his second child and held him in his arms. Big, unseeing eyes blinked up at him.

'Hey, little guy,' Archer whispered because whispering

seemed to be the only thing he could force past the emotion in his throat. A tiny hand escaped the wrap and waved wildly in front of the baby's face. Archer ran a finger over the back of it and the baby settled.

'Oh, damn,' Iris muttered from the bed.

'What is it?' Archer looked up in concern. 'Do you need the nurse?'

'No,' Iris said with a frown. 'It's just the book club was right.'

'The book club?'

'Yeah, you look really hot holding a baby.'

'I look…'

'Never mind,' Iris said, waving him away. 'We should probably name him before Olive gets here.'

Archer chuckled, thinking about how Olive would react to her new brother. Two kids. He had two kids to take care of now, two kids to love, two kids to worry about. He looked up to find Iris still looking at him, a tired smile on her face.

Two kids and a partner to share it all with.

'How about Owen?' he suggested.

'I was still kinda holding out hope for Knives, but Owen's nice.'

Archer looked down at the baby. 'What do you think, Owen?' The baby blinked. 'Feels like as good an answer as any.'

Iris laughed a little. And she looked tired and beautiful and perfect.

The nurse peeked in the door. 'We have a very excited big sister here.'

Olive burst into the room and ran straight for him. 'Let me see him,' she whispered because she felt it, too. She understood that he was too little to talk to at a regular volume. At least not yet.

'I'll keep the rest of the guests at bay for now,' the nurse told them. 'But I'm not sure how long I can hold them off.'

Iris laughed, but Archer was glad for the moment alone with Olive and Iris and little Owen.

He sat on the edge of the bed and Olive climbed up next to him.

'Olive, meet Owen.'

'He's very small,' she whispered.

'He'll get bigger.'

She ran her finger over the back of his hand and now her little hands looked so big in comparison. More emotions crowded in Archer's throat, and maybe a tear or two slipped out because Iris ran a hand over his back and said, 'It's okay, Papa Bear.' And then maybe a few more tears slipped out.

'I like him,' Olive declared.

'Good, we like him, too.'

'Iris?' Olive said, turning to face Iris on the bed.

'Yeah?'

'Is Owen going to call you Mom?'

Iris glanced at Archer before answering. 'He will, yes.'

Olive sat quietly thinking and they let her. They'd talked about it, he and Iris, over the months as they waited for the baby. Olive was officially his now, the permanent custody paperwork had all been signed. But they'd decided to let Olive take the lead on her relationship with Iris. They never wanted to erase Cate from Olive's life, but they wanted her to know that she was just as much a part of the family as the new baby.

'Can I call you Mom, too?' Olive asked, after a while.

'Of course. I love you both. You're mine, too, Olive.'

Olive crawled up the bed to snuggle closer to Iris's side. And with his son in his arms and his girls cuddled together Archer didn't think he could be happier.

Then Olive looked at him with a grin and asked,

'Dad, what's for dinner?'

He couldn't wait to get his family home to cook for them. A flood of images came to his mind: school-morning breakfasts and family dinners, holidays and Sunday brunches, cooking and baking for his kids, for his family. A lifetime of showing his family he loved them.

'How about you cook it with me, Liv?'

'Like your sous chef?' she asked, her face lighting up. He'd taught her that word last week and she'd loved it.

'Yep, like my sous chef.'

'Okay,' she said. 'Me and you will cook for Mommy and Owen.'

He definitely wasn't the only one with tears in his eyes when Olive called Iris *Mommy* for the first time, but he let them fall. They were happy tears.

'I love that idea.'

Olive beamed.

And that smile was worth so much more than any five-star review. Archer was the best chef in his kid's eyes and that was enough for him.

That was everything.

Acknowledgments

This was a tough one! I don't often write kids into my romances for lots of reasons (besides the fact that they get in the way of sex scenes). While I have kids of my own, I don't believe that kids are necessary for a happily ever after. Parenthood is complicated and messy and wonderful and certainly not for everyone, so trying to capture all of that while making sure the central romance didn't suffer was tricky! All that to say, thank you all for being here, for sticking with me through book four. I hope it was satisfying and I hope you all fell in love with this little family as much as I did.

Thank you to Charlotte and Jennie and everyone at One More Chapter and HarperCollins. Chloe, Christina, Emma and everyone else who worked on this book, a huge thank you! To Kelley McMorris for another gorgeous cover. Thank you to the Harper360 team for making sure these books are in stores in the US. It has been an author's dream come true to walk into stores and see my books on the shelves. I do a double take every time.

Thank you to the book community on BookTok and Bookstagram. Your support for Dream Harbor is a huge part of why this series has been so successful. I cannot thank you enough for using social media in ways I'm terrible at to shout about my books. You guys are truly the best!

I dedicated this book to my kids because I definitely stole a lot of tidbits about them to put into this story! My daughter really does sleepwalk, and we really do have Christmas bells on our door just in case (although she's never gone further than our bedroom). My son plays the trumpet (not in the middle of the night but definitely at the end of a long day and of course it sounds beautiful and melodious, but…let's just say it's not quiet). Neither of my kids are good at relaying health symptoms, so sick days are always a mystery. In general, they make me crazy and I love the crap out of them. Parenthood is objectively nuts. But I wouldn't trade it for anything.

Thank you to my two favorite fictional chefs for inspiration for Archer: Carmy from *The Bear* and Gabriel from *Emily in Paris*. I think I basically averaged these two to create Archer. And really this story is what I want for Carmy. I want him to chill out and make up with Claire and to let himself be happy. So, if anyone who works over there at *The Bear* is reading this, give me a call and we can workshop some stuff.

A shoutout to my brother, Steve, who actually did get lost at a Tulip Festival after a puppet show. Don't worry, we found him.

Thanks to my mom for making us pancakes every Sunday (using a mix) and for showing her love for us through food. Thanks to my mother-in-law for her from-scratch pancake recipe to make when I'm feeling fancy. And to the rest of my family for all your support.

Finally, thank you to my husband, always, but specifically for being such a great dad. Our little family is so lucky to have you as their papa bear. Oh, and thanks for the idea of naming the pancakes after the town residents. That was a good one.

And to the readers, all my love and gratitude for reading these books! Now, I should probably go work on Annie and Mac's book (it's finally coming!!).

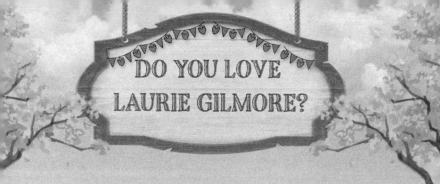

DO YOU LOVE LAURIE GILMORE?

Why not become a Dreamer
and be the first to hear
from Laurie Gilmore about:

New books
Special and exclusive editions
Additional content
Events and signings

Sign up to the newsletter or follow her at:
thelauriegilmore.com

When **Jeanie's** aunt gifts her the beloved Pumpkin Spice Café in the small town of Dream Harbor, Jeanie jumps at the chance for a fresh start away from her very dull desk job.

Logan is a local farmer who avoids Dream Harbor's gossip at all costs. But Jeanie's arrival disrupts Logan's routine and he wants nothing to do with the irritatingly upbeat new girl, except that he finds himself inexplicably drawn to her.

Will Jeanie's happy-go-lucky attitude win over the grumpy-but-gorgeous Logan, or has this city girl found the one person in town who won't fall for her charm, or her pumpkin spice lattes…

Available in paperback, ebook and audio!

When a secret message turns up hidden in a book in the
Cinnamon Bun Bookstore, **Hazel** can't understand it. As more
secret codes appear between the pages, she decides to follow
the trail of clues… she just needs someone to help her out.

Gorgeous and outgoing fisherman, **Noah**, is always up for an
adventure. And a scavenger hunt sounds like a lot of fun. Even
better that the cute bookseller he's been crushing on for months
is the one who wants his help!

Hazel didn't go looking for romance, but as the treasure hunt
leads her and Noah around Dream Harbor, their undeniable
chemistry might be just as hot as the fresh-out-of-the-oven
cinnamon buns the bookstore sells…

Available in paperback, ebook and audio!

Kira North hates Christmas. Which is unfortunate since she just bought a Christmas tree farm in a town that's too cute for its own good.

Bennett Ellis is on vacation in Dream Harbor trying to take a break from both his life and his constant desire to always fix things.

But somehow fate finds Ben trapped by a blanket of snow at Kira's farm, and, despite her Grinchiest first impressions, with the the promise of a warming hot chocolate, maybe, just maybe, these they will have a Christmas they'll remember forever…

Available in paperback, ebook and audio!

A wedding in Dream Harbor can only mean one thing, everyone wants to get involved!

With Jeanie and Logan set to tie the knot, and Kira desperate to hire out her newly renovated barn at the Christmas tree farm, everything seems to be going well. Annie has agreed to bake the cake, and Mac is responsible for, well… just being Mac. And as the whole of Dream Harbor comes together to celebrate the wedding of the year with the snow falling around them, can **Annie** and **Mac** put aside their dislike for each just long enough for the 'I Do's' or is that one request too far…

Available in paperback, ebook and audio!

ONE MORE CHAPTER

YOUR NUMBER ONE STOP

FOR PAGETURNING BOOKS

The author and One More Chapter would like to thank everyone who contributed to the publication of this story...

Analytics
James Brackin
Abigail Fryer

Audio
Fionnuala Barrett
Ciara Briggs

Contracts
Laura Amos
Laura Evans

Design
Lucy Bennett
Fiona Greenway
Liane Payne
Dean Russell

Digital Sales
Laura Daley
Lydia Grainge
Hannah Lismore

eCommerce
Laura Carpenter
Madeline ODonovan
Charlotte Stevens
Christina Storey
Jo Surman
Rachel Ward

Editorial
Kara Daniel
Charlotte Ledger
Ajebowale Roberts
Jennie Rothwell
Caroline Scott-Bowden
Emily Thomas
Helen Williams

Harper360
Jennifer Dee
Emily Gerbner
Ariana Juarez
Jean Marie Kelly
emma sullivan
Sophia Wilhelm

International Sales
Peter Borcsok
Ruth Burrow
Colleen Simpson
Ben Wright

Inventory
Sarah Callaghan
Kirsty Norman

Marketing & Publicity
Chloe Cummings
Grace Edwards
Roisin O'Shea
Emma Petfield

Operations
Melissa Okusanya
Hannah Stamp

Production
Denis Manson
Simon Moore
Francesca Tuzzeo

Rights
Helena Font Brillas
Ashton Mucha
Zoe Shine
Aisling Smyth
Lucy Vanderbilt

Trade Marketing
Ben Hurd
Eleanor Slater

The HarperCollins Distribution Team

The HarperCollins Finance & Royalties Team

The HarperCollins Legal Team

The HarperCollins Technology Team

UK Sales
Isabel Coburn
Jay Cochrane
Sabina Lewis
Holly Martin
Harriet Williams
Leah Woods

And every other essential link in the chain from delivery drivers to booksellers to librarians and beyond!